Forbidden Love

A Billionaire Next Door Neighbor
Contemporary Romance

Rachel K Stone

AS Holdings and Assets Publishing

FROM
FRIENDS
to his
RACHEL K. STONE

Your Free Book Is Waiting

GET YOUR FREE COPY – Travel delays. A fake fiancé. And trying to muffle my screams of passion...while we share a hotel room...

A high school reunion couldn't have come at a worse time. Showing up flying solo was out of the question. So, I did the next best thing and asked my best friend to accompany me as my fake fiancé — bad idea.

Bryce Howard is that bad-boy billionaire, chiseled muscle type. We have been friends since college and he is always there for me in a pinch.

Travel delays have us stuck in a city with little hotel occupancy. We have to share a room and my mind is saying, cool it, he is your best friend. But the moisture building between my thighs wants so much more.

Get a free copy of *From Friends to His*:

https://book.rachelsreaders.com/wzn85xj2po

Shop All Rachel K Stone Books:

https://amazon.com/author/rachelkstone

Contents

Chapter 1

Misti

"What I need is to be properly fucked instead of being pawed at by overgrown boys," I told Stephanie on the phone.

Stephanie was my college roommate at the University of Tennessee. We were both home for the summer and were moving into a new apartment together in the fall. I'd only been home a few days and was just as bored of the men here as I had been in Knoxville.

"You should just give them up. They're easily replaced by a vibrator or a good dildo and a woman with some stamina," she replied.

"Maybe for you, but I like dick. I like the way men smell, feel, and taste. I don't want some chick with a lubed-up rubber cock plowing me. I want a real man that knows how to do more than grab my tits and use them for leverage during the two minutes he can keep it up."

"Suit yourself, but I'm telling you that I'll stick with a woman who knows her way around a vagina and equipment that never fails. Plus, my Veronica has a tongue like a lizard."

"You're a dirty slut. Both of you are. Am I going to have to listen to you two going at it again all fall?"

"I fucking hope so. Maybe you can find some dick worth having down there in Nashville. Skip the college boys over at Vandy and look for some thirty-something dad who can't get his wife to do all those dirty things you're willing to do. They won't get clingy, and you can get your filthy little vag licked or stuffed or whatever."

"Fuck that. Those bitches don't have any money. I like nice things in between getting bent over the hood of a Bentley."

"High maintenance. That's what you are."

"True, but I'm worth every penny," I laughed as I finished getting my string bikini cinched up.

I stood looking in the mirror at myself. The bikini barely covered my nipples and snatch, but I was looking to get some sun in the backyard, so I didn't want much of it there. If Mom and Dad weren't home I'd sunbathe naked.

"Look, I gotta go. My Dad is waiting for me to come help him with his homework," Stephanie told me.

"You're going to graduate and finish a Ph.D. before that motherfucker finishes high school at the rate he's going," I laughed.

"Probably, but I love that he's gone back to get his GED."

"I do too. Tell him I love him."

"I will. Bye."

I did love Stephanie's father. He had dropped out of school to marry her mother when she got pregnant and now doted on his only daughter. I would trade dads with her in a heartbeat. They weren't wealthy but he owned his own garage and did well as a mechanic. Still, he made plenty of time to spend with his family. My father was married to his work. I could drop dead, and he'd probably only see it as a minor inconvenience that disrupted his morning meeting.

I sighed, tossing my long black hair into a messy bun on top of my head before grabbing my beach towel and making my way downstairs. My mother was in the kitchen baking something for one of her many potlucks with the other bored housewives who had too much money and not enough attention. She could afford a cook and a house staff but insisted on doing things herself, relying on only occasional help with deep cleaning or special events at the house. She scowled at me as I walked through to the patio doors.

"That bathing suit is indecent."

"It certainly fucking is," I said dismissively, continuing out the back door.

I looked at where our pool lay in a state of disrepair. It was waiting for renovations that had gotten stalled by some expensive tile work my mother had ordered from Greece. All fucking summer without a pool. What a bitch that was going to be. I turned one of the lounge chairs that sat beside it around toward the sun and laid my towel on it before stretching out on top of it.

I knew I was spoiled in a lot of ways. I'd never had to struggle for anything. My father started his company when I was a baby. He wanted me to take over one day, after college, and spend some time working with him, but I wasn't interested. Why would I want to spend my life overseeing some computer hardware empire when I could do anything I wanted to do? If he had his way I'd be giving up my summers away from school to work with him every day. No way.

All my life, my father had been married to his work and had very little time for me and my mother. She was a bored housewife, spending her days cleaning, baking, shopping, and attending any one of a number of women's groups or social causes with other bored housewives in the neighborhood. I never wanted to be like her or my father. I loved them both and they'd provided well for my life. Dad was even willing to pony up for me to go to an Ivy League school, but I'd wanted to go to the University of Tennessee with my friends.

Of course, that was another disappointment for them. They viewed me as lazy and unmotivated, but I wasn't. I worked hard in school and was at the top of my class in every subject. It was only the fact that I intended to pursue a degree in mechanical design that gave my father hope I might one day change my mind about joining the company. He saw it as me possibly building frameworks for certain aspects of his business, but I didn't want to build computer racks. I wanted to build buildings. I wanted to build bridges.

Reaching for the suntan oil, I began rubbing it on my skin, letting my grievances with my parents fall away as I tried to maximize my time in the sun. Mom had a tanning bed in the house that she used. I preferred to tan the old-fashioned way, especially if there was the possibility of being seen doing so. Of course, there was a dire shortage of eligible men in my neighborhood. The street was full of middle-aged millionaires and billionaires but hardly anyone my age.

Then again, perhaps I should consider some of them. I was only going to be here for another summer or two, at most. I'd be starting my senior year this fall and if all the classes I wanted were available, I would finish by next spring. If not, I might be stuck taking summer classes or waiting for any classes I needed the following fall. After that, I planned to pursue work and get my own place somewhere in the city instead of out here in richburbia.

So, why not just have a fling this summer? There was no shortage of divorcés around here. It was just a matter of finding one who hadn't let himself go to shit while sitting behind a desk all day. Out of shape men could rarely fuck for shit. There were exceptions, no doubt. I'd fucked a waiter at my favorite Irish pub in Nashville one time that had me coming like a fountain. The next morning, he'd run me a bubble bath so that I could soak while he made me pancakes.

Of course, when he'd asked me out again, I'd made excuses not to see him again. Sure, he was great in bed, fucking adorable and a total sweetheart but he was also clingy as fuck. Who needs that shit? The last thing I wanted was a relationship. I wasn't about to turn into my mother. In some ways, I was very much like my father, I feared. All work, no romance. The difference was that I didn't plan on dragging a family down with me if I decided to marry my job.

After that, I'd steered clear of anyone who seemed interested in anything but sex. Unfortunately, there was a shortage of college men who had any sexual prowess. They either came too soon, couldn't come with a woman because they spend too much time masturbating, or fucked like jackrabbits you thought might send your head through the bed frame before it was over. It was exhausting trying to find a guy who knew how to fuck and was just as uninterested in a relationship as I was.

A glint caught my eye as I turned my face up toward the sun. I noted a figure standing in our neighbor's upstairs window. I squinted up toward it, trying to decide if it was a person or merely something that seemed that way. Then it moved and I saw the glint again, perhaps from a watch catching the sun coming into the window. I turned my head so that I wasn't looking directly at it but continued to watch from the corner of my eye.

The shape moved again, but not far. It was a person, and they were watching me. Of course, I knew exactly who the person was—Dylan Hayward, my fifty something neighbor. I'd had a crush on him since I was sixteen years old. I can remember making excuses to go to his garage while he was working out in there because he was so fit. For an older guy, he was fucking cut.

Was he watching me?

Chapter 2

Dylan

Did she see me?

I'd felt a moment of panic as I saw her look directly at my window, or so it seemed. I tried to move but she seemed to follow my movements for a moment and then look away, so maybe I was just being paranoid. I shouldn't be looking at her, but I'd been caught off guard by her presence. Misti Bridges—I thought she was away at college.

The pool at the Bridges' estate was out of commission this summer. Martin Bridges had told me in passing that his wife, Katheryn had ordered some sort of tiles she had specially created by an artist in Greece, and he was behind schedule in getting them made. They'd had to shut down their pool renovation in the middle of things while they waited on the tiles. He'd been livid, not because he couldn't use the pool, but because he couldn't control the situation.

I chuckled at the thought. Martin had always been a bit of a control freak. I'd learned that first hand when he hired my company to design software for some of his products. It had been a successful venture, but I'd had to bite my tongue quite often during meetings and sometimes, even when I ran into him outside our homes since we were neighbors.

Of course, I also owed him for giving me a diversion from my miserable marriage to a greedy woman who decided she deserved a big chunk of the billions I'd made with my software startup I'd started nearly fifteen years ago, right after I'd retired from the Army Rangers. I'd hit the height of a boom with the right software products and was shocked at my own success.

My ex and I had never had children. She told me she couldn't, and I had accepted that. Turns out she lied and was on birth control the entire time we were married because she was vain and hadn't wanted to ruin her figure. I had wanted children then and was devastated to learn of her deception. However, now I felt like she had done me a favor by not dragging kids into our sham marriage.

Still, I was devastated by both the loss of marriage and the secrets that had come to light when she left me. I hadn't fought her. My lawyers had negotiated a healthy settlement for her as quickly as possible to just get it over with so I could get on with my life. Six months later, she was living somewhere in Spain with her new lover, and I was standing in my bedroom looking at my twenty-something neighbor.

I laughed to myself at that, pulling myself away from my thoughts of my ex and turning back to the window. Misti was gone. Fuck. She had seen me! She must have thought I was some sort of old pervert. Perhaps I was exactly that. I mean, she was over thirty years my junior, but I couldn't help but notice how she'd changed since the last time I saw her. She was packed perfectly in all the right places.

My phone buzzed on a table nearby and I went to answer it.

"Hello?"

"Hey, Mr. Hayward. This is Chevy in product testing. We have those emergency alerts finished. You said you wanted to know when they were ready."

"The prototypes, you mean?"

"Yes. The bracelets."

"And they've been tested?"

"Yes sir. They work extremely well in most circumstances."

"Most circumstances?"

"We found some limitations when the signals are subterranean."

"Define subterranean. Are we burying them?"

"No," Chevy said with a chuckle. "I mean, the signal is not as solid when it's coming from places like subways stations and basements."

"Not good enough. We need to find a way to boost that."

"Already working on it. I'll drop off some of the prototypes for you to look at anyway. There are several styles for you to look at."

"No need. I'll be in the office in the morning. I'll stop by and pick them up. Have some data ready for me to review."

"It's a lot of data to transfer unless you want to review in office."

"Just put it on an SD card for me and pack it up with the products."

"Yes, sir. I'll see you tomorrow."

"See you tomorrow, Chevy."

I hung up the phone and looked back toward the window. Misti was back out in her lounge chair. Perhaps she didn't think I was a pervert, after all. Or maybe she hadn't seen me and just happened to go into the house for something. I slid to one side of the window and began watching her again. Her long black hair was toppled across her head in a wild bunch atop her head giving an unobstructed view of her body.

The tiny string bikini she was wearing hardly covered anything. Her large, full breasts were mostly visible with only a thin strip of cloth covering her nipples. The bottom was an equally slender strip that covered a pussy that was either well-groomed or perhaps even shaved completely based on the bare skin of her pubic mound visible on either side of it. I found myself wanting to know which was the case.

Despite the bikini, she had no visible tan lines. I found it difficult to believe that she could possibly wear a smaller bikini, so I could only assume she sunbathed nude sometimes, either out in the sun or in a tanning bed. I felt a little twinge of jealousy at the thought of someone else watching her like this, which caught me completely off guard. What did I have to be jealous about?

I stood at the edge of the window watching as she rubbed more oil on her body. I could see it glistening on her lovely sun-kissed skin as she applied it to her breasts. They swayed gently as she rubbed her hands across them, making me wish I could do the same. Her hands slipped down her stomach, applying more of the oil there. I felt my cock twitch to life.

I continued watching, wanting desperately to touch myself. But I didn't want to cross that line. It was bad enough that I was sitting here spying on my neighbors' daughter as she lay mostly naked in their backyard. Whipping out my cock and masturbating while doing so was taking things just a bit too far. Still, I continued watching her until I was rock hard.

I wondered what it would feel like to slip my cock between those two well-oiled globes of hers, push them together and fuck them until I blew my load all over them and her gorgeous face. I was dangerously close to coming in my pants just from watching her lay there. I could only wonder how intense it would be to actually follow through with my little daydream.

"Fuck me," I moaned out loud to the room around me.

I couldn't remember ever being so turned on by a woman before in my life. I'd had plenty of women in my life while I was in the Army. Exotic women from all over the world, some quite beautiful and well put together. I met my wife while she was stripping in a club in Chattanooga. I was young and fresh off my last tour of duty. She didn't seem to care that I was unemployed. I had some money saved from my years in the service and a pension, so I wasn't destitute, but she made more money than I did.

I'd let her beauty overtake my brain, not realizing until it was too late that she saw me as a meal ticket. I'd thought that her sticking with me while I started my company was commitment, when it was more of a case that she saw me for my potential. As soon as I was more solvent, I'd proposed and we'd gotten married. While I worked long hours, she fucked around with men she found more exciting and eventually, fucked off with one of them. I should have already learned that getting myself all worked up over a nice pair of tits and a potentially tight pussy would only end badly for me.

Yet, there I was, watching some sweet young thing out the window with my cock throbbing eagerly against the zipper of my pants. I wanted to walk out of my house, knock on her parents' front door and just walk through their house to where she lay, demanding that she suck my cock since she was the one that had gotten it so hard. I wondered if she knew I was there. I had to wonder if she knew exactly what kind of effect she would have on me.

Was it a coincidence that her chair was aimed in my direction or had she just pointed it toward the sun? She began moving and I shifted so that I was hidden at the edge of the window or, at least, I hoped I was hidden. If she wasn't intentionally showing off for me, I didn't want to alert her to my presence. I did still have business dealings with her father and couldn't afford for her to go tell him and piss him off at me.

She stood up from the chair and stretched, her breasts rising and falling with her movements. Then, she turned and went back into the house, giving me a brief view of her shapely ass in the thong bottoms of the bikini. I was disappointed that the show was over, but knew it was for the best. I needed to find something to do besides lusting over forbidden fruit.

Chapter 3

Misti

This was my second time at the pool and I returned to the deck with a large bottle of cold water I'd put in the freezer earlier in the morning so that it was ice cold. If I couldn't get in the pool, I could at least have some cold water to drink. Of course, now that I was fairly certain Dylan Hayward was watching me from his window, I had some other ideas in mind, as well. I took a long deep sip, trying to sneak a peek toward his window without it being obvious.

"Misti, for God's sake, you tracked dirty footprints through the kitchen. Wipe your feet off before you come in next time," Mom barked at me from the kitchen door.

"If it weren't such a disaster area out here, it wouldn't be a problem. There's fucking dirt everywhere. You could have at least made them clean up before they shut down to wait on your precious tiles," I shot back at her.

She shut the door wordlessly but reappeared a few moments later with a pair of pool slippers and dropped them beside the lounge chair as I was getting back into it and then stormed back toward the house.

"I'm not wearing those," I yelled toward her.

"It won't hurt you to put them on to come back into the house," she said, stopping halfway between me and the kitchen doors.

"It will," I told her, wondering if Dylan was watching all this and worse, if he could hear any of it.

The last thing I wanted was for him to hear me be scolded like a child by my mother. I was trying to be provocative and sexy, and she was ruining my mojo. She ignored my last comment and went inside. I glanced sideways directly at Dylan's house and up toward the window I'd seen him in. It didn't look like he was there. I took another sip of my water and settled back into the lounge chair.

For a while, I drifted off. The warmth of the sun settling me into a comfortable warmth. I woke up with a start, confused with my surroundings for a moment. I glanced up toward Dylan's window without even attempting to hide it and then relaxed. He still wasn't there so hopefully he hadn't seen me sprawled out snoring or some shit. I picked up my water and drank it, thankful for the chunks of ice that had kept it nice and cold.

It was only then that I caught sight of him. He seemed to be moving around, perhaps working in whatever room he was in but not watching me. Then, he was standing still, paused by the window again. If he wanted to watch, I should give him something worth seeing. I found myself wishing my mother wasn't home so I could really show off, but I'd have to settle for subtle. That might be better anyway, to start with.

I ran my hands over my skin under the guise of putting on more tanning oil. I took my time, squirting plenty of the oil into my hands and slowly slathering it up and down my legs in long, deliberate strokes before moving onto my arms. I took my time, standing up from my chair to give him a better look as I rubbed it into my stomach and up across my breasts.

I turned so that he had a nice view of my ass, which was mostly visible on either side of the tiny string that made up the center back of my thong bottoms. Bending over, I pretended to rub lotion onto my knees as if I hadn't already well covered them. The sun wasn't out very strong today or I'd be setting myself up to be baked with all of this excess oil.

Moving my hands in toward my crotch, I took my time rubbing the oil into my thighs, keeping my ass turned toward him at first, but then slowly turning so that he got a pretty decent view of my cleavage as I straightened back up to put the cap back on the oil bottle and then bent slightly back down to sit it aside.

I lay back down on the lounge chair and put my sunglasses on so that I could watch him better without it being too noticeable. I spread my legs open invitingly and picked up the water bottle, shaking it so that the straw shed tiny drops of water along my well lubed skin. It was all a waste of time as far as the sun goes because I was beginning to lose it behind some clouds, but I seriously hoped it was doing something for Dylan.

I thought back to one time when I was barely 16 and stopped by his house to ask if he could let me use his phone because my parents weren't home and I couldn't remember the alarm code to get in. He was out in his garage with the door open. Well, if you wanted to call it a garage.

Dylan Hayward didn't use his garage like most people. There was a separate one to one side of the house with several different doors for his cars. The one attached to his house was kitted out like a full gym. When I arrived, he was sitting on the end of a bench in a pair of shorts and no shirt. His tanned muscles rippled as he lifted the barbell in his hand.

I stood there, mesmerized for a moment, my teenage hormones raging as my emerging libido took note of his raw energy and power. I could imagine those arms wrapped around me, holding me close. I shook free of my thoughts and spoke.

"Mr. Hayward, can I borrow your phone? I've locked myself out of the house."

"A teenage girl without a cell phone? That can't be true," he replied.

"I have one. It's just locked inside the house."

"I thought your house had an override code if you don't have a key. Your father has the same alarm style I do."

"Yes. That's why I need the phone. Dad changed it last week and I can't remember what it is."

"Ah, of course. Sure, it's right over there on the counter," he said.

"Thanks," I told him, retrieving it and noticing it was locked. I asked if there was a password.

"Oh, sorry. Yeah. Come hold it up to my face."

I did as he asked, feeling a bit jittery as I drew close to him and held the phone up. I couldn't help but notice his caramel-colored eyes and striking features. He was hot, but in a rugged sort of way that you don't expect. I had really never taken much notice of him before, but right now I was completely enamored of him.

For weeks after our encounter in his garage, I made excuses to be out where I could see him as he came and went from his house. I had such a huge crush on him that it was ridiculous. I even offered to cut his lawn once just to spend time over there but his bitch wife, Lydia, told me she had a professional to do the lawn and didn't need some high school kid fucking up her roses.

I wonder what happened to her. I think it's been over a year since I've seen her next door. Maybe longer. I made a mental note to ask Mom about her later.

For now, I refocused my energy on getting the attention that I craved. I continued showering myself with drops of water and rubbing it into my skin, wishing that I could do more to entice him. I could see him now just at the edge of the window. He was still moving about the room a bit, but he kept pausing to look at me.

I glanced toward the house and noticed Mom in the kitchen window that overlooked the backyard. She wasn't watching me, just cutting up vegetables in the sink. I could see her putting carrots and potatoes in a large bowl beside her from time to time. I wished she would go away so I could get a bit riskier with my little show, but she seemed to be taking her own sweet time with food prep.

I pushed her out of my head and began thinking about what it might feel like to be with someone like Dylan. I bet someone like him knew exactly what he was doing in bed. The more I thought about him, the more all those feelings came rushing back and I was once again that teenage girl wondering what it would be like to be with an older man. I could feel myself getting wet just thinking about the power those well-muscled legs of his must pack when he was thrusting his hips toward mine in long, deep strokes.

I closed my eyes and imagined his hands on my body, roaming up my legs toward my thighs and caressing them. In my mind, he was slowly slipping upward over me to cup my breasts, kneading them with his hands as he covered my mouth with his. I exhaled, letting out all of the longing building up inside of me as I opened my eyes and looked toward his window again.

I could see him standing there, watching me. He was mostly hidden by the curtain to one side of the window, but I could see him. Was he wondering what I was thinking about? Could he possibly know that I was thinking about all of the dirty things I wanted to do to him?

More importantly, would he let me do them?

Chapter 4

Dylan

It's been nearly a week since I first noticed Misti laying out in her parents' backyard. What I had hoped was just a momentary distraction had turned into a daily routine. She came out in one of her tiny bikinis and laid out until the sun gave up and went home for the day. If it didn't rain soon, I was going to lose my mind, because as long as the sun was shining and she was present, I couldn't keep my eyes off of her.

I was immersed in watching her drip water across her lightly bronzed skin that the sound of the phone ringing behind me made me jump. I walked over to my desk and picked up my cell. I didn't bother checking who was calling.

"Dylan Hayward," I said as I answered it.

"Dylan, Martin Bridges here. How are you?"

I hesitated for a moment, glancing back toward my window. I half expected him to be standing beside his daughter, looking up at where I had been watching her for days now—I mean, not constantly, but more than I should be.

"You there, Dylan?" he prodded.

"Oh, yes. Sorry. What can I do for you Martin?"

"I have a project I want to talk to you about. My hardware, your software. When can you meet with me?"

"Um, I'm not sure, Martin. Hold on. Let me check my schedule really quick."

I walked away from the phone for a moment. I felt dirty. What were the odds that he would call me while I was ogling his daughter. I had to recenter myself. I muted my microphone and then took a few deep breaths before returning to the conversation.

"How does Thursday look for you, Martin?"

"Thursday is actually pretty perfect. Say around 10 a.m.?"

"That's good for me. Your office or mine?"

"Mine, if you don't mind. I want to show you the prototypes we're working with, and I can get you any data you need while you're here if you want to take the project on."

"Great. I'll see you Thursday," I told him.

We said our goodbyes and I ended the call, standing there looking at the blank screen for a moment. It was so weird meeting one another in our formal offices when we live next door to one another. You'd think we could just hash out the details over a few beers in the backyard and then let our respective engineers and coders work out the rest, but Martin was very much a stickler for protocol. His business life and his private life were kept completely separate.

In the years that we had lived next to one another, we had never interacted as neighbors other than a polite greeting if we both turned up in our driveways at the same time. I used to think it was because he was jealous. Martin had inherited his business from his father. He'd put his own touch on it, brought it into the modern age and made it even more successful, but I had more money. He was a multi-millionaire, but I was worth billions.

So, I assumed he was blowing me off because he didn't appreciate the fact that I'd ramped up my business so fast and achieved billionaire status when he'd been working at it since he was in his teens. I couldn't have been more wrong. Martin was just all business. Based on how rarely I ran into him in front of our homes or even saw him at his house, I'd say he spent more time making a dollar than he did making time for his family.

I glanced back toward the window. That might explain why his daughter was laying out in the backyard where I could watch her sunbathe in skimpy bikinis. She had always seemed to have some daddy issues going on, but I'd steered well clear of them until now. No one was going to file charges against me for getting an eyeful of her tits now, but it still felt somehow wrong of me.

Unless she was doing it because she wanted me to watch.

I walked back over to the window and looked. She was still there, spread out across the lounge chair with her ass toward me. One of the back ties to her bikini top was untied. From the angle of her body, I could see the sides of her large tits as they pressed against the hard surface beneath them. I found myself wishing that they were pressed against my chest.

As if on cue, she rose, holding her bikini top down over her breasts and turned over, opening her legs to plant her feet on either side of the lounge chair. I could see clearly between them, her well-toned thighs leading to a pussy barely covered by the thong. I was sure she shaved bald or at least down to a thin landing strip. There were no escaping tufts or visible puffs in the material.

She situated herself on the lounger and then untied the top of her bikini. She pulled the strings to either side of her breasts, using the thin strip of material so that it covered her nipples and most of the lower part of her breasts. An ample portion was visible at the top as she reached for her water bottle and dripped more water across them.

"Fuck me," I said out loud, very much aware of my growing erection.

I walked away from the window. Did she know what she was doing to me? Was she just trying to get sun on the maximum area or was she showing off for me? I wanted to believe it was the latter. Who wouldn't want some sweet young thing putting on a sexy little show to get their attention?

I tried to walk it off. The last thing I wanted was to get caught spying on Martin's daughter when I was about to head to his office for what might prove to be a lucrative deal. It wasn't the first time we'd done business together and I didn't want to jinx it before I had a chance to find out what it was.

Still, the sight of her laying out there with her tits half out and her pussy barely clad wasn't shaking off as quickly as I'd like. Even doing mundane chores around the bedroom wasn't taking off the edge. All I could think about was what I might be missing outside that window.

My phone beeped with the low battery notification, and I connected it to the charger by the bedside table. As I laid it on the top, I glanced out the window again. She was still there, now applying suntan oil on her body. Her hands working it into her breasts in slow, circular motions. Damn she was fucking hot, and I was instantly hard again.

There was no walking this off. Instead, I slipped to one side of my window where I was mostly out of sight and took matters into my own hands, slipping off my pants and sliding my hand into my boxer briefs. I watched her out there, teasing me with her drops of water and oil slicked skin. There was no way she wasn't doing this on purpose.

It made sense, didn't it? She definitely had Daddy issues and if she was looking for an older guy to work them out on then who was I to not give her what she wanted. I stroked my cock as I thought about just how much I'd love to spank her tight ass and fuck those big tits of hers. I found myself wondering if she'd ever been with an older man before. I bet I could teach her a few things.

I continued to stroke myself, keeping my eye on her. Her breasts rose and fell with her breaths, beads of perspiration dotting her well-oiled skin as the sun beat down on her beautiful body. God, I wanted to fuck her in the worst way. I heard a sound and then saw her mother emerge from the back of the house and say something, then disappear back inside.

Misti continued to lay there for a few seconds, but then she got up, holding her top to her as she tied the back and gathered her things. She looked straight up toward my window, and I panicked a little, but I was pretty well hidden by the curtains to one side of my window. I watched as she walked away, padding toward the house, and disappearing inside.

Fuck. I was still hard and now my inspiration was gone. I turned and lay on the bed, closing my eyes and imagining her as I continued to masturbate. In my mind, it was her hand around my cock, pumping me until I shot my load all over her tits and face. I'd love to see her licking my spunk off her pretty little face, trailing her fingers through what landed on her breasts and licking them clean.

I slipped off my boxer briefs so that my cock sprang free and continued rubbing one out until I was about to come. I used them to catch my load so that I didn't get it all over the coverlet. The force was like a valve bursting open, sending a flood escaping from a dam that had been held back for far too long. I let the relief of it flood over me and lay back on the pillows, still thinking about her.

It was good to get off, but I wanted to get off while fucking her. I made up my mind—I was going to fuck her.

Chapter 5

Misti

I'd been putting on a show for Dylan Haywood for over a week now and it was getting a bit frustrating. I didn't even know if he was really watching me. I could see him upstairs in the window, but often it was as if he passed by or seemed to breeze in and out of the room. The houses here, despite the ridiculous price tags on them, were fairly close together. You paid for the neighborhood, not the acreage.

In other parts of Nashville, you might not find a house within viewing range, but we were in a gated community built up on a ridge, so land was scarce. It was sort of comical if you thought about it. Someone of far lesser wealth might live outside of Nashville on hundreds of acres that still weren't worth one of our mansions sitting on a tiny plot.

At any rate, I was close enough to Dylan Haywood that he should be able to get a pretty decent view, but was he truly watching or just glancing my way every once in a while? Even with my sunglasses blocking some of the rays bearing down on my eyes, it wasn't always easy to tell. I could only make out it was Dylan in certain light from where I was, so I couldn't really say if he was looking down at me or facing away.

Somehow, though, I believed he was watching, and he was getting off on it.

I had nothing better to do while home for the summer except lay out though, so I'd put on the show for him whether he was watching or not. If he was watching and I played my cards right, there might just be a chance of giving him a much more personal view. First, I just needed to know if he was interested.

For all I knew, he still thought of me as the little girl next door. I intended to show him just how much I'd grown up. I wasn't overly vain, but I knew that my body was damn near perfect. My tits were symmetrical DDs, and they were all natural, not a bit of silicone in these puppies. My ass was tight, and my waist was small. Though not as tall as I'd like to be, I was slightly above average at 5'6" and I could jack that up to 5'10" in stilettos.

My hair was jet black and, unlike many of the women I knew, mine didn't come out of a bottle. It hung in long loose waves unless I blow dried it straight, which I rarely did in the summer. The humidity in Tennessee would wreck that shit the moment I stepped outside, so I just kept it natural and mostly pulled up in a loose bun unless I was going out.

Between good genes and the fact that I stood to inherit millions if anything happened to my parents, most guys would describe me as a real catch. The truth was that I hated that. I didn't mind being objectified. I was a bit of an attention whore and didn't mind admitting that, but I didn't appreciate guys who were more interested in my father's money than me. The problem was that you didn't always know which they were more interested in.

I didn't have that problem with Dylan Haywood. I didn't know a lot about him, but I knew that he was wealthier than my father. I'd heard him telling my mother that once when they were talking about his wife. Mom said she was only with him for his money and constantly had stray men over when Dylan was away on business.

I had asked the other night what happened to his wife, playing if off like I was just curious because I hadn't seen her since I'd been home.

"Her? Oh, I think she finally decided to run away with some other guy. Took a big chunk of money too, I heard," Mom said.

"Why would he have to give her money if she left him for some other dude?" I asked.

"I don't think he had to give it to her. From what I heard, he was happy to see her go and just wanted her to go away already. It's not like he doesn't have plenty of it left. He's still a billionaire, according to your father."

"I wonder why he lives in this neighborhood. He could have a place anywhere he wanted."

"It's not like the houses here are cheap, honey."

"No, of course not, but it seems like he wouldn't want to stay in a house with bad memories."

"No idea. I don't think he had quite as much money when he bought the place. Maybe it's just sentimental to him for other reasons."

"Maybe," I said, letting it go. I didn't want her to get suspicious about why I was so curious.

The following day, I was laying out, putting on my usual show in hopes of getting noticed when Mom came to the patio doors and stepped out.

"Misti, your father, and I are headed to the Nashville League luncheon. We'll be gone for a few hours, so you'll be here alone."

"Okay, Mom. Thanks."

She went back inside and closed the door. I continued lying in my chair until I heard the garage door opening and the sound of tires on the pavement. When they faded away down the street, I knew that I finally had time to take my little sunbathing show to the next level. I stood up from the lounge chair and untied my bikini top, letting it fall to the ground beside me.

I stood there, facing his window so that he had a good view. With the sun temporarily behind a cloud, I had a clear view into his window. He was there and he was watching. I could almost see his face, despite the shadows that fell partially across it. I could also see that he was shirtless, but the window blocked whatever he was wearing below the waist, if anything.

Picking up my bottle of suntan oil, I squirted some of it across the top of my breasts and began rubbing it across them but not enough to rub it into my skin too much. I wanted my tits all slick and oiled up for him to see. I squirted some more in my hands and applied it, cupping my full globes in my hands seductively. I pulled them upward as if to get underneath and then rubbed the lotion downward across my belly.

I made a further production out of rubbing the oil down my legs, letting my breasts fall forward and bounce about as I rubbed it up and down my legs, around my thighs and reached around to oil up my ass. Once I was done, I lay back down on the lounge chair, my well lubed tits glistening in the sun. A light breeze came through the trees, blowing across my nipples so that they stood at attention.

I lay there, with my tits exposed and my legs open giving him a nice view of what I had to offer. After a few moments, I reached for my water bottle, squirting water across my skin and bikini bottoms. The bikini I was wearing today was very thin. The water made my bottoms almost translucent, leaving the material to cling to my cunt, which was dripping with excitement at the thought of him watching.

I sat the bottle down and lay there for a bit, letting the sun do its magic both of tanning my skin and creating little beads of sweat that glistened all across my breasts. I reached up and rubbed it into them, lifting them and playing with them a bit as I did so. If he had any doubts that I wanted him to watch me, I was about to make it clear that I wanted him to see every bit of my little show.

I wished the pool wasn't down for the count this summer. I'd love to strip down naked and go for a skinny dip. He could watch me climbing out of the pool, naked and wet for him. I wondered if he'd like that. Would that get him hard? Was he already hard? A part of me wanted to get up out of this chair and walk over to his house and just offer myself to him, but I was too afraid that this little game we were playing was one-sided.

For all I knew, I was making a fool of myself, but I was willing to take that chance. I'd decided that getting fucked by Dylan Haywood was my primary goal for this summer and the moment I had any indication that he wanted it too, I'd be in his bed waiting for him. I closed my eyes and cupped my tits, kneading them while wishing it was his hands on them.

The more I thought about him, the wetter I was getting. I didn't even need water to dampen my bikini bottoms to translucency now. I was so wet that they were sticking to my clean-shaven pussy. Could he see that from his window? Could he see the perfect outline of my pussy lips through my bikini bottoms? I thought about taking them off, but I wanted to leave at least a little bit to the imagination.

I ran my hands down my stomach and along the top edge of my bottoms, letting my fingers slip slightly inside. I thought about Dylan again.

I wanted to climb him like a fucking California Redwood.

Chapter 6

Dylan

Every fucking day, she took things a step further. Today, she'd taken off her top and given me a full view of her fantastic tits. But she wasn't stopping there. If I had been wondering whether she was just sunbathing or putting on a show, today pretty much removed all doubt for me. No one puts that much oil on their tits.

I watched as those melons of hers glistened in the sun, all oiled up and begging to be fondled and fucked. It took every ounce of my reserve not to walk over there and do just that. I suspected her parents were gone if she had grown so bold, but I couldn't be sure, and I didn't know if they had staff over there.

So, I just stood in my room and watched her, but I didn't bother trying to hide near the curtains. I stood directly in the center of my windows, angling the blinds so that no one but her could see me there. I was already in just a towel. I had been getting ready to go take a shower when I spotted her out there and started watching.

She didn't disappoint.

I had tried to steer clear ever since I had masturbated over her. I was getting way too into getting off on watching this little cock tease. Whether she knew I was watching or just didn't care if I, or anyone else, saw her, she was still a tease. But today, she was making it clear that she was putting on a show for an audience of one and that one was me.

The question was, why? She had never come on to me before. I remembered when she was younger, she came to the house a few times for random reasons. I remember Lydia teasing me that she had a schoolgirl crush, but I hadn't believed it. I mean, what use did a teenage girl have for a middle-aged married man? I dismissed it and didn't think twice about it. I certainly didn't ever think about it then.

But now, fuck. She was all grown up and all grown out and I wanted to bury my cock in her sweet little pussy all the way to the hilt. I would love to show her just how hard her little backyard strip tease was getting me. I dropped my towel and let my cock spring forward, rock hard again.

I took it in my hand, still not bothering to move away from the window, though I doubt she could see my cock due to the height of the window. I almost wished she could. I was pretty well endowed. I think she would really appreciate the view just like I was appreciating hers.

She had the water bottle out again, squirting water across her bare breasts so that it rolled down them and across her stomach, puddling in her navel. She moved her hands across her breasts, rubbing the water in and then moved down to her stomach, spreading the water downward so that her bikini was soaked, or I should say, more soaked than it already was.

I wondered how much of that was water, how much was perspiration and how much was pussy juices. I had an uncontrollable urge to smell her—just bury my face in her pussy and take a deep sniff before licking up her wetness. I could imagine her velvet folds against my tongue and her moans of pleasure as I teased her clit, gently biting and pulling at it with my teeth.

I began stroking myself as she took her time with her water play. She still had a little surprise up her sleeve though. Her hand slipped further into her bikini bottoms, leaving them on but fingering herself beneath the material. I watched as she rolled her head back, lost in fucking herself with increasing vigor.

I joined her, matching her strokes with my own. I reached for the baby oil in the drawer of my bedside table and began pumping away at my cock. She was beautiful like this, her dark hair toppled all over her head, a few strands clinging to her oil slicked shoulders. Her head tilted back with an expression of unadulterated pleasure as she finger-banged herself.

It was getting me incredibly hot watching her. I didn't even try to hold back, jacking off until I came so hard it made my knees buckle a little. I picked up the towel and wiped off my slowly wilting cock and continued to watch Misti. What would she think if she knew she had already made me come twice from watching her, three times if she wanted to count the wet dream I had about fucking her.

What was this woman doing to me? She was in my head all of the time. I couldn't stop thinking about her. I managed to put her out of my mind long enough to take care of work but anytime I found myself with an idle moment, I was thinking about her out there in her backyard in her tiny bikini. Now, I would no doubt be thinking about her in only half of that bikini.

As I continued to watch her masturbate for me, I found myself wishing that I could hear her. I'd love to know what sounds she made when she was excited, when she hit just the right spots. What did she sound like when she came?

This only made me wonder what she would sound like when she said my name. I could imagine her moaning it in my ear as I slipped my fingers into her tiny bikini and moved them back and forth through her wet folds. I'd love to feel her long nails digging into my back as I brought her to orgasm again and again.

Her hips rose from the lounge chair, meeting her fingers as they penetrated her repeatedly. I could feel my cock getting hard again as if being pulled toward her. I really wanted to fuck her and not in some soft, gentle way. I wanted to march down there, lift her up off of that chair and bend her over the patio table that sat nearby so I could impale her with my dick.

I'd love to fill her every hole with hot sticky come and then start all over again. In my mind, she was the perfect interactive fuck doll, letting me do whatever I wanted, whenever I wanted. Watching her finger-fuck herself was just making me want it that much more. I continued to watch, my cock twitching with need but I didn't masturbate again. In fact, I made up my mind that I wasn't going to masturbate to her little show again.

If she wanted to be fucked, I was going to hold out until I could fuck her properly. I just needed to figure out how to go about doing that without her parents finding out. If it weren't for our business dealings I wouldn't care, she was a grown woman and could fuck whoever she wanted. I just didn't want to ruin my business relationship with her father and well, I did have to live next to them even after she went back to school.

The first thing I had to find out was whether she was serious about wanting to get physical with me. There was always the possibility that this little tease show of hers was all she wanted. If that was the case, it was fine, but I needed to lay off of watching her so often as it was just making me want to fuck her too much.

I watched as she continued to masturbate and then she suddenly stopped, her head cocked toward the house. She jumped up, grabbing her things and making a mad rush toward the house. Mommy and

Daddy must be home. I could only assume she heard them pulling into the driveway and made a run to get decent. Definitely couldn't let them know their little angel was topless and masturbating for the neighbor in the backyard.

I chuckled to myself, looking down at my own raging hard on. It would subside. I went to the bathroom and turned on the shower, leaving the water at a low temperature to cool me down before turning it back up to get a shower. When I came back out, there was no sign of Misti. I guess the show was over for today.

I went downstairs and sat at my desk, pulling up my emails to go through them and look at the prototypes my R & D department had mocked up for our latest product. We were working with a local jewelry company to create jewelry with GPS technology. It was an innovative bit of tech, as it combined the power of GPS tracking with security alert systems that could be hidden in ordinary looking jewelry.

The tech was intended to protect women by giving them a way to ask for help if they didn't have a phone on them. If they were abducted or in a part of a building without an alarm or phone, they could access the alert embedded in the jewelry. It would automatically send out a signal to law enforcement requesting emergency assistance and giving a location signal.

It had started out as a GPS chip that would simply track the person wearing it, but market research showed concerns that it could be used by unscrupulous partners for tracking unsuspecting people. I had developed the idea to instead only initiate GPS signals if they were turned on by the person wearing the jewelry and that seemed to resonate better with potential purchasers.

I picked up my phone and called my liaison at the local police department.

"You ready for a test?"

"Absolutely, let's do this," he told me.

I focused on going through the steps with him for a bit, pushing the thought of Misti continuing to masturbate in her room or the shower out of my mind—at least for now.

Chapter 7

Misti

After almost being caught masturbating in the backyard by my parents, I had decided I was out of control and stopped laying out back there for a couple of weeks. Instead, I lay in my mother's tanning bed naked to get rid of any tan lines and avoid the urge to do naughty things for the neighbor. However, I still kept thinking about him and spent more than a few lonely nights masturbating in my bed while thinking about him.

One morning, I awoke to find my parents arguing in the kitchen about something. I came down the stairs and went inside to see what was going on.

"What's happening here?" I asked.

"Your father is leaving for the rest of the week and won't be here for the fundraiser I only signed up for because he asked me to plan it."

"Really, Dad?" I asked, exasperated.

"It can't be helped," he said, addressing both of us.

That was Dad, always super-efficient with everything, even arguing with two women at once.

"If you leave, I'm going to postpone the fundraiser," Mom told him.

"Don't be ridiculous, Katheryn," he said in a dismissive tone.

"If you leave, I'm canceling it. I mean it, Martin."

"So, you've escalated from postponing it to canceling it?" he barked.

"Yep," she replied.

"You're impossible," he said.

"As are you," she retorted.

I stood there, looking from one of them to another.

"We'll talk about this tonight at dinner. I have to go to work," Dad said.

Mom threw her hands up and stormed out of the kitchen, stomping toward their bedroom, and slamming the door. Dad just sighed and headed out the front door.

"Tell your mother that I'll be home by seven for dinner."

"I'm sure she'll be ecstatic," I snapped.

He shook his head and walked out the front door. A few minutes later, Mom emerged from the bedroom, dressed in a well-fitting sheath dress and heels. She had her hair pulled up into a sleek knot and fresh lipstick on. It wasn't hard to see where I got my figure from. Mom could still turn heads, sometimes even my father's.

"Dad said he'll be home by seven," I told her.

"When he gets here, tell him I'm not home and he can order a fucking pizza for dinner," she said, pulling a wad of cash out of her purse and handing it to me. "Go do something nice for yourself today. Take your father's Ferrari. You get bonus points if you scratch or dent it without getting injured."

"Where are you going?" I asked.

"For a drive. I'll be back tomorrow."

"That's a very long drive," I remarked, an eyebrow raised in her direction.

"It certainly is," she said, offering me nothing else. "My cell is on if you need me but don't use it unless you're dying. Got it?"

"Got it," I said. "Drive safely."

She smiled and kissed me on the cheek before waltzing out the front door on whatever angry little private adventure she was away on. I admired my mother when she was like this. She might be a pampered housewife by a lot of folks' standards but if they thought she didn't have a mind or a life of her own, they would be wrong. This version of her suited me much more than the June Cleaver act she put on for others.

I counted the money and smiled before grabbing a shower and heading out the front door with the keys to Dad's Ferrari in my hand. I knew exactly how I intended to spend my day. First, I grabbed a light breakfast and a latte, then I went to my mother's favorite spa and talked my way into a walk-in appointment. The rest of the morning was spent getting pampered from head to toe.

When I returned home, it was only just past noon. Still, plenty of time to get some sun. I smiled as I slipped off my clothes and got ready to go out. I hoped my voyeur would be there. With my mother and father out of the house for so long, I could get as freaky as I wanted out by the pool. I even considered inviting him over to really enjoy the action, but I wasn't sure I was ready for that just yet. It wasn't that I didn't want it, I was just afraid he'd say no to moving beyond our little spying game.

Walking out to the pool, I made a production of setting down my bottle of water and my tanning oil, bending over provocatively to give him a nice view of my ass. I was wearing a new bikini today. The top was little more than a ribbon that covered my nipples, and the thong barely covered my bald pussy, which was very smooth today thanks to my trip to the spa.

I glanced sideways toward his window. He wasn't there. I felt disappointed but was hopeful that he would turn up. I stripped off the barely-there bikini so that nothing would be left to his imagination and began applying tanning lotion. I took my time lubing up my arms and legs before lying on the chaise lounge and positioning myself so that my tits were catching the rays and spreading my legs for a clear view from his window.

With my sunglasses on my face, I tilted my head so that it appeared I wasn't looking right at his window, even though I was riveted on it. I waited like that, just enjoying the sun on my naked body and hoping that he would show up. It took the better part of two hours, but he finally did. I could see him as he approached the window and stopped in his tracks. He looked for a moment and then disappeared again.

When he returned, he approached from the side of the window frame, positioning himself so that he was not so easily visible. But I could still see him as he watched from the shadows of the room, taking in my body without being so easily spotted. He wanted me to think he had glanced out the window and walked away. He wanted me to think he wasn't watching, but I knew he was, and I was about to give him something worth looking at.

I started slowly, moving one of my hands down toward my stomach and letting it rest there for a moment. I picked up the water bottle with my other hand and took a sip from the straw before squirting my skin with a bit of it, letting the tiny beads of water scatter across my slick skin. I reached up with the other hand and cupped one of my breasts before using my fingers to slowly spread the water droplets across my skin. The cool water felt amazing with the heat of the sun bearing down today.

I soon forgot all about whether Dylan was watching me. I was horny as fuck and the combination of being outside in the buff coupled with the warmth of the sun and the coolness of the water re-focused my thoughts on my own pleasure. I took my time dousing myself with water and spreading it across my skin. I squirted some of it in my mouth before lowering it to squirt some directly between my legs.

Setting it aside, I kneaded my heavy breasts, pushing them together and raising them upward. I closed my eyes and let my hand wander down my midriff toward my pussy, spreading my legs and slowly rolling a single finger across my bare pubic mound before moving further down to lightly massage my clit. I moaned slightly as my fingers made contact with my aching little nubbin.

I hadn't had sex in a while outside of self-stimulation and I wanted it really badly. I thought about what it would feel like to have Dylan Haywood's head between my legs, teasing my clit and lapping at my wet folds. As thoughts of him came back into my head, I opened my eyes to see if he was still there.

He was.

I continued to stroke my clit, my hips rising upward from the lounge chair as I massaged it to a hard little button. I could make myself come in a matter of seconds, but I wanted this to last. I didn't want to cum right away and began to slow things back down a bit, slipping one of my fingers along my pink folds, letting it dip inside of me here and there as I took my time masturbating for my audience of one. I snuck peeks up toward his window from time to time to see if he was still there.

Each time I saw his slight movements by the curtains, I smiled a little to myself and returned to my exhibition. Obviously he liked what he was seeing, even if it never went any further than these illicit moments that we shared. Soon, I was completely engrossed in imagining his hands between my legs, forgetting all about whether he was watching me finger fuck myself.

I was so focused on Dylan, that it lost focus on myself. It was taking me forever to come. As much as I liked the way it felt to play with my pussy, I just couldn't seem to get off. It seemed like all I ever did anymore was masturbate. I needed to be fucked in the worst way. I needed someone who knew his way around a woman's body to drill me so hard that I forgot my own name.

I was betting Dylan was just the man for the job.

Chapter 8

Dylan

She definitely knew I was there. I'd seen her glance up toward my window more than once while she was getting off. The only question now was whether she was interested in taking this little game of hers any further. It was one thing to put on a show for the neighbor out of boredom, but another to take it further and make it physical. She might just be a tease. Either way, she was doing a hell of a job getting me all hot and bothered after having been almost invisible for the last two weeks.

I'd resisted watching at first. I had better things to do than stand at my bedroom window like some sort of old pervert. Over the last couple weeks, I'd entertained the idea that she hadn't even been showing herself off for me. She could just as easily have been feeling free to do as she pleased in what she thought was the privacy of her parents' backyard and I'd made assumptions that I shouldn't have.

When she'd vanished for a bit, I had to think that maybe she was showing off for someone else. There were other houses that could possibly see into her backyard from different angles. It wasn't inconceivable that one of them was the target audience for her little peep show. Now, I was certain that wasn't the case. She was there for me. She wanted me to watch.

"What else would you want me to do to you, Misti?" I mused aloud.

My dick was hard. I wondered what she would do if I went over and broached the subject with her. It could be exactly what she was looking for. Maybe she wanted me to make the first move. Then again, maybe she didn't. It wasn't something I could just magically know, and the thought of picking up the wrong signals from her and ending up in a colossal fuck up didn't appeal to me.

The thought of that was enough to drag me away from the window and put me back behind my desk. The drudgery of answering emails and returning phone calls would deflate my raging hard on quickly. I settled into them, pushing the naked beauty next door out of my thoughts.

"Janice? Hey, this is Dylan Haywood at Haywood Technical Services. We recently ran a test through our local police department, and we've gotten some promising results on the product you and I discussed before. I'd like to sit down with you and talk to you about them at your earliest convenience."

"Oh, Dylan. Of course. I'd love to sit down with you. When is good?"

"Are you free this afternoon?"

"I am. I can give you an hour at 4 p.m."

"That's perfect. I'll see you at your office then," I told her, quickly closing out the conversation.

Janice was a woman very unlike Misti. There was no mistaking what she wanted, and it had nothing to do with quality tech services. Every meeting with her was a careful dance around the subtle innuendo and outright suggestive comments she was prone to make to me.

Even the meeting time was exactly what I had expected. *"I can give you an hour at 4 p.m.,"* was laced with an unspoken ending. She had purposely placed the meeting so that it coincided with the closing of her offices in hopes that I'd suggest dinner, drinks, or hell, even bowing her over her desk for a good, hard fuck.

Unfortunately for her, I wasn't the least bit interested in her. She was attractive enough, but she struck me as the type of woman you'd find boiling a bunny on your stove given the chance. I wasn't interested in long term relationships. I was barely out of one as it was. Plus, I didn't need anything interfering with our business dealings. I wasn't opposed to sexing up a hot business associate, but I was both picky and careful about who I banged.

Perhaps that was the appeal of Misti. I mean, part of the attraction was obvious. She was young, hot, and free-spirited. Who wouldn't get a boner just looking at her? The thing for me though was that I suspected she didn't see me as more than some older guy she could bang while she was home for the summer and bored. In the fall, she would go back to school and things would just end naturally—a no-strings-attached summer fling—or she might just want to let me watch.

The thought of pile driving her sweet little pussy was getting me hard again, but I resisted the urge to go back upstairs to see if she was still at it. Instead, I picked up the phone and called a woman I'd been seeing on and off again since my divorce. Well, it was probably more accurate to say we'd been hooking up. She was no more interested in anything serious than I was, but she never said no to a nice dinner and getting fucked for dessert.

"Hey, Deb. It's Daniel. Are you busy tonight?"

"I've got a thing at eight, but free until then. What did you have in mind?"

"I have an appointment in the city at four, but I'll be out before five. I can pick you up at work for dinner and then we can do whatever until you need to go."

"Dinner and whatever sounds perfect. See you at five."

"See you then," I told her.

We said our goodbyes and I ended the call. I considered my next move for a moment and then picked up the phone again, finding a number and then making another call.

"Hey, Detective Philips. This is Dylan Haywood. You want to run another test tonight?"

"Sure. When?"

"I was thinking about nine. I'll be done with some other things by then and want to drive out to do some distance testing. I have the data reports on range, but I want to live test one of the prototypes myself."

"I'll be there. I'm on a split today, the last half of my shift starts at eight, so I'll boot up the test hub when I get back in. Give me about fifteen minutes to get my shit together and make a fresh pot of coffee to replace the sludge they have left at the end of the day, and you can fire at will."

"Perfect. Talk to you later."

"Yep."

I put my phone on my desk and looked toward the stairs. I felt the pull toward them, the desire to go back to the window called to me. No. I wasn't going to let some sweet young pussy drag me back up there to gawk at her. Instead, I tossed what I'd need for later in the leather messenger bag I'd bought myself when I first started my business. It was like an old friend at this point. I pulled a set of keys from the hidden security cabinet in my office and headed out the front door.

It had been a while since I'd driven the classic convertible I'd purchased after my first big payday, but it was still a favorite. I scanned my thumb print across the code box on the last bay of the detached garage and watched as the door slid upward, revealing the baby blue

1953 Cadillac convertible hidden inside. She was a beauty with her white walled tires and polished chrome. More importantly, she was just what I needed to clear my head.

I climbed behind the wheel and started her up, pleased that she was running so smoothly. Of course, I paid someone good money to keep up the cars even when I wasn't using them. Slowly, I pulled her out of the bay and pushed the fob to close the door behind us. Seconds later, we were cruising through the neighborhood on our way out to the highway, white walled tires and chrome catching the eye of passersby.

My meeting with Janice went about as expected. Of course, she was on board with creating the designs I wanted for my product. She was also on board for anything else I had in mind, but I ignored her implied propositions with the charm I was capable of when needed and excused myself promptly at 4:40 p.m. to visit the flower shop just down the sidewalk from her building before returning to my car.

It was just before 5 p.m. when I pulled up to the gates of Deb's building complex and parked my car. I texted her that I had arrived and waited. Getting into the secure area where she worked was practically an act of congress. I was quite certain that she'd run a background check on me before ever going out with me in the first place considering the nature of her job, which I actually wasn't quite certain of the details. Given that it involved working in a bunker on a government facility, I likely didn't want to know.

"Damn, this is nice," a security guard said as he walked over to check me and the car out.

"Thank you," I replied, fishing my identification and registration out for him. Even though he hadn't asked for it, I knew the drill. Despite not being inside their gates, I was still on their property, and he needed to know why. "I'm just waiting on Deborah Sunderland. She should be out in a minute."

"She is expecting you?" he asked, glancing at my documents.

"She is," I told him, holding up my phone to show him where she'd replied to my text while I was talking to him.

"Very good. Take good care of her," he said, handing me back my stuff and taking another lustful look at the car.

"I'll make sure of it," I told him.

I had to wait a good ten minutes in the parking lot before Deb pulled up beside me in her trusty BMW. I knew that it was fortified for safety. I could tell that much just from looking at it, but I had never asked why and doubted she would or even could explain. The mystery of her life is partly what attracted me to her. I felt like I was banging a spy. For all I knew, I might be.

"Look at you out here making a spectacle of yourself," she purred, slipping out of her car, and slipping on a pair of sunglasses.

I was already out of my car and opening her door for her, flowers in hand. It was all very 1950's of me, but she didn't seem to mind that at all. Despite being standoffish in some regards, she did love a bit of pampering and a lot of getting nailed. I watched as she took a seat and stretched out her long, slender legs before closing the door and returning to my side to get behind the wheel.

"Any preference for dinner?" I asked.

"Nope. Gentleman's choice," she replied with a sultry smile.

I knew it would be. It always was. I had made us reservations at Delugi's, a quaint little Italian restaurant we'd been to before and pointed my car toward our destination.

It was only later, sitting across the table from her that I realized how shallow our conversation was. Neither of us ever talked about our work. I didn't because I found work chat boring and whatever she did was certainly not up for discussion, so we talked about the weather and other polite topics while we ate and drank wine.

Usually, I didn't care, but today I was finding it all very annoying to have so little of a connection to someone. I had asked her out to let off some steam, sexually. She was usually a great outlet and it seemed I was the same for her, but today, I just wasn't feeling it. It would seem that my sexual appetite was now squarely focused on Misti.

After dinner, I took her back to her car without so much as a kiss goodnight, making polite excuses about not feeling well. I waited until she was safely inside her car and pulled away before heading in the opposite direction toward my next stop. I had hoped that the night air would clear my head but all I could think about was the naked girl next door.

"Fuck me," I muttered into the darkness of the rural highway as I made my way out toward the rolling hills of the countryside.

Chapter 9

Misti

"He left," I told Stephanie on the phone later that night.

"What?" she asked.

"Dylan, the neighbor. Mom is gone until tomorrow and Dad was at work, so I used the alone time to put on a little show for him. He was there for a while, but then he left while I was still fingering myself."

"Maybe he had to go spank the dragon," she replied.

"Spank the dragon? What sort of guys have fucking dragons?"

"Hell if I know. I don't fuck guys, but my girl has some very interesting dildos," she said with a laugh.

"Well, let me assure you that most guys don't have enough to call a dragon, but I have high hopes that he's at least above average."

"You're running out of time. Summer will be gone before you know it and you'll be back here with all these inadequate frat boys you complain about."

"I know. I have to up my game. You don't think I went too far do you? Maybe stripping naked and masturbating wasn't as hot for him as I thought it would be."

"Girl, are you kidding? I'd watch if my neighbor wanted to show me how she likes to get off. Just don't tell on me."

"But he left while I was still going. I looked up and he wasn't there. I thought maybe he would come back, but he didn't."

"He might have had a phone call or a zoom meeting. You don't know. There could be a lot of reasons he had to walk away that you have no idea about. Fuck, for all you know, he walked away because you're hot and he came watching you get off."

"I think I need to step up my game."

"How? You going to go masturbate at his front door? Or maybe ask to come in and spank your slit for him on the living room floor?"

"You have such a way with words," I teased.

"I know. It gets all the chicks," she shot back.

"Right," I told her, my face screwed into a frown. "I'm gonna go. I need to figure out my next move and find something to eat. I don't think Dad is coming home. He was due an hour ago."

"That sounds par for the course," she told me. "No wonder you have daddy issues."

"Fuck you. I don't have daddy issues," I protested.

"Says the woman masturbating for the neighbor who is twice her age and obsessing because he didn't stick around to watch her climax."

"Fine. I have daddy issues then. I'm going to order a pizza and drink whatever isn't locked up in the liquor cabinet or the wine chiller in the kitchen. I'll call you later."

"Later!" she said, ending the call.

Stephanie was well aware of my father's shortcomings. I didn't like the label, but she was probably right in saying my daddy issues were why I wanted to fuck the much older neighbor. It was sort of disturbing if you thought about it, so I chose not to. Both the booze locations upstairs were locked so I ordered a pizza on my phone app and liberated a bottle of red wine from the wine cellar while I waited.

Kicking back on the sofa, I poured myself a glass and sipped it, considering the possibilities. I could give up on Dylan and find someone more accessible. My father had plenty of rich friends who hated their wives and would love to fuck the nubile daughter of one of their equals on the side. Still, that seemed somehow whorish. I didn't want to fuck just anyone. I wanted Daniel. I just needed to be more direct.

Most importantly, my parents could not know. That made things tricky with him living right next door, but there had to be a way to spend time with him that they wouldn't pick up on. My father was gone enough that I could spend hours there without him ever realizing it, but my mother was almost always home, and she had eyes like a hawk, plus her little neighborhood cohorts were all busy bodies.

It occurred to me that the easiest way to spend time with him was to have a reason to be at his house. If I told my parents I was going to be going over there for some purpose that made sense to them, they wouldn't think twice about it. I mean, we'd known him for years. They trusted him and they would trust him not to do any harm to me.

I could offer to clean his house, but I don't think that either he or my parents would buy that I wanted to spend my summer as a maid. In fact, my mother would probably find it appalling that the neighbors might think we must be in financial peril if I needed to get a summer job. Rich kids don't work in the summer around here unless they have dropped out of college and are being taught a lesson.

It's unfair, in a way. I would love to work in the summers. It would give me something to do, and I could get a job where I could meet the kind of men I wanted to spend time with instead of incels, prudes, and dudes that came if a breeze happened past. I should have gone to Paris with some of my friends from school. Instead, I was here, bored off my ass and fantasizing about old men.

I had already finished the bottle of wine by the time the pizza arrived. I considered seducing the pizza guy. He was okay looking and well built, but he looked like he might be jail bait and that was definitely not on my agenda. I paid for the pizza, letting him get a good eyeful of my braless breasts through my sheer tank top and then sat the pizza on the coffee table in the den while I retrieved a second bottle of wine.

My phone buzzed as I returned. It was my father texting me he was going to stay in the city overnight. I threw my phone across the carpet and plopped down on the sofa to open my pizza box and pull out a slice. I took a bite and picked up the corkscrew to open the wine, tipping it back to drink straight from the bottle.

"Fucking great," I mumbled. "A night alone and fuckin' nothing to do."

I turned on the television and clicked through the channels for a while before turning it back off and turning on some music. After a while, I got back up to retrieve my phone. I opened my Tinder app, swiped left on a bunch of losers, and put it back down with a sigh before pouring myself a proper glass of wine and settling into my pizza.

I contemplated things for a bit longer before making a decision. Setting my wine and pizza aside, I got up, went upstairs to change into something a bit more appropriate for my mission, a mini skirt that showcased my legs and a tank top that was barely there. I added a pair of stilettos.

"No. Too much. You look like you're headed for a street corner to sell sex for crack," I said, looking in the mirror with a scowl.

I took the stilettos back off and put on a simpler pair of wedges. Better. This looked more like I was just hanging about the house looking fabulous and less like I was desperate and trying way too hard. I pulled my long hair up into a ponytail and let it cascade down between my shoulder blades to swish seductively back and forth as I walked away and smiled at myself in approval.

I brushed my teeth, added a touch mascara to my already long lashes and dotted on some lip gloss in the bathroom. There. Now I was the All-American girl next door. I took a deep breath, willing myself not to chicken out of this and then headed back downstairs.

I marched out the front door before I could change my mind and made my way down the drive toward the sidewalk, then turned up his driveway. I had never even realized before that there was no gate in the fences between our houses, but then again, why would there be? His front gate was open, which I found odd but I continued on, second guessing myself the whole way to his front door.

What if he said no? He very well might. But it wasn't like I was propositioning him. I was giving him an opening to proposition me—perhaps not today or even tomorrow, but hopefully soon. I felt like I was moving in slow motion toward his door, but I arrived at last, my heart thudding noisily against my chest. I was usually much calmer than this. I was way out of my league.

I almost turned around and left but then flood lights kicked on and I was suddenly bathed in blinding lights. I reached up and pushed the buzzer and waited. Nothing happened. No one responded via intercom or by opening the front door. Surely he was here with the front entrance open and all. I rang the buzzer again. Still, no one came.

Feeling thwarted and downtrodden, I turned to leave. I had only moved a few steps away from his front door when I heard a voice coming from beside me. My heart stopped and I froze, slowly turning toward the sound.

Chapter 10

Dylan

"Misti?" I said, walking around the corner of the house from the garage.

I was barely in from my failed night out with Deb and my trial run with the prototype. Usually, I would have gone in the side door, but it had caught my attention when the floodlights up front went off. I had forgotten to close the front gate and was concerned about who had wandered in at this hour, so I went around the front.

I hadn't expected to see her standing there looking impossibly perfect. She was turned sideways when I first spotted her, the minuscule skirt she was wearing barely covering what I imagined to be beautiful half-moons of her perfectly rounded ass. Her breasts were doing their best to break free of a white tank top that was so thin that the lights upon her clearly showed the outline of nipples hardened against the night breeze.

She looked even better up close than she had over by the pool—ebony hair pulled up in a ponytail that I suddenly found myself wanting desperately to wrap around my hand while she knelt in front of me. I was getting hard just thinking about it and that was what broke the spell. I couldn't walk up to her with a fucking boner. I shook my thoughts away as I finished closing the gap between us, trying to focus on her gorgeous face instead of her barely covered chest.

"Yes. Um, Daniel. How are you?" she said, sounding meek.

"I'm good. Is everything okay?" I asked, glancing at my watch as I realized it must be late.

She looked horrified for a moment, looking down at a blank wrist and then back up to me as she realized she wasn't wearing a watch.

"Yes. It's fine. I'm sorry. I didn't realize how late it had gotten. I can come back later."

"No. It's fine. You're here now. What do you need?" I asked.

I wanted desperately to invite her in, to let things unfold however they happened, but I was hesitant. I decided it was better to see what she was here for first.

"Well, I was looking for a bit of summer work, you know just to kill some time and our pool is down for the summer, so I was hoping we could strike a deal. Would you be interested in letting me clean your pool in exchange for me swimming there a bit?"

"Oh. I—well, I have a pool guy. He comes every weekend."

She looked disappointed and a little lost, but she didn't leave. Instead, she bit her lip and looked around uncertainly like she didn't know what to do next. It was incredibly hot.

"It does get a bit dirty during the week though. If you were willing to come by and just net out the leaves and things that end up in there between his more extensive visits, I suppose that would be great. You could do a quick tidy up and then swim as much as you want."

I considered telling her that she could just come and swim, but I sensed that she felt she needed more of a reason to be over here. I couldn't quite tell what game she was playing here, but I wasn't opposed to finding out. Perhaps she intended to put on a bit more of a private show for me over here and I certainly wasn't opposed to that possibility.

"Really? That would be great," she said, perking back up. "What time should I come over?"

"Whenever you want. Stop by tomorrow afternoon, say at about one? I'll give you the code to the entrance and a key to the back gate so you can come and go as you please even if I'm not home."

"That sounds great," she said, but her tone didn't match her words. I could tell that she had been hoping for more interaction between us on her visits.

Obviously, I wanted that too, but I just wanted to be careful with this. Though Misti had lived beside me for years and had grown into a very beautiful woman, the fact that she'd been so bold in her backyard the last few weeks made me question whether she was someone I could trust to be discreet.

Did I want to fuck her? Yes, in the worst way. Did I want everyone to know about it? Not so much. I needed to spend a little time with her and see who she truly was before I let things go past her little backyard shows.

"Fantastic. I'll see you tomorrow then?"

"Tomorrow, it is," she said with a sultry smile, turning to sashay back toward the front gate, that intoxicating pony tail swishing provocatively back and forth across the center of her back and her beautiful ass begging to be touched. I watched her for a few minutes before returning to the garage to lock it and then going into the house.

I sat down on the sofa with the prototype in hand and tweaked some of the settings, pulling up the readings on my computer to see how the changes were affecting its output. Tonight's test hadn't been as successful as I would have liked. The range wasn't quite what it should be once I had hit the more mountainous area where thick tree coverage blocked the GPS signal.

If this device were to work as intended, it needed to emit a strong enough signal regardless of the conditions. Women were abducted every day and taken to locations that were remote where they wouldn't be noticed by too many prying eyes. This thing had the potential to save lives, but only if it worked as intended. Otherwise, it was just an expensive piece of jewelry.

I laid it aside and let my thoughts drift back to Misti. She had crossed the bridge between us. There was no way she needed a summer job. I was well aware of how much money her father was worth and also that he would not approve of her working, for me or anyone, but I also knew that she wasn't serious about a job. She was only serious about access, which meant she was ready to take things to the next level.

The thought made me smile. I cautioned myself not to push her but to let her take things at her own pace. She couldn't be home much longer for summer, maybe a couple of months if she wasn't returning early. It was enough time for a good summer fling. I was looking forward to burying my cock in her smoothly shaved pussy—hopefully soon.

Glancing at the clock, I saw that it was getting late, and I had an early day tomorrow. I put my work away and made my way upstairs to bed, stripping down and slipping between the fresh clean sheets that had been put on this morning. A lot of men with my money would have a live-in maid. Hell, a lot of men with my wealth would live in a much bigger house on an estate somewhere. I just liked to keep things simple. I have a woman that comes in a few times a week and that is enough for me.

I lay in the dark and thought about Misti again, wondering what it would feel like when I finally got to bury my cock inside her tight little pussy. I could only imagine that she would be a wild little thing in bed. I imagined her sitting on my cock and riding me, those bodacious tits of hers bouncing up and down with every thrust. I wanted to see that in the worst way.

I was hard—rock hard. I took things into my own hands, slowly stroking myself beneath the sheets as I imagined what it would be like with her. A part of me wished I had invited her in earlier and skipped this little game of hers, but something told me she liked toying with her food. I could wait for her, but it didn't mean I couldn't fantasize about her in the meantime.

I closed my eyes and imagined her above me as I took care of business, bringing myself to a climax in a matter of minutes. It usually took me a lot longer to get off, the product of spending too much time spanking it myself instead of enjoying a proper fuck. Still, I felt optimistic that things might change soon after her visit.

If I was lucky, tomorrow I just might get to find out how serious my young neighbor was about having a bit of fun with the old guy next door. The most important thing was to make sure she wasn't a nutjob, then we could explore what all she was willing to do with me from there. As long as it didn't interfere with my relationship with her father and his company, I couldn't see why I shouldn't have a little fun. I was way overdue.

I slipped down into the covers and flipped my pillow over to the cool side. I was asleep in a matter of moments, a smile on my face and dreams of my perky young neighbor on the horizon.

Chapter 11

Misti

I felt pretty proud of myself as I settled back down onto the sofa with my now cold pizza and the rest of the wine. I finished off the wine and tossed the rest of the pizza in the kitchen for breakfast tomorrow. I chunked the wine bottles in the trash, not caring if my parents saw them. I was old enough to drink and if they didn't want to share their wine with me, they should lock it up.

I teetered back to the living room to pick up my mess. Empty wine bottles were one thing, but a mess left in the den would result in a scolding like I was still a twelve-year-old girl. I detested being treated like a child.

It was still fairly early for bed, at least for me, but tomorrow was a big day and I needed to sleep off all the wine I had drank with my pizza. I didn't want to oversleep or show up looking hungover as fuck. I intended to look like the most fuckable woman on the planet when I arrived next door. Dylan Haywood would not know what hit him once I dropped the cover-up I would have to wear over my suit in order to get past my mother without scorn.

The thought of the day ahead was enough to make me smile. I glanced at myself in the hallway mirror as I passed by and noted how disheveled I looked. Even like this, I was damned fuckable. I had come a long way from that gangly teenager who used to have a crush on Dylan. This was no crush. I had no fantasies about him sweeping me off my feet and being my first lover or any of those things that used to cross my mind when I was sixteen. This was all sex and nothing else. I wanted him to fuck me until I went back to school and then walk away.

I turned from the mirror and made my way up to my room, I stripped off my clothes and got into bed, turning on the TV to watch until I fell asleep. My thoughts drifted back to Dylan and what I hoped would be an interesting rest of the summer. I didn't want to rush things too much, but I didn't have a lot of time. It was pretty obvious that he had been watching me sunbathe, watching the little show I kept putting on for him, so he was definitely interested. Hopefully, things would just happen naturally.

I was still contemplating this when something on the news caught my attention. There was a girl named Hannah that I recognized from one of my classes back at UT. I turned up the volume to better hear what they were saying about her.

"In tonight's news, the search for Hannah Jackson continues. Miss Jackson has been missing for more than a week after disappearing from her dorm late last Wednesday evening. She was last seen on surveillance footage leaving the UT library on foot. A reward has been posted by her family for her safe return," a rather serious looking blonde was saying from the news desk.

I sat up and listened to the rest of the newscast. The blonde anchor turned the segment over to a young redhead standing in front of Ayres Hall, a well-known landmark on campus but also the arts and sciences building. That was exactly where I met Hannah. We were both taking a calculus class.

I didn't know Hannah well, but the brief interactions I had with her were pleasant. She came across as a well-adjusted, kind person. She was very similar to me with big boobs and dark hair. As I continued watching, I realized that she wasn't the only girl missing. How had I not already known about this?

"Miss Jackson is the third woman to go missing from UT in the past month, leading police to believe that there may be a serial abductor in the area. However, none of the women have been located so far, so the families of the missing young women continue to hold onto hope that they will be recovered soon," the reporter said.

The photos of the other two women popped up on the screen. I didn't recognize either of them, but I could see that they resembled Hannah. If there was someone out there taking women, he certainly had a type and it didn't exactly sit well with me that I fit his pattern, even if only in a superficial, physical way. Perhaps that was his only attraction to the women who were missing. It wasn't like most criminals took the time to really get to know random victims, was it?

"For now, many women are dropping the summer classes they had signed up for in hopes of getting ahead of the fall semester and heading home to the safety of their loved ones. While police are urging the young woman attending summer classes here at UT not to panic, they have also expressed the importance of taking precautions for personal safety," the reporter continued.

The reporter droned on about reasonable safety measures. It was the same sort of lecture I got from my parents every time I left for college or went out with friends at night. I doubt there was a woman who hadn't had it drilled into her head from the time she was able to leave home without her parents that she should never let herself be caught alone, especially in the dark. Half the girls my age had permits to carry guns with them everywhere they went, but that just felt like excess paranoia to me.

Well, it had until just now. While I was more than a safe distance from UT right now, I would be going back there in less than two months. If this wasn't resolved before then, I might have to reconsider whether I wanted to be one of those girls that packed a Glock in my handbag just to go to the gym.

"We'll have further updates as the situation develops. Back to you in the studio, Candy."

I chuckled. The blonde anchor looked like someone who would be named Candy. She spoke in a perky little voice as if she was introducing herself. It seemed out of place when she was reading a report about something as dire as women being taken from a college campus.

Clicking off the television, I pushed thoughts of missing women out of my head and refocused my energy on Dylan. I was beyond excited about tomorrow. I wondered what he must have been thinking when I turned up at his house. Neither of us had spoken about my little sunbathing activities, but we both knew what had been going on.

I was sure now that he was interested, but it still didn't mean he'd go through with anything. There was a chance that he just enjoyed looking at me and had no intention of ever touching me. I wanted this to be his choice. In my mind, I'd already been forward enough, and it was his turn to take the reins. I'd shown myself off to him. I'd masturbated for him and now, I'd given him an opening by making myself easily available to him.

What more did a girl have to do to get some dick?

That was the question though, wasn't it? My time here was getting shorter by the day. I'd already been home for a month and had less than two to go. If Dylan didn't show some sign that he wanted to do more than gawk at me from his window soon, I'd have to give up on him and settle for someone more obtainable. I really hoped that I didn't have to do that though. I had my sights set on him.

I lay there in the dark, feeling somehow still a bit unsettled from the news and oddly excited thinking about what it might be like with Dylan. Tomorrow, I might find out just how far he was willing to take our little game. My bet was he was just as interested in getting physical as I was. Not many men could resist me. I wasn't overly vain, but I also wasn't oblivious to the way men looked at me and though I couldn't quite make out any details from his second-floor window, I knew he had lingered there to watch.

Tomorrow, I would give him a more up close and personal look. I had a new bikini he hadn't yet seen. Not only was it small, but it was mostly transparent when wet. The pale pink color would stand out nicely against my summer kissed skin and the moment I got in that pool, it would not leave much to the imagination. I rubbed my left leg across the top of the opposite one, enjoying the smoothness. Thank goodness I'd gotten them waxed this week in anticipation of some fun.

I began to drift off, finding my way to a decidedly erotic dream starring none other than Dylan Hayward.

Chapter 12

Dylan

"Good morning," I said, trying very hard not to stare as I answered the door.

Misti smiled brightly and returned my greeting, seeming a little anxious despite how completely perfect she looked otherwise. She was wearing a pair of shorts that were so tiny and fitted that I wondered how she had gotten in them, much less managed to move around. The crop top she wore over them wasn't doing much to cover her generous breasts either. Between the two was a perfectly flat stomach that begged to be traveled by fingers, lips, and tongue.

I shook off my errant thoughts and invited her in, motioning her down the long hallway that led to the central foyer and then out toward the French doors that led to the patio and pool. My house wasn't overly large for someone with my assets. I had never seen the point in owning some large uncomfortable house just because I could. The gated community we lived in was exclusive enough to keep out the sorts who meant to do harm but not so pricey that only blue bloods lived here.

"I'll show you where everything is and then I'll give you the code to the gate so you can access the pool from outside the house."

"Outside the house?" she repeated, looking disappointed.

"Yes. I may not always be home when you come to clean, or I may be working and not answer the door. My lab sits in the back corner of the house, and I don't always hear the doorbell when I'm in there."

"You don't have servants?" she asked with a furrowed brow.

"No. Why would I? It's just me here. I have some folks who come by to clean, do the lawn, and clean the pool here and there. Beyond that, there isn't much for them to do and they'd be under my feet when I'm trying to work."

"I get it. We don't have any either, just some part-time help that comes in for the same reasons. Mom likes to do most things herself."

"Of course. How is your mother?"

"She's fine," she replied, enunciating the last word in a way that made me feel she wasn't.

"And your father?"

"You know Dad. All work, no play."

"Yes, he does tend to give it his all, doesn't he? He's a good man though," I told her, stepping through the doors and out onto the patio. "Everything you need is over here. There's no need to bother with any of the pump settings or anything like that. The only thing I need for you to do is to pull out any floaters on the surface, clean the sides of any debris and empty the baskets."

"Oh, I can do all that. Dad used to make me do it for our pool. Do you have socks?"

"Socks?" I repeated, confused.

"It's easier to just get in the pool with socks on my hands and feet to clean the side walls of debris that sticks there."

"Oh, socks. Yes. Of course. There are some in the pool shed. Come on and I'll show you."

She followed me to the shed that sat in one corner of the pool, looking at it with a bemused smile as we approached it.

"Is that a mermaid?" she asked.

I felt myself blush. It was unusual for me to be embarrassed by something, but that mermaid was an eyesore that my ex insisted on putting there. It was large, with iridescent scales and bejeweled eyes. Her breasts were large and her nipples hard. Lydia had her created by a local artist to obscure the small shed beside her from the pool area because she felt it was an eyesore. So, she'd hidden it behind an even bigger eyesore.

"Yes. I've been meaning to have her removed but just haven't gotten around to it yet."

"You don't like mermaids?"

"I don't like that mermaid," I said with a slight smile or maybe it was more of a grimace. "Anyway, here is the shed she is hiding. There is a skimmer and the tub beside it is full of socks. They may look dirty due to stains, but Harley, the woman that comes in during the week, washes them and puts them back out here when she comes to do laundry."

"Perfect. Shall I get started then?"

"Knock yourself out. I've got some work to do in the house, so I'll leave you to it. Feel free to use the pool as much as you want and let me know before you leave so I can give you the code to the gate to use when you come over."

"Great. Thanks."

We both stood there awkwardly for a moment as if there was something that remained unsaid and then I turned and walked back to the house, fighting the urge to look back. I could only imagine that she was stripping off her already sparse clothes to reveal an even more revealing bikini. Hell, knowing this girl, she might clean the pool naked.

Instead, I made my way to my lab. There were no windows in there, so that would keep me from giving in to the temptation to watch her.

After Lydia left me, I converted what used to be a large dark room to a clean room for working with some of the tech inventions I had going. She had never really used it anyway. She fancied herself a photographer but spent most of her time taking selfies for social media.

The hum of the bright lights that helped me see even the smallest of the components I worked with somehow soothed me. I never played music or turned on a TV here. I liked to work without distraction when I was focused on my work. Today's task was improving the range on the chip. It was a challenge due to its tiny size, slightly smaller than a micro-SD card.

Before I knew it, several hours had passed. I hadn't heard a knock on the door or anything that might indicate that Misti was done. My eyes and fingers were both tired from fiddling with the tiny chip anyway, so I took a break to check on the situation. As I approached the French doors, she was just climbing out of the pool on the opposite end. Much to my surprise, she did appear naked.

As she turned slightly, I could see that she did, in fact, have on a bathing suit, but it was so tiny and so light colored that it was easily missed. Somewhere between her beautifully tight asscheeks, there was undoubtedly a tiny string of pink thong that connected to the sliver of material that covered her pussy. The small triangles of the top barely covered her nipples and were mostly transparent.

I took a deep breath and let it out as my cock reacted to her hardened nipples. She looked nothing short of a swimsuit model stepping out of the water to have her photo taken for the cover. I knew I should move away from the doors, but I was completely mesmerized by the perfection of her form.

Her long, dark hair begged to be wrapped around my hand as I put her back in the pool and fucked her along the edge of it. I wondered what she would do if I just opened the doors and strolled out, shedding my clothes on the way to skinny dip and then invited her over to enjoy a bit of water play with me. I doubt she'd be shocked. I doubt she'd say no. She was making it pretty obvious what she wanted.

And yet, I held back. I wasn't sure what my reasons were, but there was just something that made me reluctant. Was it because of my sometimes business relationship with her father or was it something more?

I wasn't even sure what the answer to that was, but it was very unlike me to resist going after something I wanted. I didn't do that in my business pursuits, and I certainly didn't do it when it came to women, at least not since Lydia left. She'd broken me in a way I rarely allowed myself to acknowledge, and I had no desire to suffer at the hands of a cold woman again.

Besides, Misti was young—too young and too close to home. Sure, I could have some summer fuck fling with her while she was home from school, but what if she decided she wanted more? What if she wanted something real from me? Women with daddy issues, which knowing her father, I was quite certain she had, tended to be clingy. I didn't want to be the poor middle aged sod who got twisted up with the attention seeking behavior she'd already exhibited.

I was completely lost in my thoughts, watching her with a stiff cock, when I saw her turn toward the French doors. I bolted sideways before she could see me watching her, flattening myself against a nearby wall and hoping she wasn't headed directly for the door. I didn't want to explain the tent in my shorts.

Chapter 13

Misti

I had spent three days at Dylan's and still nothing. No sparks, no overtures, no mind-blowing impromptu sex. I'd gone over twice last week and was headed there again tomorrow. I'd caught him watching me on the very first day, though it had only been for a few minutes at the end. I'd climbed out of the pool, intent on approaching him. I had it all planned out in my head. I was going to walk up to him, dripping wet in my almost nothing there swimsuit and tell him that the pool was clean.

"Would you like to come in for a swim with me?" I would ask.

"I'd love to," he'd reply. "Let me get my swimsuit."

"You don't need one," I'd tell him, turning to walk provocatively back into the pool, stripping off my bikini as I walked. At the edge of the steps, I'd turn back toward him, letting him get a good long look at what I had to offer. "You coming?" I'd purr.

Instead, none of that had happened. I'd only gotten a week of cleaning the neighbor's pool like some sort of neighborhood charity case. It was obvious he didn't need the help. The pool had barely been dirty either time I cleaned it and showed no signs of being any worse off yesterday. There had been a handful of leaves and a few bugs floating about. I scooped them out and pouted for a bit before donning some socks and wiping down the sides.

The last time I was there, he had watched me a little longer. I'd seen him up in the upstairs window looking down at me while I floated about the deep end, hiding my eyes behind sunglasses so I appeared to have them closed. He'd stood there for quite some time while I soaked up the sun and observed. At one point, he walked away but he returned.

So, we were still where we always were. I had stayed outside in the sun, and he stayed inside, pretending he wasn't interested. Time was getting shorter. I had only a little more than a month left before I had to go back to school. What I needed was to step up my game another notch. I had to wonder if he was worth it. I was doing all the chasing here and he didn't seem inclined to cross any lines with me. I could settle for someone else, but I knew I wouldn't. He'd caught my eye and now I was intent on having him before I left.

I could go over there on my off days to just lay by the pool or swim. He'd given me the gate code and said he was fine with me using the pool whenever I wanted, even if he wasn't home but what good was it if he wasn't there to see me. Rather than wear out my welcome, I decided to just resume laying out in my own backyard and hoping he'd see me there, making him want me enough that he did something about it.

Of course, there was no chance of getting too out of hand. My parents were both back at home most days now. My mother's night away had turned into several days while my father had returned home the next morning. They weren't speaking to one another for whatever reasons but that wasn't unusual. It's been a recurring occurrence since I was a child that they sometimes had these little spats and spent some time apart. It was never long. Just enough time for Mom to cool down and come back home.

Dad, on the other hand, rarely left just because he was annoyed or angry. If he did, you could usually find him at the office working on something. I'd be shocked if I found out he had ever cheated on my mother or anything like that. His only mistress was his company. Mom, on the other hand, might have a lover or several. If she did, she at least had the good taste to keep it very discreet.

I glanced out the window and saw the angry gray clouds hovering in the morning sky. It was looking like a nasty day lay ahead. I wouldn't be going over to Dylan's pool or laying out in my backyard in this weather. Instead, I called Stephanie to talk for a bit. She and I were supposed to meet near campus soon to sign the lease on our new apartment for the upcoming semester. Plus, I'd gotten my schedule and wasn't happy with one of them, but I'd missed the online drop and add date. I'd have to do it in person now.

"How's it hanging?" Stephanie chirped as she answered the phone.

"Short, shriveled, and slightly to the left," I replied with a chuckle.

Stephanie was often prone to what we referred to as "dude talk" that was really quite nonsensical with both of us being women, but we found it amusing.

"We need to make plans to meet up for the lease thing," she told me.

"Yeah. When do we have to have it all sewn up?"

"I've already signed, so it's just a matter of your signature and then they'll give us the keys. A couple of weeks will be okay. Is that good for you?"

"Sure. I'll give you another call in a few days to set it up."

"You so busy with that hot neighbor of yours that you have to consult your schedule to see when you won't have your legs up in the air?" she teased.

"I wish. I still haven't gotten him past watching me from the window," I griped.

"Dude, what's wrong with him? Has he even seen you?"

"Oh, he's seen me. He's seen every single bit of me, but he just doesn't seem inclined to do more than look."

"Idiot. Well, you know, there are plenty of other men out there willing to take his place in line."

"Yeah, I know. I've just decided on this one."

"Well, you're running out of time. Good luck."

"I guess I'm going to need it," I told her glumly.

"You'll get there, chica. I have confidence in you. More importantly, I have confidence in that bodacious rack of yours. If a man can resist that set of tits, he's playing for the other team."

"Thanks. You really know how to lift a girl's spirits."

"Damn right I do, babe. Now, go out there and get that cock."

I laughed and told her goodbye before going back downstairs to pout in the den while streaming Lolita. Perhaps it would give me some inspiration.

"What are you watching?" my mother said as she stepped into the room.

"I don't know," I lied. "Some old sixties film."

She stood watching for a moment and then walked off, leaving me there alone with my thoughts. They quickly drifted back to Dylan and how I was going to push things to the next level. I needed to spend more time at his place, but I didn't need to be pushy about it. I just needed to make myself available.

Today I would wallow in my self-pity. Tomorrow, I would go back to Dylan's house to clean the pool. The weather outside right now was whipping up into a heavy storm, so it meant the pool would be full of debris blowing in with the rain. The filters would have to run, and I'd have to do some more serious cleaning, putting me there for quite a while longer than was usually required.

I contemplated how I wanted to play things with him. Perhaps my antics in my own backyard and my skimpy outfits to his house were too much for him. I decided to dial it back. I didn't want to appear desperate. Perhaps that was what was keeping him at bay. I turned off the television and went to my room, rummaging through my swimsuits until I found what I was looking for.

I stripped down and put on the suit, looking at it in the mirror. I didn't like one-piece suits, but this one did look good on me. It was neon green with a racing stripe down either side in black. It clung to my flat stomach and cupped my breasts, pushing them up so that they were nice and firm with enough cleavage visible above the top of the suit to be sexy but not indecently so.

"Not too bad, Bridges," I said aloud as I twisted back and forth, admiring myself in it.

Tomorrow, I would put on a pair of my more demure hiking shorts and an oversize t-shirt. I'd work in those and then unveil what lay beneath when I was ready to swim. The combination of unflattering clothing and a modest swimsuit should send a message that I wasn't interested but the way this swimsuit fit would remind him what he was missing out on.

I changed again and went back downstairs to find Mom and Dad standing in front of the TV looking very unhappy. Mom looked at me as I walked in and then turned back toward the screen in front of them.

"Misti, have you seen this?" Dad asked, waving toward whatever they were watching. He reached for the remote and turned the sound up so I could hear it better as I moved closer to where they stood. It was the news again. Another woman missing from Knoxville. This one was very unlike the others. She wasn't a student, but a professor teaching English and Literature. Her photo showed a tall, thin woman with sharp features.

"Yes, I've seen some reports."

"I'm concerned about you going back there and being in an apartment alone," he said.

"I won't be alone. I'll be there with Stephanie."

"Stephanie isn't going to do much to protect you. I'm thinking about sending security with you when you go back."

"Don't be ridiculous, Dad. I'm not having some muscled goons follow me around from class to class or when I go out with friends."

"I just want to make sure you're safe."

"I'll be careful, Dad. I know all the rules about personal security. I promise that I won't do anything that puts me in jeopardy. I don't want them to use some horrible picture of me on the news. As a matter of fact, can I pick out a few photos for you and Mom to give to the police in case I go missing? I want them to be flattering," I joked.

"That's not funny. You can't take anything seriously," my mother snapped, storming off.

"Is that a no then?" I called after her before turning back to my father. He scowled at me before turning to walk away. Halfway across the room, he stopped and spoke, not turning around.

"If you fuck up and get abducted, I'm going to put that horrible picture of you in a majorette uniform with your eyes closed and mouth half open on the front page of every newspaper in this country," he said in a completely serious tone.

I chuckled as he disappeared into his study. I turned back to the screen. The other women were flashing across the screen again as the report continued. I *was* taking this seriously, far more seriously than they realized. There might have been an exception—perhaps the professor wasn't even a related case to the others—but the rest of those women were far too similar to me to not consider the worst.

Chapter 14

Dylan

I was surprised to find Misti cleaning the pool in what looked like a t-shirt she borrowed from her father and a pair of loose utility shorts. Later, as I glanced out the window, she had stripped them off to reveal a bathing suit that probably had more material in it than all of her other suits combined. Even the full coverage it offered did nothing to hide the dangerous curves beneath it. Somehow, it was even more alluring than the skimpy bikinis.

I pulled myself away and went to the lab. I had a lot to accomplish today and couldn't afford to be distracted by her. At least she had a good reason to be here today, as there were all sorts of random twigs, leaves, bugs, and other trash in the pool from yesterday's storm. No doubt the pool guy would be happy about having a leg up on having to clean it all up on the weekend too.

I dismissed any thoughts about Misti and went into the lab, busying myself with trying to match up the final version of the chip we'd produced with appropriate jewelry. This project was important to me. It was odd that Misti's father was the one who had originally sparked the idea for it. I chuckled at my mind trying to pull her back into my thoughts and pushed her away from them again, focusing on my work.

The sound of the phone jarred me out of work mode. I put down the piece I was working with and went to see who it was, making a pained face as I answered it.

"Hello, Lydia," I said into the receiver.

"Dylan. I wanted to let you know that I'm getting a divorce."

"Wow, a divorce. That makes two this year doesn't it?"

"I don't need your snide remarks. I need a place to stay."

"Excuse me? What does that have to do with me?"

"I want to come home."

"Yeah, that's not going to happen."

"Look, I didn't mean to spring that on you over the phone. I guess I'm a bit out of sorts over everything that is happening. I'd like to come over so we can sit down and chat."

"No need, Lydia. That ship has sailed and I'm not getting back on board for a second voyage."

"Dylan, can't we just ta—" she started saying, but I had already ended the call.

It rang again immediately. I put it in silent mode and laid it back on the counter before returning to my work. Right or wrong, I felt invigorated by the conversation. It wasn't the satisfaction of having her try to come crawling back. It was the realization that I was over it. I well and truly didn't care about her anymore.

Sure, I still had feelings for her. If she was in some sort of real trouble, I'd probably try to help her, but she wasn't. For some women, 'I need a place to stay' might mean they were destitute or feared for their safety. In her case, it meant she was trying to manipulate her way back into a life she had already wrecked one time. She had plenty of money to get a place to stay and hire security if she didn't feel safe. In fact, she still had plenty of *my* money. Fuck her.

I went back to my work, losing all track of time as I tinkered with things like some sort of mad scientist. I picked up a gold bangle bracelet from nearby. It was styled like one of the old Gregorian slave bracelets popular with the BDSM community. It was hinged on one side and clasped together on the other. The clasping mechanism was a sort of pointed spike with a spring-loaded mechanism on one side, when you pushed it into the other side of the bracelet, the spring pushed in and then popped out on the other side, locking the ends of the bracelet together. In order to remove it, you had to use a pin of some sort to push the spring back down so it would slip back through the capture device.

I picked up a small instrument nearby and slid it into the tiny release hole to open the bracelet. It was hollow inside, providing ample space to work with. I began fashioning a small shell to house the chip and mounted it on the inside using a tiny bit of solder so that I didn't damage the bracelet and then I used a pair of tweezers to insert the chip. Once I was done, I examined the bracelet for any evidence that it had been altered. It was still flawless.

I smiled and laid it down on the table. A bit of testing and it would be good to go. I glanced at my watch. Fuck, it was almost four. It was too late to set up a test from the office. I contemplated whether I wanted to skip it and just go for a test later tonight directly with my police liaison or wait until tomorrow. I didn't want to waste his time. My impatience would just have to be checked for now. I'd do it tomorrow.

Leaving the lab, I noticed that Misti was gone from the pool. She must have finished up her work and left already. I wasn't sure if I was glad she wasn't there to further test me or if I was disappointed. There was a good chance today that I might have at least gone out there and swam with her. I could use a bit of relaxation and getting to know her a bit better couldn't hurt, could it?

Instead, I decided to burn off some of my energy by going to work out in the garage. Lydia had always complained about my conversion of the garage into a gym because she couldn't park her car in there after I did it. Never mind the fact that I had built the multi-car detached garage on the opposite side of the house and made a covered walkway just for her to connect the two. Of course, that wasn't there anymore. I'd torn it down in a fit of rage after she'd left—a protest against everything I'd done for us not ever being good enough.

Lydia. Thoughts of her again after so long without them. I'd stopped thinking about her months ago and she'd reinserted herself with one little phone call. I picked up my phone and glanced at it. There were three missed calls from her and one voicemail. I dialed the voicemail and deleted the message without listening to it before changing clothes and heading to the garage. I was well into my workout when I heard a voice behind me in the open door to the garage.

"Dylan?" she said softly.

I barely heard her over the music I had going. I turned to see her standing there in the baggy clothes she'd been in earlier, looking impossibly down to earth and adorable instead of like the sex on a stick look she usually embraced. She had her hair pulled up into a messy bun that I wanted to tangle my fingers in and a slight smile on her face.

I stood up, sweat dripping down my bare chest from the workout and the temperature of the garage. Though I had a mini split installed out here for heating and cooling, I preferred to work out without it on, if it wasn't too hot. The rain from the day before had cooled things a bit so I only had a fan on today.

"Oh, Misti. I thought you had already left."

"I did. I just wanted to come back over and ask for a favor."

"A favor?"

"Yes. I know you said I was welcome to swim after cleaning the pool, but with our pool down all summer, would you mind if I came over on days that I'm not cleaning the pool to just swim or lay out? It's so much better to lay in the sun when you can cool off by jumping in the pool every once in a while."

"Sure. Of course. You are welcome to use it all you want. You may have noticed that I'm not out there very much myself. Someone should get some use of it."

"Yes and I wouldn't want to leave the lovely mermaid out there all alone the whole summer," she teased.

I laughed and nodded in agreement. "Right. Can't have that."

"I'll only be here for another month or so, about six weeks at this point. I have to head back to UT for the fall semester."

"Of course. You're what, a sophomore?"

"I'll be a senior this year."

"Wow. Time flies. It seems like just yesterday you were a teenager selling me magazines for your class trip in this same garage."

She looked embarrassed but nodded. Though she was smiling, I could tell she wasn't thrilled about having her youth pointed out. I wasn't sure I liked the thought that I had been lusting after someone I knew at a much younger age either. There was nothing wrong with it now. She was most definitely a grown woman, but it somehow felt a little bit on the seedy side.

"I've seen that there have been some abductions there this summer. Will you be in a safe place?" I asked, realizing immediately that I probably sounded like her father.

"Yes. I'll be fine. Dad wants to send a bodyguard with me but I told him no. I didn't want to say it to him, but some of those girls looked a bit like me. The last one didn't, but the rest of them did and it was a little unnerving. I might get a taser or something to carry."

"Or a real gun."

"I don't know how to use a real gun. I'd probably just shoot myself in the foot or something."

"There's nothing to it. It's just a matter of practice. I can help you if you like."

"That sounds interesting, but I don't even know how to go about buying a gun."

"Are you kidding? This is Nashville. You can pretty much get a gun anywhere. Lucky for you though, I happen to own a shooting range with a gun shop. I have to take care of something in the morning, but how about we make plans to go down there tomorrow afternoon and pick you out a gun. I'll teach you to use it at the range and we can practice when you have time between now and when you go back to school."

"Really?" she squealed. "That would be so great of you. Are you sure it's not a problem?"

"No problem at all," I told her.

"Fantastic. Just call me tomorrow when you're ready to go and I'll meet you over here," she said, fishing her phone out of her pocket. "What's your number? I'll send you a text, so we know how to get in touch with one another."

I rattled off my number and she typed something in and then smiled, shoving the phone back in her pocket. I heard the ding of a text notification from my phone on a nearby shelf.

"Sounds like I got it. I'll call you tomorrow when I know what time I'll be done."

"Perfect," she said, sounding excited. "See you tomorrow."

I watched her as she bounded back down the driveway and stepped through the open gate, turning toward her house, and disappearing. I wasn't sure what I had just signed up for, but something told me I was headed for an adventure. Walking over to my phone, I read the text she had sent. It just said, "Looking forward to tomorrow."

I grinned widely, realizing that so was I.

Chapter 15

Misti

I woke up early, too excited to sleep. I finally had my chance to spend some time with Dylan and I didn't want to blow it. I had no idea what time he would be ready to go but I wanted to look perfect. Jumping out of bed, I showered and got ready to go out. If I got to the day spa my mother frequented when they opened, they would work me in without an appointment. I wanted to get a fresh wax and a mani-pedi.

"You're up early. Where are you headed?" my mother asked as I ducked into the kitchen to grab an iced coffee from the fridge to drink on my way.

"Spa day," I replied, heading for the front door.

"You should have told me. I could have made an appointment and we could have made a day of it," she called after me.

I was already on my way out the door and didn't respond. The fact that she would have turned it into an all-day mother-daughter event was precisely why I hadn't mentioned it to her. I'd take my chances at a work and if that failed, there was another spa not far away that I didn't like as well but they usually have a free space that they kept open for VIPs. All I had to do was name drop my father and I'd be golden.

I hopped into the candy apple red Tesla Model 3 my father had special ordered for me. He usually was much tighter with his money, but he'd splurged on this for me because he wanted me to have a safe car to drive back and forth between Nashville and Knoxville when I was in school. It wasn't my first choice, but he had a list of criteria any car he purchased for me had to meet before purchase and I'd just let him do his thing. It was just a car, after all.

I noted how empty the parking lot at the spa was this time of the morning and smiled. Looked like I was in luck! They had me in and out in under two hours. I still had plenty of time to do a little shopping. Stepping into a little boutique near the spa, I browsed through the clothes in the center rack.

"Looking for anything in particular, honey?" the saleswoman asked.

"I don't know. I have a, um, date later in the day to go to a shooting range. I want something that says 'sexy' without looking like I'm trying too hard."

"Honey, with a figure like yours, you could show up in a toe sack and get a rise out of whoever sees you. Now, if you want to just look like you're not trying, I would suggest a pair of boot cut jeans with boots and a simple summer halter. It's classy and a bit sassy without looking overdressed for a mandate."

"A mandate?"

"A man-date. One of those dates where a man takes you to something that he usually does with the boys."

"Ah. Of course. What jeans do you suggest then?"

"Something that looks like you've worn them for a while. What size are you, about a five?"

"Yes, exactly. A bit too much backside to go slimmer, but I need something that tapers in at the waist."

"Yep," she said, glancing at my midriff and then pulling down a pair of jeans from a shelf above the jeans display. "You got boots?"

"Not the kind of boots I think you have in mind."

"Come on," she said, taking me to the other side of the store toward the shoe area. On the way, she grabbed a few halters of different colors from different racks and put them on top of the jeans I was carrying. I was amazed as she pulled down a pair of black boots with a wide heel and a silver buckle without even asking my size and put them on my pile. "Okay. Give those a try and see what you think. Dressing room is over there," she said, pointing the way.

"Thanks," I told her, hurrying over to try on the things so I could get home and get myself all put together to look like I made far less effort than I was actually making.

After a couple of adjustments in choices, I left the store with three pairs of jeans, two halters, a fitted tee, and a pair of boots. That would give me some additional choices for future outings to the gun range. In all honesty, I probably had similar items already in my wardrobe, but it always made me feel sexier when I was wearing brand new clothes and I did need the boots. All of mine were more like what you'd wear to a club rather than everyday wear.

Back at home, I took another shower to remove any remnants of the wax and liberally applied lotion to my skin, enjoying the silky-smooth feel of it as my hands roamed freely. I took my time, resisting the temptation to lay across the bed and masturbate. It would take the edge off of things, but I didn't want to do that. I wanted to feel the full intensity of having him so near to me.

I looked down at my nails. They were filed a little shorter than I usually kept them, but I figured that I didn't need talons if I was going to be handling a gun. They were painted a summer peach color that contrasted nicely with my tanned skin and picked up the tones in the mixed print halter I was planning to wear. I pulled on the rest of my clothes and looked at myself appreciatively in the mirror.

I looked good. I debated leaving my hair down but then decided to pull it up in a high ponytail instead. I added a pair of small bronze-colored earrings and smiled at my reflection. Perfect. Everything about me appeared effortless. Now, all I had to do was wait.

My phone beeped and I jumped, laughing a little at how nervous I felt. Picking it up, I saw that it was Dylan telling me he would be ready to go at two. I wondered if he was already at home or if he would just be showing up then to meet me. I supposed it didn't matter. I just felt a little jumpy and felt curious about what he was doing. I doubt he was over there agonizing over what to wear but it was a bit funny to think he might be.

Now that I had time to meet him, I wondered when I should go over. Should I be a little early, a little late or right on time? A thought occurred to me that I hadn't thought of before—my car. How was I going to explain where I was going with my car still parked out front? I had told Mom I would be working over at Dylan's place cleaning the pool so that she didn't suspect anything else. She'd been surprised but didn't argue with it.

I'd asked her not to tell Dad because he'd be upset that I'd gotten some menial job working for a neighbor and somewhat of a business associate. He wasn't home enough to notice that I was gone and even if he did, he'd just assume I was out with friends. My mother, on the other hand, was nearly always home and would notice me going over at some point. It was best just to get it out in the open with her. I had told her at the end of my first week over there.

"Why would you clean a pool for money? Your father gives you a more than decent allowance," she told me.

"It's not just about the money, Mom. Our pool is down all summer thanks to you being fickle about the tiles you want installed and it's hot. Dylan is paying me to clean the pool and doesn't mind if I swim or lay out by it if I want. It helps him and it's convenient for me."

"Still, you know he's divorced now, and I just don't know how this looks."

"Looks to whom, Mom? Besides, no one is going to notice. He's not home most of the time anyway. He gave me the gate code to come and go as I please. It's fine."

I knew I was stretching the truth a bit about the situation, and I could tell she didn't like it, but really what could she say? I was a grown woman and unless they caught me slipping in and out the front gate, no one could see me over there. His house was hidden behind a large brick fence and had trees overhanging in the front, giving it a bit of privacy.

As for the pool, I'd already checked the visibility back there and determined that it could only be seen by any of the neighbors at the very front. So, I knew not to do anything I didn't want someone to see up there. Other than that, I could get as freaky as I wanted in the pool or on the back section of the deck around it without fear of being caught.

Today though, I wasn't leaving the house in a swimsuit. I would need to cover my tracks. Then it dawned on me that it was really very simple, I would simply wait until it was almost time for me to go over, drive my car down the block and then enter his front gate from the opposite direction. The trees would cover me, and I could park to the side of the house in the guest spots he had beside the garage.

It wasn't a perfect plan, but it would accomplish my mission. I waited until five minutes before two and headed out, relieved to see that the gate was open as I passed and then circling back to enter it. Dylan was outside, pulling one of his cars out of the garage when I parked up. He looked at me with a confused expression.

"Did you want to drive?" he asked.

"Not today. I just don't want my parents to know I've gone somewhere with you, so I told them I had plans and left in my car. They can't see it over here."

"I see," he said, his face bunched up in a scowl for a moment.

I wasn't sure what he was thinking. Maybe he'd back out now that he realized that I didn't want them to know about me spending time with him, even if it was technically innocent at this point. Then he smiled and waved me toward the classic convertible he'd pulled out of the detached garage. I felt relieved as he opened the door and let me climb in.

"Top up or down?" he said, eyeing my hair.

"Oh, down. Definitely down," I told him.

"Down it is," he said happily, cranking a handle to peel it back before getting into the car beside me and starting the car up.

We were on our way. My heart raced with anticipation.

Chapter 16

Dylan

Breezing down the highway in the convertible with Misti draped over the seat beside me felt exhilarating. I couldn't quite put my finger on it but there was something about her that invigorated me. I'd never felt this alive just from having Deb beside me in the car and not even Lydia had affected me like this for a very long time before our marriage ended. Perhaps it was just her youth and beauty that lifted my spirits so much.

I felt a mile tall as we pulled into my parking spot at the Gun Garage. It was a stupid name, but it had been named that when I purchased it and a lot of folks liked their merchandise portraying a cartoonish gun on wheels. It had been a bit of a random purchase shortly after my company took off. I was here to do a bit of target shooting and found out it was on the market.

The owner was elderly and had taken ill. His family wanted nothing to do with it, so they had it up for grabs at a ridiculously low price. I snapped it up and retained the existing staff. I'd made a few changes to the personnel and premises since then, but nothing of consequence. It was profitable and that was all that mattered.

I let Misti browse the guns in the cases and left it to Barnard Smith, known to most simply as Smith, the gunsmith who ran the handgun counter, to explain the pros and cons of each one. After a bit of back and forth and some recommendations, she finally selected a Glock 26 9 mm. It was small, easy to handle, and I knew enough about it to help her learn to operate it without having to hand her off to one of the experts until she was ready to get her concealed carry permit, which was a bonus.

"What will I do with it when I'm not practicing? I can't take it back home with me," she said.

"You can leave it here while you're learning to use it and once you've got your concealed carry permit, you can carry it however you please."

"Even then, I don't know how comfortable I am just having it laying around somewhere. I know girls who carry them in their purse, but I don't want to do that. Seems like a good way to lose a finger or worse."

"Smart girl," I told her as Smith nodded in agreement. "We can hook you up with a proper holster if you want to carry it on your person and I'll throw in a biometric safe for you to keep it in when you're at home or wherever."

She still looked a little doubtful. I got it. Not everyone was comfortable around guns. I wasn't about to insist that she buy one if she didn't want it. I decided it might be best to back this down a bit.

"I tell you what. Let's let you try it out before you make your final selection. Smith, do we have a store Glock 26 in stock?" I asked.

"I think so. Let me check," he said. He disappeared into the back and returned with one of the Glock 26s we used as a loaner for those who wanted to do a bit of shooting but weren't gun owners or, like Misti, just wanted to try out a particular gun. He laid the clip on the counter and turned it sideways to ensure the weapon had been properly cleared before handing it to me.

"Great. Check this one out to Misti Bridges," I told him. "Misti, he will need to see your ID."

"Will do," he said.

Misti fished her driver's license out of her pocket and handed it to him. He began filling out the form in front of him using the info on it and flipped it around for her to sign.

"And what will you be shooting?" he asked me.

"I'm not. I'm just here to teach my neighbor how to shoot. She's headed back to school in Knoxville this fall."

"Oh, right. I've heard there are some girls missing over there. A gun is a good idea."

"Right," I told him. "Alright, I'm going to take her out to the private range. Is it empty?"

"It is. I'll sign it out to you."

"Great. Give me a box of rounds and we'll get out of your hair for a bit. Just put it on my tab."

"Just one box?" he asked.

"Yeah. That'll be enough for today."

Misti stood quietly, looking doe-eyed with all the back-and-forth chatter. I picked up the gun and double checked to make sure it was cleared, not that I didn't trust Smith, it was just always a good habit of practicing gun safety. Satisfied that it was in good order, I picked up the clip and took the bullets he fetched from the cabinet behind him.

"We're ready to go," I told her, nodding toward the exit.

She looked all around curiously as we made our way down the path toward the shooting range reserved for VIPs who wanted to shoot in private without being gawked at. Staff used it to demonstrate new weapons for groups and for personal use if it wasn't booked by paying customers. It was a bit more secluded, preventing shooters on the main range from observing.

Once we were in place, I showed Misti how to load the empty clip and put it into place before also showing her how to remove it and clear the gun. Once we'd gone through the safe handling of the gun, I began showing her how it operated. Finally, we got down to the business of showing her how to hold and shoot it. I could tell she was nervous, but she was paying close attention to everything I said.

She was a quick study. I had been just a little afraid that she might be one of those flighty, careless kind of girls who might not take to the lessons very well and be unsafe with the weapon, but I had been very wrong. She picked up what I was showing and telling her very quickly and did exactly as I instructed. It was just a matter of improving her aim.

"Do you mind?" I asked, moving in behind her.

She glanced back at me and smiled. It was enough to melt a man, but I tried to keep my thoughts on the lesson at hand.

"Go ahead," she purred.

I positioned myself behind her and steadied her hands on the gun, guiding her sight and showing her how to position the gun to get a better lock on the target. I was surprised at how much she improved just in our one visit. She was a natural but I was enjoying being so close to her so I helped her for a bit longer than I really needed to just so I could enjoy how soft her skin was as I touched her hands and arms.

Her scent was intoxicating, as well. It didn't seem strong enough for perfume. I suspected that it was more of a natural combination of scented lotion, citrus based soap, and floral shampoo that all came together as one incredible scent. If you could bottle whatever she was wearing into one bottle, men would buy it for the women in their lives at any price. I know I would if the woman I desired wasn't standing in my arms.

The thought caught me off guard and I let go of her, stepping away with an uncertain smile. She raised an eyebrow in my direction, but I nodded for her to continue, watching as she took several more shots before laying the gun down in front of her.

"Are you done?" I asked.

"I think so if that's okay. I understand how to use it, but I don't really enjoy it, if that makes sense."

"It does. That's not a bad thing at all. Clear the weapon like I taught you and we'll head back to the clubhouse."

"Okay," she replied, picking up the gun and removing the clip before clearing it exactly as I had shown her earlier. I watched with something akin to pride.

"Fantastic. You're a quick study."

"You have no idea," she purred, the first indication I'd had today that she was interested in anything more than a lesson on how to shoot a gun.

"Let's get you home," I told her after retrieving everything we'd brought out with us.

"Are we still buying a gun?" she asked.

"Do you still want to?" I asked.

"Yeah. I think so. It seems like a good idea."

"Then we are. We'll do the paperwork and Smith will check you out on the database. It won't take long. You can walk out with the gun today."

"I think I'd rather just leave it for now if that's okay. We can come back and shoot some more before I take it off-site. I'd like to get the concealed carry permit, so I don't have to carry it out in the open."

"Fair enough. Smith can store it in a locker for you until you're ready for it to leave the premises."

"Thank you."

I left her with Smith to fill out her paperwork and went to do a quick round of the facilities while I was there. Everything was in good order, but I hadn't expected it to be otherwise. My staff here ran a tight ship. This place had been an excellent investment, it ran like a well-oiled machine thanks to the people who worked for me. I owed them a debt of gratitude. When I returned, Misti met me at the front door of the clubhouse with a huge smile on her face.

"I passed!" she said gleefully. "I'm a gun owner now."

"Excellent. Did Smith sign you up for the concealed carry course?"

"He did."

"Fantastic. I guess we'll head back home then. What time are the folks expecting you?"

"No certain time. Why?"

"Want to stop off for a bite to eat?"

"That would be wonderful. I'm starved."

"Me too."

We left the gun range and went to a little Italian place I always stopped off at when I came out this way. I usually went there alone so it was extremely nice to have company for a change. Over an early dinner, we sat and chatted comfortably with one another. It was surprising how little we knew about each other after having lived side by side for years, but I'd always been a private person and she had been a kid to me—at least until recently.

It was the woman she had become that I was beginning to find completely mesmerizing.

Chapter 17

Misti

I woke up several mornings later to find a message on my phone from Dylan saying that he had gotten called away on business and would be gone when I came to clean the pool. I was disappointed. Since our trip to the gun range, he had taken to coming out and talking to me while I worked. The last time, he had even gotten into the pool, and we'd talked and drank beer until he'd had to leave for a meeting.

When I arrived at the pool, it was quite dirty. The filter would need to be run for a while to help the water circulate and clean itself. I walked toward the shed and stopped dead in my tracks. She was gone. The mermaid was gone. I looked around to see if she'd just been moved, but there was no trace of her. He'd finally had her taken out. In her place was a simple brick wall that hid the ugly shed that sat behind it.

I smiled and went inside to switch on the pump. It roared to life and then shut down. I tried a few more times but it failed each time. Finally, I sent a text to Dylan to let him know that something was wrong. Rather than texting me back, he called.

"It's been on the fritz for a while," he said. "Can you do me a favor and call the pool guy? I don't have his number with me but it's in the card file on my desk."

"Um, I don't have access to your house," I told him.

"You will in a moment. I'll give you the code to get in the back door."

"Oh. Okay. Are you sure?" I asked.

"Yes. I'll be done here soon but if I call them too late, they might not be able to get to it and it might take more than a day or two if I have to get an electrician involved. I have some people coming over this weekend and don't need it looking all brown and contaminated. I could really use the help."

"No problem. I'll take care of it," I said, feeling a little hurt that he was having folks over and hadn't invited me, but I couldn't really expect him to. We seemed to have become friends, but it wasn't looking like it was going to go beyond that and a bit of idle flirtation. He just wasn't willing to cross that line.

"You're a peach. Thanks, Misti."

"Sure," I said. He gave me the code and I entered it into the box on his back door as he spoke. The door clicked open, and I went inside, disarming the system with a separate code while he was still on the phone. He told me where to find the book and who to look for before a woman started calling his name in the background.

"I've got to go, Misti. Thank you so much for this. I'll make it up to you," he said before hanging up.

"Yeah, but not how I want you to," I replied into the deadline.

I called the pool company and told them there was a problem with the pool and they didn't really seem to care until I told them who I was calling for. As soon as I gave them Dylan's name, they told me they would get someone out immediately. I wasn't sure when he would be back, so I decided to wait for them.

I realized I hadn't been inside the house since I was a kid and came over with Dad a couple of times. It seemed different but I couldn't put my finger on exactly how. I walked around, examining everything. The one thing I noted is that it didn't seem terribly lived in. Everything was pristine and polished, nothing out of place.

The only exception was his office and desk, where there were scattered files and papers. I didn't look at those. His business wasn't really something that concerned me. What I wanted to know about was far more personal. I went to the kitchen and looked into his cabinets. They were mostly bare except for some protein shakes and cans of tuna. Looked like Dylan was a bit of a health nut.

Opening the fridge, I saw only fruits and vegetables, containers of juice and iced coffees. I helped myself to one as payment for my extra efforts. I didn't think he'd mind since I was waiting for his pool people on his behalf. The freezer had pre-prepared meals in containers that made it clear a professional had packed them. I assumed he had a personal chef come in from time to time.

There was a wine chiller and a liquor cabinet, both locked. Of course, I wasn't planning on lifting anything from either one. Helping myself to a cold latte was one thing. Drinking from someone's alcohol stash was just tacky. I was a lot of things, but tacky wasn't one of them.

However, I was curious, and I didn't mind snooping a bit. I continued to look around while waiting, only abandoning my explorations when the doorbell rang. I crept to the front door and looked at the video screen beside it. There were two men in pool uniforms standing there so I opened it.

"Hey, we're here to look at your problems with the pump," one of them told me, carefully averting his eyes from my bathing suit top. I realized that I had stripped off my T-shirt when I had been planning to clean and hadn't put it back on. The other guy wasn't so modest. He was fully checking out my rack and then smiled at me, his eyes full of mischief.

"Yes. It's out back," I told him.

"Of course. We know the way. If you'll open the back gate for us, we'd rather not come through the house."

"Right. Of course. I'll meet you around there."

The other guy continued to smile at me for a moment before bounding off behind his partner. I closed the door and headed out the back door to unlock the back gate and let them in. They made quick work of the repairs, finishing up in less than thirty minutes.

"It was just a loose wire. Looks like it got disconnected. Did something get moved recently?"

"Yes. A statue."

He glanced over his shoulder toward the shed area and nodded his head, turning back to me with a smile.

"Ah, I see now. Gloria has been removed."

"Gloria?"

"Yes. I've been servicing this pool for nearly ten years and the mermaid was here the first time I came. She just looked like a Gloria to me. I'm almost sad to see her go."

"She was a bit of an eyesore."

"So she was, but she had more character than that brick wall," he laughed.

"I suppose she did," I replied.

"Tell Mr. Hayward that we'll send him an invoice for the service charge and Charles will be back this weekend to do the routine cleaning."

"Will you be here?" the other guy asked suddenly.

"Are you Charles?" I asked.

"Yes."

"I might be," I replied, flashing him my best smile.

His partner shook his head and motioned for him to follow. Charles did so, glancing back at me as he exited the pool gates. I had to admit that he was hot. I'd guess early 30s. He was tall and athletic. His hair hung in thick black curls on top with faded sides. He might just be the fun I had been looking for if Dylan wasn't going to play.

Once they were gone, I put on my headphones to listen to music while I worked. I skimmed the larger debris from the pool. I would need to let the filter run a bit longer before getting back in to clean out what it didn't get. While it finished doing its job, I went back inside the house to venture further. One door downstairs was locked with a code box so I ventured upstairs to see what was in that second floor room he had once enjoyed watching me from.

I wasn't at all surprised to find out it was his bedroom. Like the rooms downstairs, it was remarkably pristine. I stepped into the bathroom and noted how perfectly arranged the items on the sink and counter were and how clean the shower was. I had to say that I was impressed by how tidy he was. There was no doubt he had someone come in from time to time, but I was guessing they never had very much to take care of when they did.

Moving back out to the bedroom, I noticed a shelf full of books. I went to look at them, noting that several were photo albums. Unable to help myself, I pulled one free and began leafing through it, running my fingers across some of the pictures of him when he was probably my age. He had played football and baseball in college from the looks of it. That explained why he liked to keep up his fitness. A lot of former athletes did like to maintain a physical fitness regimen.

I quickly lost track of the time as I continued to peruse his photos, enjoying seeing him on what looked to be a number of adventures. I found myself wishing that I could be one of the things he found a need to explore.

Chapter 18

Dylan

Dylan

"Comfortable?" I asked, a wry smile on my face.

Misti flew up off my bed with a stricken look on her face. Pulling her ear pods from her ears and stuffing them in a pocket. Her face was flushed with embarrassment.

"I'm so sorry. I didn't mean—" she started to say, but I held up my hand to stop her.

"It's okay, Misti. I'm not mad. What are you doing in here though?"

"I, um, the pool people came to fix the pool and while I was waiting for them, I wandered around a bit. Then, they left and um, I guess I wasn't done. I just wanted to see your place and then I noticed the photo albums and started looking at your photos and oh, man. I'm so sorry. I'm so ashamed. Are you sure you aren't mad? I'd understand if you were mad."

"Misti. Stop," I said, chuckling at her nervous babbling.

She looked sheepish, but a small smile spread across her face.

"I just feel bad for being nosey," she said.

"I know. What are you looking at there?" I asked, noting the open photo album on the bed.

"I'm not sure. I just opened that one," she said. "Looks like some sort of travel photos."

I reached for the book and picked it up, flipping through a few pages. I could see why she would think they were travel photos. They were taken on a cross country trip to start basic training in the army. I sat down on the edge of the bed and motioned for her to sit down beside me.

"It's a scrapbook I kept from my time in the army."

"You were in the army?" she said. "So, that's why you know so much about guns."

"A little but not really. I learned some things about guns in basic training, but most of it I learned after I bought the gun range. Smith is the expert, not me. He's taught me quite a bit to help me not sound like an idiot when I'm talking to customers there though."

"So, what did you do in the army? Were you in combat?"

"Combat? No. I rarely even saw daylight while I was in the army. I worked with a bunch of tech stuff. Things I can't talk about."

"Ooh, covert ops and stuff."

"That sounds cool, but it wasn't really like that. I was just working on some tech stuff."

"Why do I have the feeling that you are dumbing down what you actually did?"

I smiled and flipped the page to show her some of the photos, suddenly reliving those early days of my manhood. I was fresh out of college. Just a big dumb kid who didn't know his ass from a hole in the ground. I'd traveled from my hometown of Pulaski, Tennessee, to Fort Moore, Georgia for basic training and officer candidate school.

"I'm not dumbing it down, it's just not anything fascinating. I worked with onboard computer systems that guided the navigation of vehicles. The tech itself is classified so I can't get much into what it entailed but I basically just worked to get guys where they were going and making sure their leaders knew their locations, but their enemies didn't."

"Is that what your company does now?"

"I suppose some of it is like that. I'm working on a design right now that I hope will help people in need of assistance get it right away."

"Like the 911 system where they call for help?"

"Yes and no. This system won't require them to call anyone. It won't require a phone. It's more like pushing a button to call for help. Nothing sounds, no one knows, but help is on the way immediately."

"More like life alert then."

"Similar but no intercoms, no need to be in a known location. You can be out in the middle of the woods and push the button for help. The signal will be tracked via GPS technology using existing infrastructure."

"Like satellites and cell towers?"

"Yes. Like those."

"That sounds really cool. You gave up your military career to start your own company and make stuff like that?" she asked.

"Something like that," I said, looking back down at the album and turning the page to show her a set of photos of me graduating from officer candidate school. It brought back a flood of memories.

I'd completed both basic and officer training with flying colors but had given it all up after my parents died in an accident. My first urge had been to run, to accept the furthest post I could and pretend I wasn't devastated by their deaths, but fate had led me to Lydia, and she had led me to Nashville. It was far enough from Pulaski to put my past there in the distance, but not far enough that the memories didn't linger every time I saw familiar haunts from family trips.

I had finished my time in the army but had not signed up for another tour. Instead, I had taken the money left to me by my parents and started my own tech business. They weren't rich, but they'd had decent enough life insurance policies and assets to afford the startup costs. The military had pushed me forward by giving me a handful of contracts through one of their programs designed to promote startups. From there, things just sort of took off and eventually, so did Lydia.

Though it was clear now that I was finally over Lydia, that time in my life took me back to a place filled with so much sadness. I'd met her two weeks after their funeral. She worked as an assistant in the real estate office I'd consulted about selling their home. I'd left it in their hands when I returned to active duty.

Lydia had kept me up to date on things and eventually I'd asked her to meet me for dinner while I was on leave a few months later. Things had happened fast after that, and I hadn't wanted to be apart from her. I was still grieving, and she was my life raft. What I hadn't realized was that it was never love for her. She only saw my potential as a provider, and I had exceeded her wildest dreams in that regard.

I glanced at Misti, curious if she could see the melancholy that had crept into my eyes, but she was looking down at the page I had opened, dragging a single finger slowly down the length of a photo of me in uniform. She let out a slow breath and smiled, finally tilting her face up towards mine.

"You were very hot," she said.

I looked at her face, unsure how I should respond to that.

"Well, still are hot," she added, not taking her eyes off of mine.

It was a clear invitation. I'd been resisting this for far too long and now, here she was beside me, propped up on the edge of my bed and practically begging me to make a move. Only a fool would say no to her, and I was certainly no fool. I pushed my sad thoughts aside and pulled her toward me, letting the photo album fall open on the floor below us as my mouth covered hers in a deep kiss.

Her mouth was hot and wet. She had that same crisp, clean smell I'd noticed when we went to the range and tasted like my favorite iced latte. What were the odds of that? Our tongues danced a delicious tango as we kissed. I hadn't felt this kind of sexual chemistry in a very long time, and I was eager to see where it would take us.

I pulled away, realizing that I had lost control. My eyes met hers again. They were darker, full of a lust that I could appreciate but nothing had changed other than the kiss. She was still my neighbors' daughter, and it could create complications.

"Misti, I don't think that we should. I'm not sure that this would be good for either of us," I said, not even believing it myself.

"That's the problem with you genius types. Y'all always think way too much," she replied, moving toward me, and pulling me back toward her in another kiss.

My resistance was gone. Now that we had crossed that line, there was no going back. Her mouth on mine only pushed me to want more. She shifted as she kissed me, pushing her body against mine, her breasts firmly resting against my chest. I could feel my cock throbbing against my jeans, begging to get out. I wasn't sure if I wanted to take things that far, but my body had no reservations about it at all.

Reaching forward, I tangled my fingers in her hair, giving in to what I had been wanting to do since the first day I had seen her laying out in the backyard next door.

Chapter 19

Misti

Dylan pulled away again, studying my face. We were both quiet unless you counted the heavy breathing between us. I studied his face with all of its masculine angles and his intensely dark eyes. He even smelled divine, some combination of sandalwood and spice. I broke eye contact, glancing downward for a moment and smiling as I noted the outline of his cock pushing against the crotch of his jeans.

Shifting myself on the bed, I lay down across it, leaving myself open to whatever he wanted to do with the opportunity. Instead, he reached out and pulled me forward to sit beside him, then he stood and faced me before pulling me up onto my feet. I thought he was going to send me away but instead he kissed me again, his hands roaming softly down my arms and around my back, pulling me closer to him. When he let me go, he studied my face for a moment, a soft smile on his lips.

"This has to stay between us, Misti."

"Ashamed of wanting to bang the young coed next door?"

"No, not at all. We're both consenting adults. However, I do have business dealings with your father, and I don't want to get on his bad side."

"I can understand that. This will be our little secret."

"Good. And not to be dreadfully unsexy about it, but are you on birth control?"

"I have an implant. I'm good to go at the drop of a hat."

Rather than responding, he bent down to kiss me again. Soon, we were a whirlwind of flying hands and clothes, stripping one another down to our underwear. I stepped back to finish removing mine, letting him get a nice view of what I was offering. I knew he'd seen me naked before in the yard, but not like this—up close and personal.

He looked me up and down appreciatively, taking in my full breasts, tiny waist, and smoothly waxed pussy before stripping off his boxer briefs. Now it was my turn to be impressed. Not only was he gorgeous and in great shape, but he had what might possibly be the most perfect cock I'd ever laid eyes on. The length and girth were worthy of a porn star. If he knew how to use that thing, I would be in for the time of my life.

I could feel myself getting wet as I continued to look appreciatively at the carefully manscaped balls beneath his sizable erection. I was looking forward to feeling them slapping against my hungry cunt but first, I wanted to feel it in my mouth. I moved down to my knees in front of him and went to work, looking up at him as I began slowly licking and sucking at the tip of his bulbous head.

"Mmm," he moaned, tilting his head backwards to enjoy the sensations. His hands reached for me, guiding my movements as I slipped more of him into my mouth. I loved the way his dick throbbed inside of my mouth, twitching, and pulsating heavenly against my tongue.

"That feels amazing," he groaned. "Don't stop. Suck my cock."

I loved hearing him talk dirty to me. It only turned me on that much more. I opened my mouth wider, clamping my mouth over more of his monster cock. He let me move at my own pace, bobbing up and down until I was taking every delicious inch down the back of my throat. I gagged a little, but I kept going, enjoying the way he tasted as he face fucked me eagerly.

"That's so good, but I want to fuck that sweet little pussy of yours," he said, pulling me upward off his dick and moving me back toward the bed, kissing me deeply. As the back of my legs touched the bed, he pushed me down across it, his hands reaching down to massage my breasts for a moment before leaning across me and sucking at my already hard nipples. He took his time, kissing and licking his way across my tanned globes appreciatively and then smiling up at me.

"Absolutely beautiful," he said before slipping downward and pulling my legs apart. I could feel the coolness of the air-conditioned bedroom blowing across my exposed clit for a moment and then it was replaced with his hot mouth. My hips bucked forward, eager for the warmth it offered. I gasped as his tongue touched my aching pussy lips, parting them and lapping at my juices. A loud, primal moan formed in the back of my throat and seemed to just slip free involuntarily as he licked my pussy in long strokes with a hard, flattened tongue.

My hands reached for him, but he was just out of my grasp, his head buried between my legs as he ate me out enthusiastically. I grasped the covers on either side of me instead, grunting and moaning as he explored me thoroughly, pushing me closer to climax with every stroke of his tongue.

His mouth enveloped my clit, sucking at it—milking it like a tiny little cock against his tongue until I could do little more than pant and squeal with ecstasy. He slipped two fingers inside of me and began finger fucking me as he continued to tug at my hard little nubbin with his teeth and mouth.

I let out a loud cry, my hips bucking forward as my orgasm spilled into his mouth, giving up a creamy reward for his efforts. My body quaked and rocked until I finished shattering against his open mouth and collapsed against the bed, trying to catch my breath. No one had ever pleasured me like that.

"That was fucking amazing," I told him.

"Oh, we're just getting started," he replied, half whispering, half growling.

I smiled as he flipped me over, putting me on all fours so that my ass was up in the air toward him. I felt his cock as he centered it at my pussy and began rubbing the head of it back and forth along the opening. Despite having just cum, I was eager to have him inside of me, but he didn't seem in any hurry at all as he continued to tease me.

"Please. I want you inside of me," I begged.

"Oh, I will be," he said, his voice deep with want.

I groaned as he dragged his heavy cock across my virgin asshole. I wasn't sure I was prepared for having something the size of his cock in my tiny little sphincter, but I was willing to let him fuck me there if he wanted. I waited, eager to see what he had in mind. He moved his cock back downward, pushing the head of it just inside my hot folds.

"Yes. Please," I begged, pushing back against him, trying to get more of him inside of me.

"Not yet," he replied, his fingers digging into my asscheeks, spreading them apart as he eased just a little further in and then pulled almost free again.

I moaned loudly, trying to relax and not anticipate so much. I did my best to just let him take his time with me. Wasn't that always my complaint? That guys my age were like jackrabbits and done too soon? Now, here I was trying to force this one to get on with things. It wasn't that I wanted it to be over quickly, I was just so horny. I wanted him to fuck me so badly.

I screamed as he suddenly shoved his hips forward, pumping the full length of his cock inside of me with one swift thrust. It didn't hurt. It just caught me off guard as his fat cock filled me to the hilt. He rolled his hips and then pulled back again before slowly inching his way back inside of me.

My moans filled his bedroom as he began fucking me in long, fluid strokes. Our bodies rocking back and forth against one another as his hands roamed across my ass and then slid upward to grasp my waist. He held me there for a moment, using it to push and pull me back and forth onto his cock.

"Tell me what you want?" he said softly.

"I want you to fuck me until I come again. I want to feel you come inside of me," I panted.

"How do you want me to fuck you? You want it hard or slow?"

"Hard. I want you to fuck me like a dirty little slut."

"Is that what you are?" he grunted, picking up the pace of his strokes.

"Yes," I told him.

"Say it," he replied, accenting his words with a hard thrust of his cock.

"I'm a dirty little slut."

"I know you are. I saw you in your backyard. Who were you showing off for?" he asked me.

It was the first time he had mentioned my little backyard sex productions. It made me smile.

"I was showing off for you."

"Why?"

"Because I'm a dirty little slut and I wanted you to fuck me. I wanted you to see me and want me," I replied in words stilted by his heavy thrusts.

"I know," he replied and then he was silent.

The room was filled with nothing but our grunts, breathing and the sound of our naked bodies slapping against one another. He leaned forward and grabbed my breasts, his fingers biting into my bouncing globes as he ground his cock deep inside my center. I could tell he was close, but he was holding back. He was waiting for me.

He let go of one of my breasts and slid that hand between my legs, rubbing my clit as he pile drove me in hard, deep strokes. I was on the verge too. My orgasm kept building until I wasn't sure how much longer I could hold back.

"Come for me, Misti. I want to feel you explode all over my cock," he said, panting with need.

He didn't have to tell me twice. I let go, exploding all over his hot, pulsating cock. He was right behind me, releasing a sticky load of cum inside of me, our juices mixing together as he continued to fuck me until neither of us had anything left to give. He lay against my back for a moment, his cock slowly deflating inside of me and then he pulled free of me with a wet plop.

I turned around in the bed and draped my head over the side so that it was upside down in front of him. I took his deflated cock in my mouth and cleaned it thoroughly with my tongue, licking him clean of all of our juices while he watched me, groaning slightly as I finished.

"Delicious," I said, wiping my mouth with the back of my hand and moving back across the bed so that I was laying on my side. He climbed in beside me and pulled me close to him, kissing me softly again. I felt the electricity all the way down to my toes.

He held me there for a while until we both drifted off to sleep. It was the most peaceful rest I had enjoyed in a while. When we woke, we had sex again. This time he took his time, exploring my body with his hands, mouth, and fingers and then fucking me so slowly that it felt like something much more than just a summer fling, but I knew it wasn't. What surprised me was that I felt just a little sad about that.

"I guess I need to get home before someone misses me," I said finally, not wanting to leave but knowing it was best.

"Right," he replied, twirling his fingers through my hair.

"I did get your pool clean while I was here," I said.

"Come back tomorrow. We'll fuck in it."

I smiled and kissed him on the lips before getting up and dressing. We said our goodbyes and then I hurried home, darting in the front door and going up to my room before anyone got a look at how disheveled I was. Once I was inside, I stripped off my clothes and lay across my bed, touching my sore pussy. I could still smell him on my skin, and I liked that. Sex with him had been so much more amazing than anything I'd ever experienced before, and I wanted to let his scent linger for a while longer.

Chapter 20

Dylan

Misti was in my head. She consumed me. Just as I had been drawn to her while she lay out in her parents' backyard and showed off for me, it was even stronger now that I knew I could have her whenever I wanted—which was all the time. Lucky for me, she wasn't doing anything this summer but enjoying her time away from school and part of that enjoyment seemed to center around letting me fuck her brains out.

I almost hated that things would end soon. She would go back to school, and I would go back to lackluster sex with whoever came along. Deb was definitely off the menu after the way I'd shrugged her off the last time we had gotten together and I was fine with that, but it sucked knowing that I would soon be forced to give up my little trysts with Misti.

Just the thought of her made me hard. Her breasts were perfect, and her pussy hugged my cock like it was made for it. She was eager and willing to try everything. In the past couple of weeks, we'd fucked in every room of my house and some places outside of it, including the pool and on the hood of my convertible in the middle of a secluded field outside of town.

Today she was coming over to clean the pool, though she didn't actually do that anymore. Still, it was what her parents thought she was doing, so we kept up the charade. Instead, she was coming over to lay out naked while I attended a meeting with some of my team via Zoom in my lab. I knew she'd be ready for me when I was done.

It was all I could do to focus with the image of her laying out there all oiled up, her pussy dripping with anticipation while I did my work inside. My cock jumped to attention at the thought, and I willed it down as I dialed into the meeting and waited for others to join. I could cut it short and just go do what I wanted to with Misti, but this was a part of the game with us, and I loved how wanton she got when I made her wait. She was like a wild animal when she finally got what she wanted.

I pushed her from my thoughts long enough to get through the meeting and then walked up to my room. The same window that overlooked her backyard looked over my pool. I expected to see her laying on the lounge chair, but she was swimming instead. I watched as she climbed out, completely naked and padded back over to the chair to lay back down.

"Glad you're cooling off so I can come heat you up again," I said aloud.

I watched her for a moment, enjoying the way she spread out on the chair and touched herself. She cupped her breasts for a moment and then moved one hand down to her pussy to massage her clit. I continued to watch her for a moment. It was almost like old times—her masturbating while I watched from afar. The difference was that now I could do something about the huge tent forming in my pants.

I turned and walked out of the bedroom, stopping by to pick up a gift box I'd left on the kitchen counter. I carried it out the patio doors and crossed the pool area to stand looking down at her. She continued to play with herself as I watched.

"How was your meeting?" she asked.

"Lonely," I replied.

"Good thing you're out here with me now then," she cooed, pushing her hips forward and closing her eyes as she hit just the right spot. I let her continue, watching how she bit her lip with pleasure as she began finger fucking herself, her lovely legs spread wide open to expose the engorged pink folds of her cunt.

"I brought you a present. You want it now or should I let you finish?" I asked.

"Ooh. A present? I want it now," she said, pulling her fingers free and making a show of licking them clean for me. She then lifted the back of the chair so that she was sitting up, her gorgeous mouth very close to my throbbing cock.

I stripped off my clothes and handed her the rectangular box I'd laid down beside her chair when I walked out. She smiled and untied the string that kept it closed and pulled out the contents. She smiled at it and looked back up at me for a moment.

"It's beautiful. You want to use it on me?"

"Maybe, but not right now. Right now, I want to watch you ride it."

"Ride it?" she asked, looking back at the large black rubber cock in her hands.

"Yes," I replied, taking it from her and helping her up from her chair.

I led her over to the patio table and pulled one of the armless chairs back, taking the dildo from her hands and sticking it to the seat using the suction cup on the bottom. I reached between her legs and gathered some of the juices pouring from her hot little box to lubricate her new toy and motioned for her to take a seat.

I watched as she straddled it, biting her lip provocatively. She began easing down on it little by little, taking more of it each time until she was seated fully onto it. Beads of sweat appeared across her skin, the warmth of the sun and the heat from her exertions dotting her smooth sun-kissed skin with perspiration. It was beautiful to watch.

I stroked my cock only inches from her face while she enjoyed fucking herself with her new toy. My hand reached out for her breasts, pinching her nipples playfully. She bit her lip, trying to be quiet so that no one who might be outside could hear her getting off, but I knew she wanted to squeal. I loved it when she was vocal, but we always tried to be quiet out here and that was fun too.

Soon, she was bouncing up and down the length of the cock, getting herself off. Her body jerked and seized as it hit her most sensitive spots. I could tell she was getting close to coming and I sped up my own pace, jerking myself off heavily so that I could come with her. I watched as she convulsed, the throws of an orgasm taking control of her body.

"Open your mouth," I whispered.

She did as I asked, still fucking herself as the climax sent shockwaves through her body. My hips lurched forward as my climax surged forward, my cum spilling into her mouth and spilling down her chin in the proverbial pearl necklace before dripping down her perfect tits. I milked every drop of it out onto her and watched as she finally came to a halt, the dildo still buried in her center.

Never taking her eyes off of me, she used her fingers to retrieve the cum that missed her mouth and then licked them clean. She dragged them across her chin and her chest, making sure she got every single drop before finally sliding her body upward so that the big fake dick inside of her slipped free with an audible sucking sound. It was soaked with her juices.

"Did you like that?" I asked her as she stood up and moved toward me.

"I did," she said.

"Good. It's yours to take with you when you go back to school."

"That's very thoughtful of you. Can I leave it here until then? I'm sure we can get a lot of great use out of it between now and then."

"I'm sure we can," I said, pulling her to me and kissing her passionately.

After a few moments, I scooped her up and tossed her in the pool. She let out an unexpected scream of surprise and then immediately looked around nervously. I laughed and jumped in beside her, diving under the water and then coming back up behind her so that my body was pressed against her back and my hands were cupping her breasts. I enjoyed the weight of them in my hands and the way the water lent buoyancy to them when I let them go.

"I want to spend the night with you," I whispered against her ear.

"I don't think my parents will allow me to have a sleepover with you," she laughed.

"Silly," I teased. "I mean away from here. Come away with me for a weekend."

"Really?" she asked, leaning back against me as I planted little kisses on her shoulders.

"Yes. Really."

"I think we can manage that. I'll just tell my parents I am spending the weekend with friends. We can go wherever you want."

"Perfect. I'll set it up and give you the details."

We lingered in the pool like that for a while. There was no need for any words when we were just holding one another like this. I'd learned in the weeks we'd spent together that Misti wasn't lacking for conversation. In fact, she was a lot more than just a fuck buddy. She was smart, witty, and infinitely interesting.

However, our time was short, so I tried to focus on just the sex. No matter how hard I tried to convince myself that this was still just a summer fling, I knew it had become more than that. Somewhere between trips to the range and spectacular sex, I'd started to fall for her and that wasn't something either of us needed in our life right now. I pushed the thought from my head and turned her around, her breasts pushed against my chest as I kissed her.

"Let's get a shower and talk about your schedule before you go," I told her as I pulled away.

"That sounds like fun, but I have to get home," she said, and there was something in her tone that gave me pause.

We began making our way out of the pool, climbing up the deep level pool ladder rather than walking out the shallow end where we might be seen from her house if anyone were looking. The clandestine nature of our relationship that made it so hot now seemed to wear on me. I just needed to refocus on the fun and let the rest go. I watched as she slipped into the bathing suit and t-shirt she'd worn over before she kissed me on the cheek and told me goodbye.

Whatever I was feeling, I think she might just be feeling a bit of it too. Or was that just wishful thinking?

Chapter 21

Misti

"I've got to meet Stephanie this weekend to sign our lease and get keys to the new place," I said as Mom walked into the kitchen.

"We'll go with you," she replied.

"You mean *you* will go with me."

"No, I mean that your father and I will go with you," she replied dryly.

"We both know that he won't. You will make all the plans for a family adventure of taking little Misti back to college and then he will announce that some work thing has come up. Of course, he won't be able to leave it in the hands of anyone else. So, you and I will end up going alone and you'll sulk angrily the entire time. Just spare me the nonsense and let me make my own plans, Mom. I'm just driving back to Knoxville for the weekend. It's less than three hours and I make the trip all the time," I barked.

There was no way I could allow my parents to go with me to Knoxville because I was only going to be there for about an hour. Dylan was going to take me and then we were going to spend the rest of the weekend in Sevierville at a mountain cabin one of his friends owned. It would be our last chance to spend any serious time together and I wasn't about to let my parents fuck it up.

Still, that wasn't what annoyed me about her suggestion. She always did this. Her desperation to be a normal family was disturbing. I supposed I should have felt sorry for her, but I didn't. As absent as my father was in our life, she could have left him and found someone who would treat her the way she wanted years ago. She didn't stay for love, and I was an adult now, so she didn't stay for me.

No, my mother stayed here because of the money. She traded her happiness for status, and she'd been happy enough to share that misery with me all of my life.

There was no reply to my outburst. Instead, she turned back to the pie she'd been working on when I came in and pursed her lips, keeping her thoughts to herself much as she did with my father. It would seem that I had somehow become merely an extension of him for her. Annoyed by it all, I started to leave but she surprised me by speaking up again.

"There's a serial abductor, maybe a killer, in Knoxville," she said flatly.

"And?"

"I just thought it might be best if we went. We haven't seen this new place of yours or where it is. I'd like to know you are in a safe location."

"It's a safe location, Mom. You can look at it and check the crime rate online. Dad's paying for it, so he has the address already. He's probably already done all of that. The two of you should actually talk to one another someday," I snapped before walking out to the kitchen.

Anyone that didn't understand my family dynamic might think I was an asshole, but they'd have no idea how many times similar discussions had taken place. The endless plans that had been canceled despite my mother's good intentions. It wasn't her fault that my father was a dick that preferred working over spending time with his family, but it was her fault that she put up with it. I'd been forced to cope with the disappointments due to her not wanting to make waves with the man who provided her comfortable lifestyle.

Like my father, my mother had come from money. Unlike my father, she'd not been able to hold on to it. Her father had lost his business due to some shady business dealings that had cost him everything. Whether she and my father had ever loved one another was debatable, but I did know she had hidden the fact that her family was destitute. She'd even been devious enough to opt for an elopement to cover the fact that her family couldn't afford an elaborate wedding.

My mother might come off to her friends as a loving mother and wife who dedicated herself to her family, but I knew the truth about her and had for a very long time. I'd been hearing the arguments between them for years and during visits to my father's family back in Manhattan, I'd heard a lot more from his sisters. Mom was a gold digger and that was a terrible thing to say about the woman who gave you life, but the truth was the truth.

It was one of the main reasons I had no desire to chase some man around. I didn't need one to take care of me. Yes, my father took care of me now and some might say that contradicted my need to be independent but that is what fathers were supposed to do, wasn't it? It was part of their duty to raise their children to be independent adults. I didn't feel bad about taking money from a man who gave me very little else, at least until I was finished with school. Then, I would cut the ties that bind me and get on with things the way I saw fit.

Back in my room, I began contemplating what to pack for the trip. Friday would be here before I knew it and I wanted to make sure I had everything in order. I might even buy a few special things for the trip. In fact, I was pretty certain that I would. I found that I was very excited about the weekend, far more than I had anticipated.

A part of me had become attached to Dylan. I hadn't intended for that to happen, and I didn't have room for it in my life right now. I still had a year of school to go and now that I'd gotten a taste of what being with an older man was like, I didn't see myself going back to guys my age, but I could easily see myself enjoying the company of a lot of older types. The last thing I needed was to have my senior year stilted by a ball and chain back home.

Thinking of him like that instantly made me feel bad. He had done nothing to deserve such an indignity. He was more than understanding of my need to remain free and seemed to want to do the same himself. However, I would be lying if I didn't feel some special bond with him. Perhaps it was because I had known him so long or maybe it was because he was my first real lover. Everyone else had just been an interlude that was unsatisfactory and short-lived.

As the week passed, there were more discussions with my mother, who was still pushing for a family trek to my new place. However, my father had not uttered one peep about being on board and I took that as a clear sign that it wouldn't work out. Even though I had no intention of allowing them to escort me to school due to my plans, I still found it disheartening to deal with at all. I was grateful when Friday finally rolled around. I packed my car with my things for the weekend and my mother saw me off. As usual, Dad was nowhere to be seen.

"Your father said to tell you he loves you and to drive safely," she said but I could tell she was lying.

I suspected that my father had said no such thing. He likely told her that he would be back from whatever fire he had to rush off to put out in time to tell me goodbye. When he didn't make it, she covered for him. I could make a stink of it, but I could tell how down she seemed and let it slide. Instead, I just hugged her.

"I love you, Mom. I'll be back late Sunday evening."

"Okay. Let me know if you get delayed and I know you girls probably have big weekend plans for getting the apartment all set up and going out but drop me a text here and there to let me know you are all right."

"I will. Don't worry," I told her.

"I do worry. Be careful," she said. "I love you, Misti."

"I know," I said, starting the car and backing out of the driveway.

I drove away, giving my mother enough time to disappear back into the house before backtracking and pulling into the drive next door. I pulled quickly around the house where Dylan was waiting for me with one of the car bays open. In a nearby visitor's spot, sat a sleek Mercedes SUV. He motioned for me to pull into the bay and then came over to help me transfer my weekend bags to the SUV before closing the garage bay door.

"No convertible?" I asked.

"Not this time. The Mercedes will be more comfortable for you to stretch out in, and the ride is a lot smoother."

"Can I drive it?"

"No," he laughed.

"Why not?" I asked.

"Because I won't let you," he replied with a smirk.

"Sounds like misogyny to me," I teased.

"Yeah? Seems like you're taking that whole 'fuck the patriarchy' thing a bit literally then," he retorted.

"Ouch. That was quite good," I laughed.

He winked and opened the passenger side door, giving me a playful slap on the ass as I climbed in and then leaned in to kiss me. I noted that the windows were tinted, so I didn't worry much about being seen with him once we left the house. He pushed a button on the same remote that controlled the garage doors and we were on our way to Knoxville.

I had intended to be in and out to just sign the lease and get the key, maybe show Dylan the place before leaving but earlier in the week, I'd gotten my fall schedule and found that one of the classes I'd signed up for had been full. I'd got my second choice, which I really didn't like because it started at 6 a.m. on a Monday and would be my only class that day. I needed to find something else to pick up in its place and today was the time to drop or add a class for those of us who had registered late and not had time to do so online.

My new apartment was only a few blocks from campus, so Dylan and I made our way there once I had my keys. Stephanie was already there, unpacking her things. She was excited to meet the man she'd been hearing about rocking my world the past few weeks. I left the two of them to get acquainted while I walked back to campus and made my way to Professor Gregory Simmons' office. There were several grad students there processing drop and add slips and I approached one of them to get things sorted out.

"What do you know about this professor?" I asked him.

"Not much. He's new. Started back in the spring while Professor Houser was on maternity leave but now he's taken over for the teacher that is missing until they—find her," he said, after a short hesitation.

"Oh, right. Wow," I said, knowing that no one believed she—or the other missing women—were still alive.

"I heard that he's very witty and charming," a man said as he approached us in long-legged strides from the opposite side of the room.

"Is he?" I asked, flashing him my best smile.

"Yes, I am," he replied.

"Ah, Professor Simmons, I assume."

"Very sharp. I love it when my students can figure out the simple things for themselves."

I studied him for a moment. He was quite witty and charming, but he was also very attractive. He looked like he was probably in his early forties, with a shock of blonde curls and shockingly pale blue eyes. His tanned skin and athletic build gave him the look of a surfer, but the fine lines around his eyes revealed that he was older, perhaps in his mid-forties.

"And I love it when my classes are on Wednesday after lunch instead of early on a Monday morning," I replied.

"Then I'm your guy," he told me before redirecting his attention to the grad student watching awkwardly from between us. "Sign her up, Tyrone."

I finished my paperwork and thanked him before heading for the nearest exit. By the time I returned to the apartment, I had forgotten the momentary attraction to him, instead more interested in getting the weekend with Dylan started. He finished helping Stephanie hang a photo in her bedroom and then we left for the cabin.

I was tingling all over with anticipation.

Chapter 22

Dylan

"Here we are," I announced as we stepped into the cabin.

I could see Misti looking around, her brows furrowed together as if puzzled by something.

"This isn't what I was expecting," she said finally.

"What were you expecting?" I asked.

"I'm not sure. I guess something a bit, well, bigger."

"Are you disappointed?" I asked.

"No. Not at all. It's cozy. I just wasn't expecting it to be an actual cabin."

I laughed. "What were you expecting then?"

"I guess I'm just used to pretentious people. They say they have a cabin and then you get there to find out that it's more like a resort."

"And that is pretentious somehow?"

"Well, yeah, because they act like it's some tiny place so that when you get there and see it, you are impressed rather than critical. If they said that they have some fabulous cabin and then you get there to find it isn't anything special, they can't change that. However, if you just say you have a cabin, anything beyond four walls and a cot exceeds their expectations."

"That is a helluva observation," I told her.

"Yeah," she said, looking sheepish.

"Let's get our stuff unpacked and I'll show you just how fascinating I find you," I told her.

I wasn't surprised that she was taken aback by the cabin, for just the reasons she mentioned. I suppose that when I told her we were staying at my friends' cabin, she hardly expected it to be a one room a-frame built with rough sawn wood by hand. It didn't belong to one of my newer set of friends. It belonged to an old army buddy who had ended up in places I never saw and came out for the worse on the other side.

While I was having a weekend in the woods with my sexy neighbor, he was away at a treatment facility he thought was being paid for by the feds. I had told him I would take care of the place for him while he was gone. He had been trusting me with it since I'd taken over his loan on the place. It had taken some convincing to get him to accept my help, but it was all he had, and I couldn't let him lose it.

I brought in our bags and dropped them on the living room floor. Rather than unpacking, we went straight for one another. Although I was eager to spend some real time with her this weekend rather than just spending afternoons in bed exploring one another sexually, that didn't mean I didn't want to fuck her right here and now. I pulled her to me in a heated kiss and then scooped her up to carry her off to the bed.

It was nice not to feel rushed. I could take my time and truly enjoy her. I slowly undressed her, peeling off what little clothes she was wearing so that she stood naked before me. My mouth drifted away from hers as I began planting butterfly kisses down her neck and across her shoulders. She moaned as I lightly ran my tongue along the soft, dewy skin that covered the hard protrusions of her clavicle bones.

"Such perfection," I mumbled against her skin before devouring her beautiful breasts. Cupping them in my hands, I moved from one to the other, licking and softly biting the skin there. I pulled a deep rose nipple to my mouth and suckled at it, enjoying the way she tilted her head to the side and closed her eyes, lost in the moment.

My hand stretched down between her legs, my fingers feathering lightly across her pubic mound. I could smell the earthy scent of her excitement as I moved downward and parted her pussy lips, letting my fingers slip into the wetness that had already formed. She was always dripping with desire when we were together.

"I love how wet you get for me," I whispered as I moved back up toward her mouth to kiss her again.

"Always," she managed to reply, half moaning it into my mouth as I parted her lips with my tongue and explored her hot mouth.

She whimpered loudly as I began massaging her pussy with my fingers, her hands draped around my neck and her nails digging into my back. It was nice to hear her be so vocal. I loved how loud she sometimes got when we fucked. Our kiss lingered as I continued to explore her dripping pussy. I was completely lost in her.

Finally, I pulled away, leading her over to the bed that sat in one corner of the cabin and yanking back the covers to place her on the cool sheets beneath. I stood over her for a moment, just admiring her body as she lay sprawled provocatively in front of me, waiting to see what I would do with her. I continued to admire her as I stripped off my clothes, my cock springing forward in anticipation but I wasn't ready to take my prize just yet.

Instead, I knelt down and ran my hands up her legs, slowly caressing her ankles, then calves and moving up toward her knees. I pulled them apart and began kissing my way up her thighs, taking my time to enjoy the golden valley in which I found myself. She moaned loudly each time my mouth drifted across a sensitive spot. Her hips bucked forward wantonly as I reached my destination and brought my mouth to her center.

Slowly, I suckled her clit until it was a hard little button against my tongue. I pulled at it ever so slightly with my teeth, enjoying the way her body seized forward with delight and her fingers moved down into my hair to pull me further into her. She loved being eaten out and I loved the way she tasted.

"Mmm, Dylan," she moaned.

My name on her lips was ecstasy. It spurred me on as I pushed my tongue into her pussy and began lapping up her juices before bringing my fingers inward and pushing two of them into her slippery hole while I refocused again on her clit. She was writhing and moaning as I pleasured her. It was beautiful.

"Cum for me," I told her, my mouth still on her pussy. I let the words vibrate across her clit as I repeated myself, "Cum for me, Misti."

I took my time, letting her excitement build until she couldn't hold back anymore. She drew her hands back up to her breasts, digging her nails into the soft globes as her body shattered into a million pieces, filling my mouth with a powerful orgasm, but I didn't stop. Instead, I kept going, giving her orgasm after orgasm until she had no more to give.

Pulling away from her, I wiped my mouth and climbed into bed with her, pulling her close to me and kissing her, letting her enjoy her pussy juices on my mouth. Then, I pulled her on top of me, piercing her with my hard cock and letting her ride me so slowly it made me want to cry tears of joy. She was a vision as her hips rose and fell, tilting forward and back as she fucked me. Her hands cupped her large breasts, kneading them and tweaking her own nipples as she took what she wanted in the most exquisite way.

By the time I finally came, I was certain of one single thing—I was in love with Misti. As she climbed off of me and lay again by my side, I pulled her closer to me and held her, my nose buried in her long, dark hair. One arm wrapped around her waist as we just lay there and enjoyed one another's breathing. This was perfect but it would end soon and the thought of that filled me with a melancholy I'd not felt for a very long time.

After a little nap together, the two of us finally climbed back out of bed and threw on some clothes while we finished unpacking. I unpacked the cooler of food and drinks I'd brought for us into the fridge, and we settled in to make dinner. This felt right and it only became more perfect over the course of the weekend as we split our time between hiking, swimming in the nearby lake, and making love to one another.

"I don't want to leave," I confided to her on Sunday afternoon when it was time to go back home.

"Me either," she replied, reaching up to softly touch my face.

"We could just run away and never return," I told her, perhaps only half kidding.

"Wouldn't that be nice? Too bad we both have a life outside of this cabin."

"Do we?"

"What? Yes, of course we do," she said, looking just a bit confused by the statement.

It occurred to me then that I might be the only one in love. Misti seemed to enjoy our time together, but that didn't mean she had fallen for me in the same way. I was tempted to say the words, to get them out into the open. Something told me that it was a bad idea though. Maybe not forever, but for now, I should keep that to myself. Let her finish school. Let her live her life. She'd let me know if this was more than just the summer fling it started out to be.

I thought about our relationship a lot on the drive back home. The more I considered it, the more I knew that I was right. It was a sad truth that the person we loved didn't always love us back and I might have to accept that about Misti just as I had once had to accept it about Lydia. Time would tell if she had feelings for me and I wasn't in any hurry.

At least that is what I told myself.

Chapter 23

Misti

After our incredible weekend at the cabin, the fact that I would have to leave Dylan behind soon really began to sink in. I had planned on things with him being no strings attached and in some respects, it had been, but it was also apparent that we shared a bond I hadn't anticipated. He was willing to let me go to live my life, but I wasn't sure I wanted to, and I couldn't be certain he was okay with it.

Though he had said nothing about our imminent parting, I could see what seemed like sadness in his eyes when he was looking at me and thought I wasn't looking back. If he loved me, he hadn't said it. If I loved him, I wasn't willing to admit it. To do so would mean too many changes in my life. So, whatever we felt for one another, we both treated it like a fling and ignored anything beyond that.

We spent the last week of my being home having sex constantly. We also laughed together and talked about our plans for what we called "post-summer life" though we both knew that really just meant the end of us. It seemed like the time flew by and before we knew it, we were spending our last day together. We made love so slowly that I wanted to cry but I held my emotions back as we said a very physical goodbye to one another.

As I got dressed and prepared to leave Dylan's house for one last time, he surprised me with two boxes sitting on the table in his breakfast nook.

"Open the bigger one first," he told me.

"Dylan, this wasn't necessary," I told him, a little anxious about whether whatever was inside might finally set the tears free.

"It's nothing. Just a little something to help you when you're back at school."

I smiled and picked up the larger box. It wasn't huge but it was quite heavy. Pulling off the wrapper, I found a black wood box inside with a logo I didn't recognize. I pulled the top of the box and saw another black box inside, this one made of black steel. I pulled it from the outer box and sat it on the table.

"What is it?" I asked, my brows furrowed together.

"It needs to be set up. You can open it with a key, a code, or a fingerprint. Here's the key," he said, holding an odd little stubby key out to me. I took it and found the keyhole in the box to open it. I opened the lid to find blue LED lights illuminating the contents—the gun I'd purchased at the gun range, two clips, and a box of ammunition.

"Oh! It's a gun safe," I said, feeling oddly excited by it.

"Yes. There are instructions on setting it up with your fingerprint and the code so you can get it open quicker without having to locate the key. It'll make sure no one accesses your gun but you."

"Thank you. I love it," I told him.

We had brought the gun back from the gun range on our last trip there and he'd put it in his gun safe until I was ready to take it. I'd gotten my concealed carry permit so I could carry it but I had forgotten that I'd need my own gun safe to protect it. It was thoughtful of him to take care of that for me and didn't make me cry, so that was good. Still, I had another gift to go.

"I'm glad. Now you can open the other one."

This box was much smaller and lighter. It wasn't wrapped. Instead, it was in a deep red velvet hinged box with a silver ribbon wrapped around it. I slid the ribbon off to open the box and drew in a sharp breath.

"Oh, Dylan. It's beautiful," I said, feeling very near those tears now.

"I had it engraved," he told me.

I tilted the bracelet in my hands. The engraving was on the inside where it wasn't easily seen. It read, "Misti Ann Bridges" and had a QR code imprinted on it. I looked up at him, puzzled once again.

"Here, put it on," he told me, taking the bracelet from me and picking up a small silver stick from a tiny pocket in the top of the box. He pushed the stick in a tiny hole in the bracelet and it popped open, exposing some tiny mechanism embedded inside. The clasp was an odd one for a bracelet. It was shaped like a pointed bullet that pushed through an expanding metal mechanism and then tapered so that it couldn't be reversed.

"It's gorgeous, but it's not just a bracelet, is it?"

"It is not. It's one of the prototype pieces for the ones I was telling you about."

"So, you can track me wherever I am?" I asked, not certain I felt good about that.

"No. It doesn't allow anyone to track you. This bracelet will only function if you want it to," he said, snapping it into place around my wrist and putting what I understood was a little release pin back in the box. He turned my wrist over to show me the delicate little paisley pattern that went around the bracelet, trailing his fingers along it until he came to an imperfection.

"See this tiny little dot here?"

"Yes."

"It's an activation point. It's not easy to press down, meaning you can't just brush it across something and accidentally activate it. You will need to push it against something hard, like a wall or the floor, for it to push in enough to activate and once it is activated, it cannot be turned off by anyone but my team."

"So, if I get in trouble. I just press the button and this thing turns on until someone finds me?"

"That's correct."

"What if I'm not wearing the bracelet though?"

"Well, there is that. You can take it back off if you want, but it is purposely designed to look like an ordinary piece of jewelry and one that isn't easily removed. You have to have the key or at least something small enough to go in the pin hole to unlatch it."

"What exactly happens if I activate it? I mean, I know it gives out my GPS coordinates like some sort of beacon but how does that work?"

"The moment you push that button, an alarm goes off. Eventually, that will be through a system accessible to whatever police department is closest to your coordinates. For now, it is a singular station here in Knoxville that I'm working with for developing the product and my team. So, response time will rely on us then contacting the police wherever you are."

"How will I even know if I've turned it on? Is there a light or a beep or something?"

"There will be the tiniest clicking sound that won't be noticeable to anyone unless they are listening for it. So, there is that and you'll see that the tiny dot that activates it remains pressed in. It won't pop back out once it's activated. It locks into place, activates the signal and it will stay that way until the bracelet is physically back in the hands of someone who has the tools to return it to its normal position."

"How remarkable," I said, turning the bracelet back and forth on my hand, letting the pretty paisley pattern etched into the silver bracelet catch the light. "What is it made of?"

"This one is made of titanium. I tried it with gold and silver but those are too prone to damage. This one will go the distance."

"What about the battery?"

"It's a new technology that is virtually endless. The battery remains out of use unless you activate the bracelet and once you do, it will continue emitting a signal for years beyond when you would need it."

"And no one can use it to follow me around? I mean, I know you wouldn't do that, but no one can hack the system and find me. Say like a stalker or something?"

"No. There is no way for anyone to track that bracelet's location—your location—unless you activate it from your end. In the future, that may change. I want to build a backup failsafe in case there are women who are abducted and can't, for whatever reasons, activate the bracelet. That is a future version once I can develop a system that will not allow women to be found without their consent."

"How would that work?"

"That's the thing. I don't know yet. The moment you give someone access is the moment they will try to abuse it. Stalkers can, like you said, find a way to hack into it. Law enforcement would use it to find those on the wrong side of the law. I won't have that. I designed this tech to protect women, not bring them harm. I want to eventually develop it further to protect children who can't push a button."

"What about men?"

"Sure, men too. Once I get the system up and running, we will also develop men's jewelry lines and probably other devices that can act as vessels for the tech."

I nodded, smiling. He was protecting me in the only ways he knew how from afar. He was making sure I had quick access to a weapon and that I was equipped with a beacon to guide him to me if I was in trouble. Perhaps he hadn't said the words, but Dylan Hayward loved me. I loved him too.

"Thank you," I said, holding back my emotions.

"Do you want me to take it off for you?" he asked.

"No. I will keep it on. It's too lovely to sit in a box and I feel very comforted by it."

"You are my very first recipient. I had hoped it would make the women who have it feel that way so thank you for confirming that," he said, sounding victorious.

"It does," I told him.

"Well, I guess that is us done then, isn't it?"

"I suppose it is," I replied.

He nodded and looked at the floor for a minute before moving toward the table to pack my gifts back up and place them in an innocuous looking shopping bag for me to take back home. He sat them on the table, his back turned to me. I could hear him as he took a deep breath and then slowly exhaled. Turning around, he forced a smile and handed me the bag.

"I'm going to miss you terribly, Misti."

"I'm going to miss you just as much, Dylan," I replied, taking the bag from his hand, and sitting it on the floor beside me before stepping closer for a hug. We held each other for a moment before he pulled back and kissed me—one kiss filled with a longing I knew wouldn't soon pass for either of us before I left.

"Goodbye," he said in a choked voice as we pulled apart again.

"Goodbye," I told him, retrieving my bag and hurrying for the door before I said three more words that I shouldn't. I opened it and made a beeline for my house, never looking back.

Chapter 24

Dylan

I wasn't sure what I expected to happen after Misti was gone. I had it in my mind that it would be a clean break. Summer was over and so were we. Instead, I got a text from her the very next day.

"Made it to Knoxville just fine. Will stay safe thanks to you."

It wasn't overly personal, but it made me feel better that she wasn't just cutting ties completely now that she was away. I started to reply and then stopped. I didn't want to seem too eager. Instead, I laid the phone to the side and dove back into my work. After a while, I picked up the phone and replied.

"Glad you're back safely. Stay that way."

Rather than sitting in my lab and feeling lost, I decided to go for a drive to clear my head. I picked up my keys and headed out to the garage to fetch the convertible. As I sat down in it, I noticed a small black object in the passenger seat. Reaching over, I picked it up. It was a bobby pin.

I smiled at the thin sliver of metal, remembering seeing Misti pushing several of them in her hair to hold back strands of hair on numerous occasions. I opened the ashtray and laid it inside with a collection of other items I stored in the otherwise unused space and started the car.

As the weeks passed, I found that it was just as hard to resist Misti from a distance as it was when she was next door. We continued to text one another in an increasingly provocative series of messages. I let her take the lead, not wanting to push myself on her but more than happy to be there when she wanted me. It was about two weeks after her departure when I got a text message from her that seemed fairly innocent at first.

"*What are you doing?*" she texted.

"*Just got home from a meeting,*" I texted back.

"*That sounds incredibly boring.*"

"*It wasn't too bad but I'm glad to be home and it's always good to talk to you.*"

"*Yes, but it was better when we could talk in person.*"

I hesitated for a moment. Did she mean just what she said or was she alluding to something else we may have done in addition to talking? I didn't want to overstep any boundaries, so I kept it neutral with my reply.

"*Talking in person is always preferable.*"

"*How about a video chat instead?*"

"*Sure. When?*"

Rather than answering, my phone began to chime. I smiled and answered, smiling as her lovely face filled the screen. She was wearing a tank top without a bra, her hard nipples visible through the thin material. Her hair was pulled up into a messy bun and her skin looked like it was positively glowing.

"Well, there you are. And you look amazing. I take it that school is being good to you?"

"It is. Busy, but it's good. How are things with you?" she asked, reaching up to push some hair back that had escaped one of the pins. I noticed that the bracelet was still intact.

"Things are good. I see you still have the bracelet on so that's great."

"Oh, yes!" she said, holding up her arm again to look at it and for me to see. "I've gotten so many compliments on it from people. They all want to know where I got it. I didn't know if I was supposed to talk about it, so I just told them it was a gift."

"Ah, good. Yes. I hadn't thought about that. I'm not quite ready to do any big reveals yet and probably don't want to advertise what one looks like really."

"I can see that. So, do you miss me?" she said, biting her lip provocatively.

What was she up to and was I opposed to it? I wasn't quite certain, but I got a sudden feeling that this wasn't exactly a platonic call. I smiled at her and nodded.

"More than you know," I answered.

"Show me," she said.

"Show you? What did you have in mind?" I asked, wanting to make certain there were no misunderstandings about what was going on.

Rather than responding, she began pulling her tank top over her head, slowly revealing more and more of the breasts that I missed so much. She reached upward and cupped them in her hands, pushing them upward seductively. She licked her lips and smiled, her lips curled into a sensual curve and her eyes darkened with desire.

"Are you going to just watch or participate?" she purred into the camera.

"Oh, I'm in," I told her, popping my phone into a nearby stand so I had use of my hands.

I watched as she slowly undressed, matching each piece of clothing she lost with one of my own until we were both naked and exploring our own bodies, turned on by one another's needs. I had never had cam sex before. I'd never even had phone sex, for that matter. It had always seemed kind of silly, but now I was totally getting it.

"Tilt the screen down. I want to see that big cock of yours," Misti cooed as she did the same, spreading her legs open for me to see the familiar wetness I'd enjoyed many times. She slid a single long-nailed finger down her stomach and pushed apart her pretty pink folds, never taking her eyes off of me.

I tilted my phone downward to show her how hard I was for her, my rock-hard boner standing at full attention. What I wouldn't give to bury it in her right now. I wanted her so badly, but she was out of my reach. Still, this was better than nothing. I watched her finger herself, slowly dragging her fingers across her pussy entrance before slipping two of them inside.

"Mmm," I groaned, enjoying the way she closed her eyes and tilted her head back, her long neck exposed and begging to be kissed and caressed. Her breasts heaved slowly up and down with the movements of her hand as she panted and moaned with pleasure.

"Do you like what you see?" she asked.

"I lo-ike it a lot," I replied, catching myself.

"Do you get off by yourself thinking about me now that I'm away?" she gasped between her own manipulations.

"Sometimes. How about you? Do you touch that sweet pussy of yours and wish it was me?" I asked.

"All the time," she said, leaning back forward to look at me again.

We were silent for a moment, both of us just enjoying the show the other was putting on for the camera, for the person on the other end of the camera. I was mesmerized by her. We'd texted here and there while she was gone, but it had seemed like those letters you get from an old lover who keeps in touch for a while and then fades away. I was surprised by her video call and even more surprised at how it was going.

"I want to come," she moaned, fingering herself harder and faster. She closed her eyes again, biting her lips and leaning slightly forward so I had a nice full view of her tits. She raised her body and pulled the suction dildo I had given her from behind her, fashioning it onto the center of the chair and then slipping down onto it.

"Glad to see you are getting used to that," I told her.

"Plenty of use," she grunted as she lowered her body, impaling herself on the big black latex cock and began slowly slipping up and down the length of it, squeezing her breasts and pinching her nipples between her fingers until they were red and hard with excitement.

"Fuck me, you look amazing. I am so jealous of a dildo right now."

"Don't be. I'd much rather have your cock," she groaned.

I was so close to coming but I wanted to hold back until she was done. I slowed my pace, stroking myself in long, fluid paces while I watched her get herself off. It didn't take long. Soon her beautiful body was rocketing up and down on her toy. I could see her head roll back as the first wave of an orgasm rippled through her body.

"Such perfection," I moaned.

"God, I'm coming. I'm coming so hard," she screeched.

"I'm coming too," I told her, my dick pulsating with thick spurts of semen surging upward, eager to escape.

She had lost all control as he body spasmed with a powerful orgasm. I began jerking my cock to spill my load, letting it splatter upward across my fist and onto my stomach so she could see it.

She finally settled, slipping the cock free of her body, and pulling it free to set aside somewhere off camera. She sat back, her legs still open as she dragged her fingers through her thick juices and slowly licked them clean while looking directly at me. It was enough to get me going again if I had anything left to give.

"Now you're just trying to give an old man a heart attack," I teased.

"Nothing old about you. You could run circles around most guys half your age."

I smiled and watched as she picked up a thin pullover t-shirt and pulled it over her head, her tits pushing the thin material to its limit. She didn't bother to put on any bottoms, content to let me see her heated pussy for as long as I liked.

"That was very nice. Thank you," I told her.

"Are you really thanking me for cam sex like I just served you a hamburger or something?" she teased.

I laughed out loud. It was the first time I could recall laughing since she left, and I wondered if I would laugh again. Was this a one-time thing on a lonely day or would there be more of these digital sexcapades for us to share?

Time would tell, but for now I said a regretful goodbye and we ended the video chat. I sat looking at the blank screen for a long time before I finally stood up and went to take a shower, thinking about how she and I had showered here together dozens of times. Life was dull without her. I was going to have to find a way to let her go.

Chapter 25

Misti

As much as I enjoyed the naughty video chat with Dylan, it made me realize that I was far too hung up on him. Since I'd returned to school, I had not been on one single date. All my time was spent going to class, studying, and hanging out with platonic friends. There had been a number of guys who had shown interest and I had shot them all down. It wasn't that I was so in love with Dylan that I couldn't move on, it was more that I felt like it was just going to be a disappointment to go back to guys my age.

Then I met Tucker at a study group for one of my classes. He was the image of perfection with his chiseled jawline and muscular body. I loved that he wasn't the sort that raced off to the gym every day. Tucker was from Georgia, and he'd earned his muscles on his family farm. Summers filled with hauling hay, mending fences, and tending cattle kept him tan and fit.

He caught my eye as he leaned casually back in his chair. His steel blue eyes surveyed the other students and finally rested on me. I met his eyes unabashedly and held them until a smile began to form on his face. He'd gotten up and came to sit next to me. I quickly saw that he was full of the southern charm that drove even us fellow Southerners wild.

Things just seemed to happen quickly between us after that. We flirted in class and study group a few times and then he asked me out. I was elated that we clicked together so well but a part of me also felt guilty, like I was somehow betraying Dylan and his feelings for me. I pushed it aside, knowing it was just my own shit and not his.

"I made us a reservation at that Italian place everyone is always talking about," he told me when he came to pick me up for our date.

"Really. I've heard it's great," I lied.

"You haven't been?" he said.

"Not yet," I lied again.

In fact, I had been there many times with many different men. It was where every guy with no originality took his dates. It was nice enough to not look like you were cheap but not so expensive that it would break the bank. The food was mediocre and the wine sub par. I was hardly a food snob, but it just wasn't anything special. More importantly, it showed zero thought or imagination.

"So, I'm surprised you don't have a boyfriend," he said as we eventually settled into our pasta and wine, chatting between bites.

"Why? Are women required to always have a man by their side?" I asked, feeling a bit combative suddenly, though I couldn't quite figure out why.

"Of course not. But you—you're like a work of art. I bet guys fall all over themselves to get your attention."

"I don't know about all that. I'm busy most of the time," I told him, wondering how I had missed the signs and ended up here.

"I bet you know exactly what I mean," he said with a somewhat sickening grin.

"Tell me about your family's farm," I said, trying desperately to change the subject.

"Not much to tell. We have about a hundred acres that my grandfather left us. The family has owned it for hundreds of years. Our house is one of those big antebellum things that still has slave quarters on the property, but you know, we don't use them for that."

"I would hope not," I replied, appalled by the entire concept.

"Mom had an idea to turn them into little Air BnBs, give folks a real experience of living in an old slave hut."

"People pay to do that?" I asked, feeling disgusted by the notion.

"Hell yeah. She also rents it out to film folks doing documentaries and historical type movies."

"Interesting," I said.

I could at least understand documenting the history of such places but not profiting off the horrors experienced there. He seemed oblivious to the fact that someone might find it distasteful, and I wasn't inclined to hash it out with him. The charming guy that had garnered my attention had just as quickly lost it.

"How about your family? I hear your old man is loaded."

"I don't really talk about my father's business with strangers," I said, transitioning from feeling a little annoyed to completely ill at ease with him.

"Oh, come on. I'm not a stranger. We've been flirting for a couple of weeks. I just think we should put our cards on the table here. I like to know who I'm dealing with in my personal life."

"I don't see how my father's finances have anything to do with us being on a date," I told him, hoping my tone sounded as cold as I intended.

"Now, don't get all worked up. It was just a question," he said, seeming oblivious to how crass he was being.

I didn't respond, instead toying with the food on my plate and drinking my wine. I just wanted to get this over with, get home and shower off the stench of this night. He continued droning on about various uninteresting topics while I nodded and smiled, sometimes interjecting a word here and there until dinner was finished.

"I was thinking about having dessert, but I don't suppose you need any of that. Can't keep that gorgeous figure eating Tiramisu."

Under normal circumstances, I would have ordered a double helping of it and eaten it with my fingers just to piss him off, but there was something dreadfully off about him. Rather than provoke him, I decided to instead just get done with this huge mistake I'd made as soon as possible.

"I'll pass on the dessert," I said. "If you want some, go ahead but I'm going to excuse myself to the restroom for a moment."

I didn't wait for a reply. Instead, I stood up and picked up my bag with my keys and phone in it. He began motioning for our server the moment I was up so I wouldn't have long. I hurried to the bathroom and pulled out my phone, requesting an Uber to pick me up. I'd slip out of the garden seating area and meet the car to the side of the restaurant to avoid any chance of confrontation.

I'd have to deal with him tomorrow in class and I'd probably have to quit the study group, but I'd deal with that when the time came. Perhaps I was overreacting, and he was just a jerk, but I just couldn't shake how uncomfortable I felt with him now. It was so strange considering how we'd hit it off so quickly.

I put my phone back in my bag and hurried back out of the lady's room, careful to avoid returning toward the direction of the table where he would be waiting for me. Instead, I slipped around the wall on the opposite side to make a hasty exit, but I froze in place as I heard his voice behind me.

"What are you doing?" he asked.

I looked around, acting confused. "Oh, I, uh, I just got turned around."

"Right. Well, anyway, I've paid the check and was looking for you so we can go. I decided to skip dessert myself. Can't have it bogging me down during any strenuous activity we might get up to later," he said with a sickening smile and a wink.

I felt sick. Did this asshole really think that I had any interest in fucking him? There was no way in hell, but how did I get away from him?

"I'm sorry, Tucker but I got a text from my roommate, and I have to get back home. I'll just take an Uber from here and save you the hassle of dropping me off."

"What? Why? What happened."

"She's locked out, so I have to go let her in."

"That's fine. I'll take you. I wouldn't mind seeing your place," he replied.

"No, really it's fine. I'll just wait for the Uber."

"Don't be ridiculous. Who knows how long it will take them to get here on a busy night. I'll take you. Come on."

I looked around uncertainly before finally following him out. I really didn't want to get back in the car with him, but I told myself I was being overly paranoid about him. He was a jerk, but I had no reason to believe he would do me any harm. He seemed like a complete asshole, but I doubted he was a serial killer. Besides, would a serial killer take his victim out in such a public fashion if he intended to kill her?

I finally gave in and followed him out to the car, noting how he bounded around to the other side to get in without even attempting to open my door just as he'd done when he picked me up. I guess chivalry truly was dead, especially with this one. I opened my door and slipped into the passenger seat.

We were only about a few miles from the restaurant when he pulled the car into an empty parking lot beside a closed strip mall and turned to face me. I looked around nervously. We were far enough away from the city to be away from any traffic. I was alone with him here, locked in his car. My heart sank and I chastised myself for not having brought the gun after Dylan went through so much trouble to make sure I had it in case I needed it.

"What are you doing?" I asked. "I told you that I have to get home."

"Oh, come on. We both know that was a lie. All you girls are the same. You lead us on, let us buy you dinner, bat your eyelashes a bit, but when it comes to putting out, you lock your fucking knees together like you've got gold in your cunt."

"That's not—" I tried to say but he cut me off.

"I was all set to rock your world, but you act like you're too good for me," he said. "Just because you have a set of nice tits makes you think you can get by with whatever you want."

He reached out and grabbed my right breast, squeezing it hard enough to hurt. I cried out and he laughed. I was more terrified than I had ever been in my life. My mind went into fight or flight mode and fight quickly won. My arm shot up as if it had a mind of its own and knocked his hand away from my breast. He jumped back, acting surprised.

"What the fuck is wrong with you, you crazy bitch," he screeched at me. "Get the fuck out of my car. I take you out. I buy your dinner, and this is how you act? Get out!"

I didn't hesitate, yanking open the door and climbing out of the car. I had barely pushed it closed when he squealed off, leaving the stench of burnt rubber behind. I coughed and looked around. There was nothing here. My phone buzzed in my hand, and I looked down at it. My Uber was at the restaurant.

I laughed at the absurdity of it all and redirected the Uber to pick me up in front of the shopping center. My apartment was only about five miles from here, but it was dark, and I was hardly dressed for a walk. I waited anxiously for my driver to arrive, noting a shadowy figure lurking at the opposite corner of the parking lot.

"Hurry up, Uber,' I whispered into the night, and they apparently heard me, showing up a few minutes later and pulling into the entrance where I stood.

"Weird place to wait on an Uber," the driver told me when I got in.

"I agree," I replied.

All the way back home, all I could think about was Dylan and how much better things had been with him. I didn't usually have this much grief from a date with a guy my age, but this was certainly the straw that broke the camel's back.

Chapter 26

Dylan

As the weeks went by, my life seemed to finally be moving on without constantly missing Misti. I had a new project on the go developing some high-tech weapon's system for a government contractor. Between that and the continuing improvement of my safety jewelry, I stayed pretty busy. Today, I was working with local police to put a more formal system into place for tracking distress signals.

"How are we doing, Seth?"

Seth was with the IT department at the station. He was helping me to implement the software that would work with their system. We'd been using a mobile unit I'd built for testing purposes, and I'd finally gotten permission to put the full system into place. It would still be a while before it was up and running, but we wanted to get it properly in place for further testing.

"I'm good. How is the signal boost going?" he replied.

"It's doing pretty well. I've tweaked a few things so I'm hoping for better results. We'll see how I did once we get this system up and running for final testing."

"How far are you from going to market with this thing?"

"It'll still be a while. Once we've established that everything is a go here, production can ramp up with the final version of the chips.

We've got the market entry designs created and will add more to the line as it takes off."

"But aren't we the only department who can receive notifications?"

"Yes, for now, you are the only ones who will receive the notifications directly. Anyone outside of this area will go through our team. Once a notification pops up, the police department nearest to the signal's location will be notified. Of course, that's just a temporary fix. I'm in meetings with the powers that be to run it through the 911 system. If I'm lucky, I'll get that sorted in time to go live with the release of the product and skip my team's involvement in emergency situations.

"Sounds like a lot of work," he said, shaking his head.

"It has been and there's still a lot to be done, but it's worth it. I want women to feel safe when they go out. If anything happens, I want them to have the tools they need to get help."

"I mean, there are some pretty cool emergency protocols in place on cell phones these days and there are those air tags you can put in your stuff."

I nodded, following him down the hall toward the server room which also held his desk. It was like his own private computer mecca. He was quite good with the systems, but he wasn't as knowledgeable about the actual crimes that came across the desks of the officers in other parts of the building.

"That's true, but the first thing some guy is gonna do if he snatches a woman off the street is take her phone. It might get broken in the fray. It might get left behind. It might just go dead. This eliminates all of those problems. There is nothing active in this bracelet until it is activated and then it will start emitting that signal I trigger for you to check during our drills."

"I get that. But wouldn't those air tags do the same thing?"

"You might find someone using those, but they have a short range, and you have to be looking for them. This gives someone a way of getting immediate help the moment they know they are in trouble without anyone being the wiser that they've triggered an alarm. Plus, it keeps the stalker types from using it to keep tabs on someone."

"I get it. What about men? Kids?"

"We'll get there. I've started with women because they are the most likely attacked victims. We'll eventually create designs for men and children, but I've got a lot of work to do with kids because it relies on them to trigger the device. There's a lot of room for failure there, especially if they aren't able to trigger it because they are too young or perhaps cognitively challenged. It might depend on a parent triggering it remotely and that opens up a whole new set of concerns."

"Yeah, I can see that. It's a great idea though. I hope it helps. I don't get involved in the cases here in my position, but I read the news and I hear these guys talk. Probably a lot of women out there that go missing that might have had a chance if they'd been wearing one of these. I might get one for my wife if they aren't too expensive."

"They won't be. That's one of my key criteria. I don't want anyone to be priced out of their own safety."

"Well, let's get this sucker online and get you one step closer to saving the women of the world," he said, firing up his computer and taking a seat in front of it. He motioned to the chair sitting to one side and I took my place, working with him to get the software installed.

My phone buzzed while he was adjusting some code to marry my system to his and I picked it up to look at it.

"What are you wearing?" the text said.

I smiled broadly but didn't answer. I'd answer her when I got home and had time to pay attention to her instead of being distracted by work. She was used to me waiting to answer if I was busy.

"Who is she?" Seth asked.

I looked back up to find him smiling and nodding toward the phone in my hand.

"Just a woman I was seeing over the summer."

"Was? Didn't work out?"

"It did, but she was only here on vacation," I lied. "She had to go back east. I've not seen her since she left."

"But you could," he said.

"I suppose, but she hasn't said she wants to see me. I don't want to be the kind of guy that makes her feel like she needs one of my bracelets," I said with a chuckle.

"I see. I'd work on that though. She's still contacting you, so she obviously ain't mad. A man who smiles like that at his phone when it beeps has found someone he needs to spend more time with."

"Ah, if only things were that simple."

"They are when it comes right down to it. I mean, unless she's married. Is she married?"

"No. Nothing like that."

"Well, then hang in there. Women like to be chased."

"I don't know that all women do like that, but I'll keep it in mind."

Seth shrugged and finished up, running me through a demo of the program to show that it was working. We did a short-range test and then I left to do a longer-range test from some different locations, driving out to some spots I'd picked out just for that purpose.

I was tempted to text her once I got home, but I got a call from my research and development guy about some problems they were having with the weapons contract, so I ended up getting sucked into that instead. By the time I was done, it was nearly bedtime, but I didn't want to go to sleep without texting her back.

"Sorry. I've been all over the place with work stuff today. Just now getting a chance to respond," I texted her.

I waited a bit for a response but finally gave up and went to take a shower. It would help me relax before bedtime. When I came back out, there was still no message on my phone. I was disappointed but I couldn't very well expect her to immediately respond when I'd waited for hours to reply to her. I hoped she didn't think it was on purpose.

I threw on some shorts and a T-shirt before going to the kitchen and pulling out a bottle of wine and a clean glass. With a full glass of chianti in my hand, I did something I rarely ever did. I went to the den and turned on the television, setting the rest of the wine on the side table and sinking into the overstuffed sofa there.

I found a movie to stream and settled in for some much-needed downtime. I woke up hours later to find the movie had gone off and was playing previews for suggested films to watch next. I couldn't even remember watching the one I'd selected, Kelly's Heroes, past the first ten minutes or so. I'd seen it several times before so that was no big deal, but I must have been really tired to doze off so quickly.

I picked up my phone immediately and found that Misti had still not responded. It was after midnight, so she was probably in bed by now. I found myself wondering if she was out and if so, was it with a guy? The thought of someone else touching her was something I just couldn't think about. I hated the idea of that so much.

I left my unfinished wine on the side table. At least I hadn't still had it in my hand to pour all over the place when I fell asleep but I couldn't really remember putting it over there. I climbed off of the sofa and went upstairs to sleep. My bed was empty without Misti. Though she'd never spent the night in it, she'd been here enough during our daytime trysts for me to miss having her in it.

I fell asleep with her still on my mind, letting her settle into my dreams with her lovely body and sweet smell. This was the one place where she was always mine.

Chapter 27

Misti

After the horrible experience with Tucker, I had been reluctant to return to class. I had been right to be wary too. He had already started a campaign with the guys in the class labeling me a "cock tease" and a psycho who tried to hit him. It was the other women in class that put a stop to it by pointing out that he was a Neanderthal. I was apparently not the only one who had been on a decidedly uncomfortable date with him.

Eventually, it all died back down, and things went back to normal. However, it had left a bad taste in my mouth, and I just stopped dating altogether for a while. Instead, I continued to text Dylan here and there, flirting and sometimes more. I wasn't sure that was fair to him or to me, when it came right down to it, but I was lonely, and he felt safe to me right now.

So, I think I surprised even myself when I started daydreaming about my handsome literature professor. I'd noticed him when I'd picked up his class, but I'd been too involved with Dylan then to think much more about it than just that he was nice to look at. It had only been once I was in his class that I truly saw how appealing he was. From the first day, I was mesmerized by him.

"My name is Dr. Gregory Simmons. This class will blend fact with fiction, history with imagination and criminals with criminally bad writers."

There had been scattered laughter throughout the class and then he had continued, explaining what his historical fiction class would cover and his expectations of us. Watching him as he walked around the front of the room speaking, I had been struck by his eloquence and grace. His sandy blonde hair had been shorn on the sides but toppled about atop his head as he moved his sinewy frame from side to side to address students. A lovely pair of pale blue eyes had twinkled with good humor as he spoke.

The more I listened to him, the more I watched him move, the more interesting he became to me. I knew from discussions with other women in the class that he wasn't married and didn't seem to have a girlfriend that anyone knew about. That made him fair game. I decided that he was mine for the taking. I decided to make myself available to him outside of class and see what happened.

"Fancy meeting you here," he said to me as he pulled into his parking space outside the building a few days later.

I couldn't quite tell if he was seriously surprised or being coy about the fact that I'd obviously placed myself there to run into him. I'd gotten up early, taken my time curling my hair into long curly tendrils that feathered about my face and done my makeup to perfection. I'd opted for a white button-down blouse and a short skirt instead of the T-shirt and jeans I usually wore to class.

I'd made my way down to where I knew he parked so I could walk into the building with him, timing my approach to match his arrival once I saw him pulling into the parking lot.

It was a bit stalkerish, I supposed, but it was an isolated transgression. It wasn't like I was following him around or building a shrine.

Mainly, it just gave me an opportunity to speak to him one-on-one without having to frame it around class material. I didn't want to have to make an appointment and act dumb about some assignment. I wanted him to see me looking yummy outside the classroom setting.

"It's quite a miracle, what with us headed to the same place and all," I quipped, giving him my most winning smile.

"Indeed," he said, pulling a briefcase from the backseat of his car and joining me on the sidewalk. "Shall we proceed?"

"We shall," I said, turning to walk with him as he approached.

"So, Miss Bridges, is it?" he said.

I was impressed that he knew my name with so many students in his class. Perhaps I had already made a bit of an impression on him, after all.

"Yes, but Misti is fine."

"Very well, Misti. How are you enjoying the class so far?"

"It's great. I find the intersection of historical fact and related fiction fascinating," I said, trying my best not to sound like an idiot.

"Yes, it is an interesting crossing of paths. What, in particular, do you find compelling?"

I had hoped to avoid this. I didn't want to talk about school things. I wanted to talk about more personal things, but I should have expected that I couldn't just launch right into that.

"I think the most fascinating part is the liberties people take with history. You see all the time that something is based on a true story and many people take for granted that it follows the actual truth of the situation, but it doesn't mean that at all."

"No, it doesn't."

"People can take the tiniest shred of truth and build on it to make it complete fiction."

"Yes. They are looking at history as no more than a writing prompt. They see a beautiful young girl in a white shirt and short skirt, and she inspires them to envision a story about what her life is like. There is absolutely no truth to their story other than they based it on the fact that they saw you walking with me on this sidewalk."

There was no mistaking the compliment hidden in the comment, and I smiled but wasn't sure if I should thank him for it or just let it be. Luckily for me, we arrived at the door, and he encountered a colleague looking for help with something.

"Professor Simmons," the other man said, "I need to talk to you for a minute before you start your lecture."

"Oh, of course, Gordon," he replied to the man before turning back to me, "I will see you in class, Miss Bridges. Would you let my assistant know that I may be just a tiny bit late and go ahead and start class if I'm not there on time? Could you do that for me?"

"Yes, Professor Simmons," I said politely, internally sulking about the interruption as I walked toward the doors, leaving them behind on the steps to have whatever discussion was needed.

It was frustrating that I had worked so hard to facilitate our being able to talk briefly and just when he seemed to be broaching something more personal than shop talk, it had been cut short. It wasn't like I could keep showing up at his car without looking pathetic and obvious.

I went into class and spotted his assistant, a student instructor named Todd. I relayed the message to him as requested and then took my seat. A guy near me stared idly at the generous cleavage visible at the top of my blouse. I scowled at him, and he looked away, his cheeks flushing with embarrassment. Poor bastard probably didn't even realize he was just staring.

I ran into that sort of thing a lot. It was like my tits had some sort of ability to hypnotize men. In some cases, I had found that useful. It got me out of a lot of speeding tickets. It got me free stuff at stores and events. It didn't really bother me like it did some women. There was no harm in noticing them as long as you weren't creepy about it and didn't overstep any lines in the sand.

Professor Simmons showed up for class about fifteen minutes late and motioned for his assistant to continue rather than him taking over. He sat in a nearby chair looking over some papers in his hand, occasionally looking up at his stand in and nodding as if to confirm that what he was saying was correct. From time to time, he looked out across the class from student to student, but paid no special attention to me. It appeared that I had blended right back into the crowd.

When class ended, I picked up my books but lingered, hopeful that he would approach and strike up some sort of conversation, perhaps just as a way of apologizing that we were interrupted earlier, but he showed no signs of doing so. Instead, I filed out with the rest of the students and made my way down the hallway and out of the building to attend my next class.

If I wanted attention, I certainly got it there. Though he no longer made comments about me, Tucker wasn't opposed to glaring at me across the room. He had been shut down and he wasn't happy about it. If the truth were to be told, he scared me a bit. There were a lot of things he could have done to me while we were alone in his car, worse things than just putting me out in the dark. He had dialed it back in the end, but now he had been publicly shamed about his behavior. He blamed me for that, and he seemed like just the type to seek some revenge. I just did my best to steer clear of him—and I'd started carrying the gun that Dylan gave me.

Unlike my exit from Professor Simmons' class, I didn't linger once class ended here. I hurried out in order to avoid any chance of crossing Tucker's path. Several of the other women in the class had noticed that I no longer chatted with them after class. I told the ones who asked about my experience with Tucker, explaining that I just didn't want to tell anyone how afraid of him I truly was. I honestly felt him capable of violence and with a short fuse that could push him to spiral out of control.

I'd also talked about what happened with Stephanie the day after it had happened. She was furious. Her suggestion was that we go over to his frat house, find his room, and chop off his balls, but I convinced her that might be a bit excessive.

"Think of all the jail pussy I'd get though," she joked.

"That might be fine for you, but not so much for me," I replied.

"I bet there are some hot guards," she said, grinning.

"I bet there are some men who just get off on controlling women in those uniforms. I think I'll stick with staying clear of any horsemen of the patriarchy."

"I guess that's smart," she said, "but I'm still pissed off about it."

"Yeah, it sucks but I'd rather be safe than sorry. Better to just avoid him and let him cool down. Hopefully, I won't wind up in any more classes with him."

"Just be careful and just know that if we need to get the scissors out, I'm your girl."

I nodded an acknowledgment, laughing as I grabbed a bottle of water out of the fridge before going to my room to study.

Chapter 28

Dylan

With my safety jewelry in production and the weapons contract in high gear, I'd had my hands full with work, but I'd begun noticing that the texts from Misti had become fewer and fewer. We'd stopped having the naughty cam chats completely. A part of me was relieved.

A relationship centered around a digital tether wasn't sustainable. Plus, we both knew that she was less than three hours away. If she wanted to see me, she could drive home, ask me to come there, or meet me somewhere in the middle. She kept me at a distance and that was probably best for both of us.

I was walking through the park, something I'd taken to doing since she'd been gone. Today, I'd grabbed a steak gyro from a nearby food truck and planned to sit on a bench near the large lake that sat to one side of the path and enjoy them out in the fresh air. I was glad to find it empty when I arrived and had a seat, spreading out my food on my lap. That's when the shit hit the fan.

"Samson! No!" a woman screamed as a large black and white dog of questionable heritage came bounding down the path nearby. She held a leather leash in her hands as she tried to catch up to him before he got too far away.

Before I could react, the dog pounced on me, snatching the gyro from my hands. He ran toward the grass across the path in front of me to scarf it down. Caught by complete surprise by my furry mugger, I stood up and began knocking off remnants of shredded lettuce that had shaken loose onto my clothes. The woman arrived in time to get the leash back on her dog and get him back under control.

She immediately turned back to me and looked me up and down, presumably for signs of serious damage done. Finding nothing horrific, she looked somewhat relieved but embarrassed. She wound the leash around her hand and snapped at the dog to sit down. He hesitated, still licking the flavor of my lunch from his lips happily.

"I am so sorry. I took him off his leash for just a second to get it untangled and he just took off," she told me, her eyes pleading for mercy.

"He ate my gyro," I told her, though I really wasn't angry. In fact, I was a bit amused, and she was extremely attractive. Her large blue eyes looked shocked and then she glanced down at the dog as if he could explain himself before looking back up at me.

"I'll pay for it. I'll go buy you another one. Where did it come from?" she said, already reaching into her pocket, presumably for cash.

"It came from the food truck, but he's already gone by now and I'm still hungry," I told her, noting that her ring finger was devoid of a ring.

"Oh. I, uh. I'll just give you cash for more lunch. Would that be okay?"

"No. I'm going to require more contrition than that," I told her.

She stared at me, looking wary as she asked, "What do you want? You aren't going to file a report are you? He's really a good dog. He's just not mine and I'm not used to him."

"Did you steal him?"

"What? No. Of course not! He belongs to my brother," she said, squinting her eyes at me as I began to grin mischievously.

She dropped her head and shook it back and forth before looking up at me again, the sun now shifting so that it shined into her impossibly blue eyes. They were stunning. All of her was stunning really. She squinted against the light, a smile slowly spreading across her face.

"You're just fucking with me, aren't you?" she said.

"I most certain am just fucking with you. However, "Clifford" there did eat my lunch and I demand restitution. I will settle for you letting me take you to dinner," I said, feeling hopeful about this little happenstance encounter.

"I don't know. You might be completely famished by then. What if you are too weak to even show up. I detest being stood up."

"I think I can probably find another sandwich to tide me over. "Clifford" won't be joining us to eat my supper too, will he?"

"No. Clifford, whose name is actually Samson, is going to the pound as soon as I leave this park."

I laughed. Hopefully, she was kidding.

"Well, that sorts that out then. My name is Dylan Hayward, by the way. You can google me when you get home to make sure I'm not on any lists."

"You expect me to tell you my name so you can cyberstalk me too?" she replied.

"Yes. It's all the rage with modern romance," I quipped.

"Very well. My name is Gretchen Saintfield."

"Is that your real name?" I asked.

"You'll find out," she purred. "825 Hillview. Be there at seven sharp."

"Seven sharp. Got it," I told her.

"Come on, Clifford," she said. "We've got to get you home before you do worse things than get me a date."

I chuckled and watched her walk away. Rather than heading home, I went to a nearby deli and ordered a Reuben on rye and a bottle of water. I sat down at a nearby table and pulled out my phone while I waited.

"Okay, Gretchen Saintfield, let's see who you are," I said, googling her name.

My eyes widened as the results popped up. There were no social media links, no journals, no op eds or blogs. Instead, there were numerous articles about the woman I met in the park. She wasn't just Gretchen Saintfield. She was Superior Court Judge Gretchen Saintfield.

"Reuben on rye?" the deli worker called out.

I put away my phone and retrieved my sandwich, sitting back down at my table to enjoy a Clifford-free lunch and ponder what sort of woman the beautiful Judge Saintfield might be. If the news reports about some of her cases were accurate, she was quite a force to be reckoned with. I was looking forward to finding out more.

I pulled up at the front of her house with a couple of minutes to spare. Now that I knew she was a judge, I understood that a lack of punctuality was likely a huge turnoff for her. There was no sense getting off on the wrong foot with her. I parked the car, a Rolls Royce Ghost Black Badge I'd purchased last year, in the circular drive just outside her front doors. The car was a bit ostentatious, but I'd not been able to resist its sleek lines and smooth handling.

I wouldn't normally drive it to a date. I didn't like to flaunt my wealth, but I was willing to bet that the good judge had already thoroughly researched me and wouldn't be surprised by the expense of my car. Moreover, it just seemed more appropriate for a date with her than one of my flashier cars.

I rang the bell and waited, expecting to be greeted by my radiant looking date for the evening. Instead, I found myself looking at a rather large man in a dark suit. I asked to see Gretchen and he scowled.

"Name?" he said dryly.

"Dylan Hayward," I replied.

"Are you armed?" he asked.

"Are you serious?" I replied, taken aback.

"Yes. I'm quite serious," he replied.

"Harlan, he's my date. You're not at the TSA anymore," she said, appearing beside him and waving him away from the door.

"Hello Judge Saintfield," I said with a large smile.

"Ah. I see you've done your homework."

"I have. I trust you have done yours, as well."

"Someone did," she replied, her way of letting me know that not only did she know all about me, but so did those who protect her best interests.

"Well, here we are then. Shall we leave our jobs at the doorstep and go be people?"

"I'd like that," she replied.

"You look lovely, by the way," I told her, walking her to the car and opening the door.

"Thank you," she replied as she sat down inside.

It was a lovely beginning to a promising relationship, but it quickly went sour. After a half dozen dates and a few coffees between her court sessions and my meetings, we eventually found ourselves in an awkward situation. It was at the end of a wonderful evening of dancing and mingling among guests as a fund raiser she'd invited me to as her plus one. The problem arose when I took her back home.

"Do you want to come in?" she asked.

"I don't think so. I have an early day," I told her.

"I'm beginning to think you are never going to come in," she replied.

"Goodnight, Gretchen," I told her, kissing her softly on the lips before turning to go.

"Dylan?" she called after me.

I turned around, one eyebrow cocked in silent question.

"Is there someone else you are seeing?"

"No. I'll call you tomorrow," I told her.

This time, she didn't respond. I heard her front door open and close behind me as I reached my car and got in. For a moment, I just sat down behind the wheel and contemplated what I was doing. Gretchen Saintfield was a good woman. She was smart and beautiful, but I just couldn't get as excited about her. I considered how much of that was about her and how much of it was about Misti as I pulled away from her house, knowing I would likely never return.

Tonight wasn't the first time she'd asked but I'd always declined, not wanting to get physical too soon. I told myself that I just wanted this to last. I wanted to solidify our relationship a bit more before getting overly involved but deep down I knew it was more than that.

Gretchen was beautiful. Despite being in her late forties, she was in great shape. She had the athletic body of a runner, something she did every morning before work. Her breathtaking eyes and smooth pale skin contrasted with her ebony hair, though I suspected the latter came from a bottle. Most men would bed her in an instant if they got the chance, but not me.

The truth was, she had her flaws. She was very opinionated about the lines between right and wrong, though that likely came from being a former lawyer turned judge. Though her intelligence was intoxicating, it could also be off-putting. She had no room for differing opinions. It could make the conversation one sided at times.

Still, was that enough reason to lose interest in her? Maybe. Maybe not. Right or wrong, I was in love with Misti and until I got past that, I couldn't move on, even though it was growing clearer by the day that she had.

Chapter 29

Misti

"Well, this is quite unexpected," a voice said from behind me.

I turned to see Professor Simmons standing there with a shopping bag from a nearby hardware store in one hand and a journal in the other. He smiled broadly at me.

"It is unexpected. I didn't think anyone knew about this bookshop," I told him.

"It is a well-kept secret but one of the other professors let me in on it," he replied.

"What did you find?" I asked, nodding at the book in his hand.

"Oh, this? It's just a journal but it's antique. I came by earlier but discovered they don't take cards, so I had to go get cash to hurry back to buy it. I'm looking forward to filling it with words."

"You're going to write in it?" I gasped.

"Yes. Why wouldn't I?"

"Because, as you said, it's an antique."

"All the more reason to finally let it see its purpose. This book was handcrafted by someone. It was put together with careful stitching and hand pressed pages. That person spent hours of their life making this book so that someone would fill it with words, not put it on a shelf to collect dust."

"I guess I never thought of it that way. Most people I know buy journals and then don't want to spoil them by writing in them."

"And you?"

"Me what?"

"Do you write in your journals?"

"I don't really own any," I admitted. "I have a few notebooks that I keep school notes or grocery lists in but that's about it."

"Nothing wrong with that. Not everyone feels the need to catalog their thoughts. What are you looking at there?" he asked, pointing toward the book in my hand.

"Poetry. 100 Love Sonnets, Pablo Neruda," I replied.

"I love you as certain dark things are to be loved, in secret, between the shadow and the soul," he said, quoting one of my favorite poems.

"Sonnet XVII," I said, hoping to display my knowledge of Neruda's work.

"You know your Neruda. Very nice."

"He wrote such beautiful poems. I'm hoping that once I complete another semester of Spanish, I'll be able to read it in its original form and understand it. I hear it's even more incredible in his native tongue."

"It is. I'd be happy to read it to you in its original form, but if you don't have a firm grasp of the language, you are right, it won't really have the same impact."

I was flustered, not really sure how to respond. The thought of him reading me love sonnets in Spanish while cuddled together near a roaring fire invaded my thoughts and left me speechless for a moment. I merely smiled and tried desperately to find some words instead of looking like a moron.

"Listen, I've got to get going but we will talk again soon," he said.

"Sure. I'll see you in class," I replied, still feeling a bit stupid.

"You will, but perhaps we could explore Neruda together some more instead—outside of class."

"That would be wonderful," I said, trying to sound interested but not desperate.

"Meet me here again on Thursday. Same time?" he offered.

"I'll be here," I said.

"Oh, and Misti. I'm sure you are smart enough to know this already, but let's not mention it to anyone. It would look bad with me being your professor and all."

"I understand," I told him.

That was the beginning of everything.

Within the week, Professor Gregory Simmons was simply Greg, and we were carrying on a torrid affair.

"I want you to come up to my place this weekend," he told me as I got dressed in his apartment one morning.

"I thought we were at your place," I told him.

"This is just a place I keep to be closer to the school. I have a house about an hour or so outside the city toward Grandview. It's pretty rural, surrounded by trees with a large pond out back. You are going to love it."

"It sounds amazing. I'd love to go."

"I'll meet you at our usual spot on Friday after your classes. What time do you get out?"

"I'm done by two," I told him.

"I'll be ready by four, so that will give you time to get packed up and get there," he said, pulling me into a kiss before I left for my place.

"I'll be there waiting for you," I said as he let me go and stepped back.

"See you in class," he said.

I smiled and opened the back door to exit the small townhouse where he lived. We were always super careful not to be seen together. It could cost him his job. I had come to learn since we'd been fucking that he was quite wealthy. He hadn't really elaborated on it, but I knew his parents were dead, so I assumed that maybe they had left him minted. I couldn't imagine that he'd gotten rich as a nontenured professor at UT.

Since we had been seeing one another, he had spared no expense. We weren't really able to go out in Knoxville where we might be seen so he drove us to places in neighboring cities where no one would see us. Most of them were exclusive, so there was very little chance of any other professors or students running into us. Anyone else wouldn't have any idea who we were to think twice about it.

I was bursting to tell Stephanie, but I didn't. It was only after she kept pushing me that I even admitted I was seeing someone. No amount of her prodding could get me to tell her who though.

"Come on. Since when do you keep things from me? I know all about you and your billionaire neighbor stud. What's so secret about this new guy?"

"I really can't say anything about who he is. I will tell you that he is older, hot, and fantastic in bed," I told her.

"Better than the neighbor?"

"Not better, but still very talented. We have a good time."

"I just bet you do," she said.

"How about you? Do you have anyone in your life since the big breakup?"

"No. I've just been laying low, going out with some easy bitches from the club. You know, lick 'em and leave 'em."

"You have such a way with words," I joked.

"It's the way I use my tongue," she quipped, winking at me.

"Incorrigible," I scolded.

"You know it," she said, grabbing a soda and heading toward her bedroom. "I've got a trig test tomorrow, so I'll be in my room studying if you need me."

"I'll be as quiet as a cat stalking a mouse," I said.

"Okay, pussycat."

She disappeared into her room and I grabbed the bottle of vodka we kept in the freezer, pouring it into a glass and topping it off with some pink grapefruit juice. I sat at the table and sipped it, thinking about the upcoming weekend with Greg. It reminded me of the last time I had gone away for a few days with a man.

The thought of that weekend in Sevierville filled me with melancholy. Even though I was having a good time with Greg, Dylan seeped into my thoughts all the time. I missed him and a part of me wanted to return to him, but I knew it would be a mistake. I wouldn't want to leave again. I knew that I had to let him go in order to follow my own dreams and I had no right to ask him to wait while I did so.

I downed my drink and poured myself another before going to my room. I sat at my desk and opened my laptop, doing an internet search for Dylan out of wild curiosity. There was an assortment of company profiles and articles about his business that popped up, but one caught my eye. He was finally releasing the jewelry. I twisted the bracelet that I still wore on my wrist as I read the article with something that seemed like pride, though I had no right.

Clicking off of the article, I moved to another. It was an article about a charity event. Dylan was smiling broadly up at a cameraman, his head tilted toward a gorgeous woman who was listed as Judge Gretchen Saintfield. Another photo was a long shot of the attendees. Dylan could be seen dancing with the judge, his arm around her as he looked down at her. I couldn't see his face, but she was all smiles.

So, that was it then. Dylan had moved on. I would move on too. Greg and I couldn't be seen together now, but if we continued to see one another there was a chance my relationship with him would grow beyond just clandestine meetings. Perhaps I hadn't really been looking at it as long-term because somewhere in the back of my head I was still holding back. I felt so conflicted about the way I was constantly fighting my feelings for Dylan but seeing this picture of him with someone closer to his age—someone he seemed happy to be with—made me realize that I needed to stop talking about letting him go and actually do it.

Chapter 30

Dylan

After the continued lack of communication between us, I had come to the realization that Misti was well and truly lost to me. I went a little out of control. I began frequenting a local bar that was usually coming down with women. Over the course of the past few weeks, I had banged a string of women half my age, in some cases more than one in the same night or at the same time. Tonight, I was back for another round of drowning my sorrows in pussy.

"What's your name, sailor?" a long-legged redhead purred as she sat down by me at the bar.

"Does that line work on many dudes?" I asked, turning slightly to look at her.

"I don't know about the line, but these tits seem to do that trick," she said, reaching up to cup her ample breasts.

"Well, those are impressive but I'm going to pass on whatever it is you have in mind," I told her.

"At least buy me a drink?" she said.

I eyed her again, noting the tired look in her eyes. She was close to my age and dressed in clothing that looked like it had seen better days.

"I'll make a deal with you. I will buy you all the drinks you want if you tell me about yourself," I told her.

"Yeah?" she said.

"Yeah. Just the truth though. No lies. Okay?"

"Okay. I'll play your little game. Drink first though," she said suspiciously.

I turned back to the bartender, who I had come to know by name lately.

"Juan Carlos, whatever the lady wants is on my tab tonight."

"Dylan, I don't think," he started to say, but I held up my hand to stop him.

"It'll be fine. Just get her a drink and another for me," I told him.

"Southern Comfort on the rocks," she said, adding "and a shot of tequila."

"That stuff is poison. Why don't you order something nicer?" I told her.

"Nah. No use getting used to stuff I can't afford," she replied.

"Okay, well I'm Dylan. What's your name?"

"Dorothy Rose, but you can call me Dot," she told me.

I could imagine that Dorothy Rose had once been a pretty woman. That was obvious from her bone structure and her figure, but she led a hard life. She told me that, by day, she worked as a server in a seedy diner frequented by hungover locals. At night, she mostly sat in this bar hoping men would buy her drinks to help her forget how horrid her life had become. Her honesty about who she was and what she did was brutal, with no apologies or attempts to sugarcoat things.

"I married young, not even out of high school. He was handsome, popular, and ill-tempered. I was a cheerleader, and he was jealous of anyone who looked at me in the skimpy uniforms we wore. I thought it just meant that he loved me so much that he didn't like anyone disrespecting me," she told me, her words followed by a bitter laugh.

"But you married him anyway?"

"Yes. Like I said, I was young and stupid. I had dated some guys but all they wanted was to get in my pants. He was the first who wanted more than that from me. He told me he loved me, and I believed him. We eloped. Three months later I was pregnant, and he forced me to quit school. He said I could go back later but I never did," she said, looking incredibly pained.

"Do you want to stop?" I asked her, motioning toward Juan Carlos for a refill on our drinks.

"No. It's just a bad memory. I made a deal with you, and I'm not done drinking."

"Listen, Dot. Don't worry about the deal we made. If this is causing you pain, we can stop. I'll still cover whatever drinks you want."

"I'll keep going. We're almost to the end anyway. I lost the baby. I mean, I took care of myself the best I could without proper healthcare, but it wasn't enough. We didn't have much money and what little we did have, he spent on liquor. Anyway, he blamed me for losing the baby and he beat me. I couldn't see for three days, and I could barely walk."

"Jesus…" I said.

She waved her hand dismissively and finished her drink, accepting the fresh one Juan Carlos brought to the table, telling me how this had gone on for years. He'd get drunk, beat her, and then disappear for a few days while she healed up. Things would be okay for a bit, but he wanted another baby and took out his anger on her even more now that she wasn't getting pregnant again.

"The truth was, I was stashing birth control pills one of my friends got for me. She went in and got a prescription in her name so he wouldn't know. I started working and was saving up money to try and get away from him. Then, one night, I came home from my job, and he was holding them in his hand. He beat me so badly that I was sure I was going to die."

"God, Dot," I said, horrified. "Didn't you have family to help you? The police?"

"I was scared. He threatened my family. Told me if I left he'd kill me and whoever helped me. I'd removed my friend's name from the birth control pills and told him I got them from the free clinic so he wouldn't bother her."

"What about the police?"

"I called them a few times when it was bad, but I'd always get scared and drop the charges. I was afraid they'd let him out on bond, and he'd kill me or that I would lose the case and he would come after me."

"I get it. You were young and scared. I'm sorry that happened to you. How long did it take you to get away from all of that?"

"That same night. He got scared after what he did to me and took off. He crashed his car into a telephone pole and ended up a vegetable. I unplugged the bastard while I still had a broken arm, a cracked jaw, a concussion, and the bruises he'd left all over me," she said, a weary smile on her face as she tossed back the last of her drink.

"So, you were free," I said.

"No. I'll never be free. I have lived the past 35 years being completely fucked up in the head. I work a shitty job, go home to a crappy RV, and come here to drown my troubles."

"And instead, you find me, and I make you relive it all."

"You didn't make me do anything. I've kept that story to myself for all these years. It felt pretty good just to get it off my chest. I could use another drink though."

I motioned toward Juan Carlos to refill her drink and leaned back in my chair, eying her for a few moments before making up my mind. I leaned forward, looking at her in her somewhat glazed eyes.

"Tell me something, Dot. What keeps you from going back to school?"

She laughed and shook her head. "I don't have any time for school. I work constantly just to pay the rent on my shit hole camper and eat. I guess it could be worse, at least I don't have kids. The damage my ex did...this is the funny part, it left me unable to have kids at all," she said bitterly.

"Do you have any job skills other than waiting tables at a diner?"

"Not really. I took some typing in school, but no one wants to hire someone without a high school diploma."

"I do."

"What?"

"Dot, I came here tonight because I was feeling sorry for myself. I lost someone I loved and she's not coming back. Then, you told me your story and I realized that other people have real issues in their lives that are a lot more important than just a relationship that didn't work out."

"Okay..." she said, looking at me to see what I would say next.

"I own a company. We have a position open for a receptionist. I know you can deal with the public if you wait tables. Can you answer phones? Direct calls? Take messages?"

"Well, yes," she said tentatively, no doubt waiting for the catch.

"I want to hire you as my new receptionist. I can pay you 40K a year, but you do need a high school diploma."

Her face fell. "I already told you that I don't have one."

"I know. That's why I'm going to pay for you to get one. You can come to work for me with the agreement that you will complete the night courses you need and pass the GED test. I will pay for all the costs associated with that on top of your salary. Plus, you will have health insurance, vacation pay, sick pay and access to a 401K program."

She looked at me, a puzzled expression on her face. "Why would you do that?"

"Because I can, Dot."

"And you don't want anything in return?"

"Yes. I want to see you smile."

She forced a smile on her face, and I shook my head back and forth.

"No, Dot. I don't want to see you smile because I told you to do it. I don't want you to ever feel like you have to do what a man tells you to do again. I want to walk in the front doors of my office building and see your beaming face at my front desk. I want a real smile. I want you to have a chance to be happy."

Tears began falling down her face and she reached for a napkin to dry her eyes. I smiled softly at her and reached my hand over to cover hers.

"It's going to be okay, Dot."

"You don't know me. How do I know I can trust you?"

"You don't. I don't know if you'll show up for work every day or if you'll be passed out drunk in your living room from the night before. All I can tell you is that I've spent too many nights in this bar picking up women half your age and I don't remember any of their names. Why? Because I was sad, and I wanted them to make me feel better."

"Did they?"

"Some of them, for a little while—but it was a temporary fix to a heartache. Just like you coming in here and drinking after your shift at the diner so you don't have to go home to a shitty camper is a temporary fix to your pain. I'm filthy fucking rich, Dot. You and I are going to have one last night of drinking here in this bar and then tomorrow, you are going to get up and pack your belongings."

"Pack? Why?" she said, sounding a little alarmed again.

"Because tomorrow I'm going to send a car for you. The driver will take you to a little house I own not far from the office, just outside the city."

She looked down at her hands. I could almost read her mind.

"Dot, I'm not putting you up to take advantage of you. The house was rented out, but the last tenant recently moved, so it's empty now. All of the utilities and cable are included, so you'll have everything you need to get started. I have too much money and you have none. Why? Because I had better luck with my life than you did. Plain and simple. Let me do this for you. I promise you it's for real. Now, would you like another drink?"

"Maybe just one for the road. It sounds like I need to get some sleep. I don't know what to say," she half croaked.

"Don't say anything. This is just our little deal between the two of us and we don't need to even discuss it again after tonight. I'll get everything set up for you tomorrow before I send the car. Two p.m. good for you?"

"Yes," she replied.

I got her address and sent her home in an Uber. Once she was gone, I had a couple more drinks before paying my tab and catching another car back to my place. Tomorrow was going to be a busy day. Dot wasn't the only one who needed to sleep it off.

Chapter 31

Misti

"Look at you. You look like a million dollars. You're practically glowing," Stephanie gushed as I returned home from the weekend at Greg's house. "Oh, God. You aren't pregnant are you?"

"What? Don't be ridiculous. Of course I'm not pregnant. I just had a really good time. His house is amazing. It's one of those old Victorian homes out in the middle of nowhere, not another house around for miles."

"That's great. I'm glad you had a good time. I still can't believe you won't tell me who this guy is though."

"I just can't but you'd shit a brick if I could."

"I guess I'll just have to take your word for that," she told me.

I could tell she didn't like it. She felt like I didn't trust her, but that wasn't it at all. People had a way of revealing things to others in confidence and then that person told others without their permission.

I wasn't worried about Stephanie telling the general population, but she tended to be loose-lipped with her lovers. There was a good chance that someone she might meet was also a student. It could very easily turn ugly, so she'd just have to be a little upset about it. I wasn't taking that risk.

Greg and I were really hitting it off. It was a pain having to keep everything quiet and being limited as to where we could go together, but if we kept seeing one another, that wouldn't be forever. Once I was out of school, there would be no reason we couldn't date. No one had to know it started while I was still a student.

The house in the country became a regular thing for us. Greg invited me there every weekend so that we could both get away. Sometimes, he had to grade papers, one of them my own. He was fair with my grades, despite our relationship. No automatic A's, but I was a good student so I did pretty well without any special favors.

I used the time that he was busy with grading to do my own studying or venture around the property. He hadn't told me about the garden before we came here. It was a bit overgrown. In fact, the entire house was a bit rundown. It was clean and still very lovely, but it showed sides of its age with its outdated wallpaper and worn flooring.

"I haven't put a lot of work into this place. My mother left it to me, and she'd let it get a bit out of hand in her later years. I'm working with a design architect to make some updates and bring it back to its former glory," he'd told me the first time I visited.

"It's still a beautiful place," I'd told him.

"Yes, it is," he'd agreed.

I had suggested that we should work on the garden ourselves, but he didn't seem interested. He'd shrugged it off and pulled me closer with a broad smile.

"I can think of much better ways to spend our time."

We had made love out in the open, our bodies mingling together on the large deck that jutted out from the back of the house. I had come away from it with a few bruises and maybe a splinter, but it had been great sex. It was wonderful to be out here where no one could hear us or see us. We could do whatever we wanted.

Since then, I'd come to love this place. It was like a sanctuary for me, and I suspect, for him too. While we spent a lot of time here making love, we also enjoyed the peace and quiet. Today, I was reading quietly out on the deck while he finished reading some essays inside. Later, we were going to grill steaks.

"Hey, Misti. I've got to run back to the city and grab some papers I forgot," he said, emerging from the house. I could tell that he looked frustrated. I'd already learned that he didn't like it when things didn't go smoothly. He could get agitated and snippy over what he viewed as others wasting his time.

"What? I'll go with you," I told him.

"No. That's not necessary. I'll be back in a few hours. I just have to go in, get the papers and I'm going to stop on the way back to pick up something delectable for dessert. There is a little diner on the way here that makes a killer key lime pie."

"That sounds great. Are you sure you don't want me to go?"

"No, just stay here and enjoy your reading. Take a nap or go for a walk around the property. I'll be back just as soon as I can."

"Okay. I'll miss you," I told him, tilting my head up toward his for a goodbye kiss.

He gave me a soft, lingering kiss and tangled his hands in my hair, pulling it slightly as his mouth devoured mine and then he stood back up, smiling down at me.

"Just a little sample to hold you until I get back," he told me.

"Something to look forward to," I told him.

"Certainly is. Be good while I'm gone so you can be bad when I get back," he told me, bouncing back into the house.

A moment later, I heard the front door open and close as he went back out to the car and left. I continued to read on the deck for a while, but it began to rain a little, so I went inside. I went to the kitchen to check the ingredients for dinner one more time. If anything was missing, Greg could grab it on his way back.

Everything was there except for wine. We hadn't picked any up on our way in because Greg said he had plenty down in his wine cellar. I could go ahead and bring that up to save him the trouble, but I knew he kept the door locked to keep it safe when the house was empty. I hadn't noticed a key for it anywhere.

I pushed it out of my head for a moment and sat down on the sofa, turning on the small television there. Greg didn't care much for television, but the cell signal out here was pretty non-existent. He didn't even have internet here, just basic cable. I tuned to the news and saw that another woman had been taken. I stared in shock when I saw her image on the screen.

If most of the other women looked similar to me, this one had them all beat. She could have been my twin. I sat looking at her in shock and I suddenly found that I felt uneasy alone here in this big house without another soul in sight.

"Mary Anne Housley is a freshman at the University of Tennessee. This was only her first semester at the college, her first time away from home and now the unthinkable has happened. Mary Anne was reported missing early this morning after she didn't return from classes yesterday afternoon," the anchor was saying.

She then turned it over to a field anchor standing in a parking lot not far from campus. It looked familiar but I couldn't quite place it. Then it hit me. It was the same parking lot where Tucker had pulled over and put me out of the car. Was it possible that he was involved in this girl's disappearance?

Or perhaps the shadowy figure I had seen from a distance before my Uber arrived had something to do with it. I felt like I should report what I knew to the police, but I couldn't do so with my cell signal barely hitting one bar. It would have to wait until Greg got back. I would tell him, and he would know what to do.

Time seemed to stand still as I sat terrified in the big, empty house. The rain outside had begun to pour down, causing the old place to creak and rattle with the wind. I turned away from the news, avoiding the ongoing reports of missing women and found something a bit more lighthearted to watch, old episodes of I Love Lucy.

I needed to relax. I was completely on edge. I got up and went to the kitchen to prowl around. After looking through a few drawers, I finally noticed what I was looking for hanging on a nearby wall, partly obscured by the leaves of a fake green plant that had seen better days.

"Yes! Wine!" I exclaimed, hoping this was the right key.

I felt a bit of relief when I put the key into the lock and heard the tell-tale click of release but pushing the door open only gave me the creeps again. I felt along the edge of the wall and found the light switch before descending the stairs. I was surprised to find that the cellar had been converted to what looked like a fairly modern wine cellar with freshly built shelves and even a chilling unit. I guess Greg had gotten started on at least some upgrades.

To one side of the wine racks was a small room that appeared to be empty. I couldn't see any light inside other than what shined in from the one in the cellar. I assumed it was probably storage and that if he had been fixing things up down here, he'd probably emptied it for some purpose.

Walking over to the back wall, I began looking through the wines, trying to avoid any that looked rare. I found a small section of a vintage I recognized from our shelves at home and knew it was a fairly common merlot. As I pulled a few bottles from the shelves to take upstairs, something caught my eye behind the shelf.

It looked like one of those small dumbwaiters used in older houses to send food to different floors. I wanted to see if I was right, so I grabbed the small handle at the bottom and slid the door upwards. It disappeared into the wall, exposing a fairly large space. Inside, there appeared to be two boxes, but I couldn't quite see what they were. I fished out my phone to shed some light on them.

The first box was just an open wooden one. Inside, there were several hand tools for digging. They were similar to your ordinary garden tools, but they seemed larger and sturdier than what I was used to seeing. Beside them lay a compact shovel with serrated edges along one edge. All three of the tools had some sort of dark mud stuck to them in various places.

The second box was also wooden but this one had a top on it. I pulled it outward a bit and propped up the phone to get a better look at it. Inside there were photos that made me gasp in horror. How had these gotten here and was Greg even aware of them?

The thought that whoever put them here might still be lurking in the house chilled me to the bone as I stood flipping through the collection of photos and mementos I'd found hidden in the wall, horrified by what I was seeing but unable to make sense of any of it.

Chapter 32

Dylan

I was up early the day after meeting Dot in the bar despite my massive hangover. I had a quick breakfast of toast and eggs washed down with a Bloody Mary to get me going. I felt like I was moving in slow motion as I dragged myself into the bathroom for a long hot shower to help shake off the fog.

By the time I was dressed, I felt a little more cognizant but there was still a bit of a funk that seemed to have settled over me. Last night had been a real eye opener for me and I was still contemplating how I felt about a lot of things, but this morning wasn't about me. I had made Dot an offer and I fully intended to see it through.

I had plenty of time before the car would bring her over, so I set about cleaning the place. I could have sent someone to do it, but I could use the distraction. It wasn't in bad shape; the rental company had kept it fairly presentable for showings to potential renters, but it could use some freshening up. Normally, a decently sized house in this location would be snatched up within hours of being posted. Instead, this one had sat empty for nearly a month without explanation.

"I think it's because they rezoned this area," my realtor, Pam Steele, had told me after there was no immediate movement on the house.

"Rezoned?" I asked.

"Yes. There was a rezoning measure that passed last year but took effect this year. Most of the people who would be interested in this style house and yard are young couples with a family or looking to start a family, but they always want to know the school district. The house was zoned for a school that sits only three blocks away. Now it is zoned for a school that is nearly two miles away and not as well funded."

"How did that happen?" I'd asked.

"You know how it is, someone with money had an agenda and made it happen. Don't sweat it. It might not rent fast, but it will rent. An older couple will fit right into this neighborhood or perhaps even a young couple with no kids that just appreciates the quiet, safe neighborhood."

The memory reminded me to call her and let her know I was taking the house off the rental market. I dialed her number and gave her the news. She wasn't happy about losing the listing, but there was hardly anything she could do about it. She would bill me for her time and wait for me to give her something else somewhere down the line.

I finished up the house and ducked out for a little shopping spree. By the time the car I had sent for Dot arrived, I had the place spotless and ready for her to move in. She arrived with nothing but a battered old suitcase and a large garbage bag.

"Is that everything?" I asked.

"Everything I plan on taking out of that dump," she replied.

"Good enough. Just drop it somewhere and I'll take you on a tour of the place."

She put her belongings on the living room floor and followed me from room to room as I showed her the place. It wasn't a huge house, but it was more than enough space for a single person and there was a nice yard both in the front and back of the house. I noticed that she looked a little bothered by something.

"What's wrong?" I asked.

"It's nothing," she said. "It's a really nice place."

"But…"

"No. You've done more than enough. Thank you."

I looked around, puzzled about what could possibly be bothering her that she wouldn't say. Then it hit me. I redirected her to the kitchen and motioned toward the counter.

"I bought you a bottle of champagne and a fruit basket as a welcome gift. There is also an envelope with some money in it to get you started on groceries, essentials, and such."

"Dylan, I can't…" she started to say.

"You can and you will. I knew that there was a good chance today that I would get a call from the driver I sent saying you weren't coming. Maybe because you were skeptical or decided you didn't want a hand up. Who knows why people choose things. Instead, you chose to let me do this for you. You got up, probably as hungover as I was, but you packed your life up and waited in hopes that I wasn't full of shit," I said, pausing for a moment to smile at her.

"Yes," she said, her voice barely audible.

"You accepted my help because you needed it. I helped you because I needed to do that. Now, we are in this together, Dot. If you think I'm going to dump you in this house without the things you need to be happy here, you are wrong."

"I just feel like a charity case."

"You shouldn't feel that way. You are letting someone help you and that is brave. You have been given every reason not to trust a man and here you are, trusting me. I won't betray that trust."

I could see she was near tears and that wasn't the way I wanted this to go. Instead, I changed the direction of the conversation.

"So, there is $1000 in that envelope for groceries. Do you have a cell phone?"

"No."

"Then your first project for today is to grab the bus into town. There is a bus stop about two blocks to the right after you walk back out the front door. You need to get a phone, food and whatever else you need. You also need furniture. There is a card for a decently priced place with a good selection in that envelope. Go there in person and pick out what you want or set up your cell phone and order it online if you want. They have instructions to charge it to my account and deliver whatever you asked for to this address."

"It's too much," she gasped, crying anyway.

"It's not too much. It's a lot of money to you, but not to me. I spend more money than this on a weekend vacation. You aren't under any obligation to take my help. You don't owe me anything if you do. I've already told you that, but I'm telling you again."

"Okay," she croaked, drying her tears away with the back of her hand.

"Good. So, buy whatever you want at the furniture store. That includes all the furniture and any decor you like. I believe they have TVs too. Get a big one. Get surround sound. Go wild, Dot. I want you to make this place your own. Feel free to paint if you feel the need. You have the rest of the weekend to get yourself in a little bit of order before you start work on Monday. Can you do that?"

For the first time, I could see her shoulders relax. I could see that she was still a bit uncertain, perhaps even apprehensive, but she seemed to be finally embracing what I was telling her. We went over a few more details about starting work and I left her with my business card so she could call me if she needed anything else. Afterward, I left to go home.

What Dot did with the opportunity I had afforded her was up to her now. My goal was to give her a fighting chance and I'd done that.

Once I arrived at my place, I decided to lie down for a while. I usually handled my liquor pretty well, but I was dragging some serious ass today and there was something that was gnawing at me. I couldn't put my finger on it, but I felt like something was amiss. I drifted off to sleep after a bit of tossing and turning only to wake up less than an hour later feeling like I was having a panic attack.

Misti came immediately to mind. I had this completely unreasonable idea that she was somehow in trouble, and I was failing her. I tried to push it aside. If Misti were in trouble, she would push the button on her bracelet. There was always the chance that she had taken it off, but I didn't think she would.

Every time I had seen her on camera since she went back to school, she was wearing it. Still, I was convinced that she needed me. If I was wrong, there wasn't any harm in calling her was there? At the very least, surely she still considered me a friend. Unable to talk myself out of it, I hit the speed dial. Her phone rang a few times and went to voicemail. I tried again, this time leaving what I hoped sounded like a light hearted message.

"Hey, Misti. I was just trying to reach out while I had some down time. I've been so busy lately and we haven't had a chance to talk. Give me a call when you get this and let's catch up a bit."

I hung up and sat looking at my phone for the longest time, as if willing it to ring. Unable to shake off the feeling that she was in danger, I called one last time. This time, it went straight to voicemail. Either she was on the line, or she had turned her phone off. Either way, I guess it meant she was fine, and I was acting like a crazed ex. I started to walk away but was stopped by the message chime. I picked it up and read the message, finding it hard to believe she would send me such a response.

"*Stop calling and texting me. Leave me alone,*" it read.

I stared at the screen for a ridiculous amount of time before finally walking away. I felt hurt and confused but she was certainly entitled to her opinion and thoughts. I just couldn't imagine what I might have done to spark such a callous response. I spent the rest of the evening in a funk, marveling at how good I had felt earlier in the day helping Dot get back on track to a good life compared to how shitty I felt now.

I considered going back to the bar and drinking, but Dot and I had talked while I was showing her around her new home. We'd both decided that it was a bad place for us. Drinking wouldn't solve either of our problems. Helping her get a decent place to live and a job that pays a livable wage would go far in helping her with her issues, but it wouldn't fix everything.

Both of us needed to do a lot of work to overcome our emotional issues. It had taken me meeting her to realize just how far down that rabbit hole I had fallen. While her story was far more dire than anything I've ever experienced in my lifetime, it helped me see how much baggage I carried around too.

Lydia leaving me had been devastating. She had hurt me in ways that I wouldn't even admit to myself and though I had convinced myself that I was past all of that, I wasn't. I was over her. I didn't miss her. I didn't pine for her. But I did still feel the effects of her betrayal. It is what had kept me from really pursuing another relationship since she had been gone.

I felt disillusion after my divorce. The truth was that I had felt numb long before Lydia left, because I knew she was unfaithful. I knew that my money meant more to her than my love for her. I was well aware that the woman I married when I had so little to offer had stopped loving me, but I didn't understand why.

Then, Misti came along. I'd never planned to fall in love with her. All those days I had watched her from the window of my house, when she was deliberately trying to get me to notice her, seemed like a lifetime ago already. It was hard to accept that it had only been a couple of months since we'd gone from an exhibitionist/voyeur association to a torrid sexual affair that had consumed me.

It was even harder to accept that somewhere in the middle of what was supposed to only be a summer fling, I had fallen head over heels in love with her. What was not to love? She was beautiful, sexy, smart, and funny. She made me feel something after being dead inside for a very long time. Perhaps that was what had drawn me in and made me fall so hard for her.

Now, she was gone and wanted nothing to do with me. That hurt more than I could express. I had hoped that she was just focusing on her studies and would miss me too. Somewhere in my mind, she would invite me to her graduation, tell her parents she was in love with me, and we'd live happily ever after. Instead, her communications had grown sparse and then ended. Now, she was telling me to fuck off.

Misti owed me nothing. She'd set out to have a tawdry affair with the man next door while she was home for the summer. She'd never had any intention of it going any further than that. Neither had I, but it had. Was that really so one sided? I found it hard to believe that she had no feelings for me. She'd seemed to want to keep in touch for a while and I'd taken that as a good sign.

I couldn't believe I'd been so wrong.

Chapter 33

Misti

I stood there, frozen in place as I sifted through the photos. These were the missing women. I recognized them from the news. In some photos, they were naked and looked unconscious—or dead, my mind screamed. In others, they were awake, chained to a metal bar in a room that appeared to be dark based on the flash pattern. Each of them looked terrified.

Strewn around the box with the photos were their school IDs, mostly students but with one custodian and one professor. Someone had abducted these women, stripped them naked and taken photos of them. What else had they done to them?

"What else had Greg *done to them?"* my mind corrected.

For a moment, I felt like I couldn't breathe. The last ID belonged to Mary Ann Housley. She had just gone missing yesterday after class. There was no way that Greg could have taken her. He was in class himself and then here with me after that. Of course, this couldn't be him, but that meant that whoever had done it had been here. Who were they and where were these women?

What if they were still here somewhere? Or what if they came back to find that someone had been in their things. I needed to put everything back and talk to Greg when he got back. A nagging thought at the back of my mind told me not to do that, to make an excuse to get home and get out of here, but how would I do that? I didn't even have a signal on my phone to say someone called me and Greg knew that.

I had to consider that somehow Greg was a part of this. Maybe he had taken the girl and hadn't been in class at all. I didn't know his full schedule and I couldn't check. It was also possible that he had a partner and that his trek back into the city was just some sort of excuse to meet up with them for whatever they were doing. I realized that Greg could have put Mary Ann's ID down here while I was reading on the patio.

That thought made me shudder. I was still staring at the items I'd found in disbelief when I heard a noise from upstairs. It sounded like the front door opening. That was what finally got me moving.

I put everything back like I had found it or at least as close as I could remember. I wasn't sure how long I'd been down here, but Greg was bound to be on his way back soon. Once I had everything back in place, I pulled the door closed again and picked up the wine I had set aside when I'd noticed it.

The door above me creaked open and I stopped in my tracks, my heart racing wildly as I heard footsteps coming down the stairs leading down to where I stood. As he cleared the overhang that hid him from view, I saw that it was Greg. I found myself wishing that his return was a relief, but what I felt was far from that.

"Misti? Are you down here?"

"Ye-yes," I stammered.

"Are you okay? You look like you've seen a ghost."

"I'm fine. I just didn't realize you were back and then someone was coming down the stairs. I was scared."

"But what are you doing down here? It was locked," he said, sounding annoyed.

"I thought I'd bring up some wine for us to have with the steak. You told me there was a wine cellar down here," I squeaked, trying desperately to keep my voice even.

"Where did you get the key?"

"In the kitchen. It was hanging on the wall, silly."

"Ah, of course," he said, letting out a little laugh. "I forgot that Mom kept a spare beside that hideously ugly plant of hers. I don't know why I haven't thrown that thing out."

All the while he was speaking, he was coming further down the steps while I was moving closer to them, putting some distance between us. As I reached the bottom, he scooped me up in his arms and kissed me. I thought I was going to vomit while trying not to let on that anything was wrong. When he let me go, I smiled as pleasantly as I could muster.

"Ready to get upstairs and start dinner?" I said.

"In a minute. I think I'd like a different wine first," he replied, looking over toward the shelf where the bottles of wine had been as he took the bottles from my hands.

I looked too, immediately noticing that in my haste, I hadn't pulled the door fully down into place. There was just the tiniest sliver of space at the bottom. Greg's eyes lingered on it. He had noticed it too.

I bolted for the stairs behind him, desperate to get up them and out of the house. I was barely on the bottom step when I felt his hands on the back of my shirt, pulling me backwards. I cried out, screaming as loudly as I could.

"Shut up! Shut up, Misti. No one can hear you out here anyway," he barked at me, slinging me sideways. I collided with the wall behind me so hard that it felt like my bones rattled inside of me.

I began kicking and scratching to get free. There was no way I was going on that list of missing women. I just needed to get up the steps and get out of here. I didn't know where I would go, but I knew that the first step was getting out of this cellar. I aimed one of my boots for his ribs and kicked, catching him squarely where I intended. He stumbled back and I seized the opportunity to bolt up the stairs again.

"You're a fighter. I always thought you would be," he grunted. "Mary Anne was a fighter too."

I felt his hand on my ankle and the weight of one of the wine bottles hitting the back of my head with a sickening thud. Then everything went dark.

I woke up in a dark room, unsure of how long I had been there. My head was throbbing, and I could feel something wet and sticky when I reached back to see how bad the damage was. I winced as my fingers met the tender spot back there. The cut seemed superficial, but it was hard to tell without being able to really see it.

I reached for my cell phone to light up the room around me and discovered it was gone. I began feeling around me. It was a very small room with no light switches and no hanging fixtures. It had to be some sort of empty storage room. As the fog from the blow I had suffered lifted a bit, I realized I must be in the small room I had seen when I'd first come down. I was still in the cellar.

Feeling my way around for anything that might be of use, my hands landed on an iron pole running up one corner of the room. It was far enough away from the adjacent walls for me to get my hands behind it, but I couldn't budge it. I pulled at it until I was weak, not sure of what I thought getting it loose would accomplish but seeing it as my only hope.

Suddenly, the room lit up with a creepy blue light. I looked around me and could see what looked like splatters illuminating the surrounding walls. The bottom of the room was full of them, but the upper half had only some light sprays. As quickly as it had come on, the light shut back off. Horror filled my brain as I realized that this was the room from some of the photos. The pole I'd been trying to dislodge was the same one they'd been chained to in the photos.

A scream welled up in my chest, but I knew there was no point here. I needed to save my breath for when it might, but I was terribly afraid that there was no one to find me here. No one knew about my affair with Greg. No one knew where I was this weekend. My phone had no signal here to call anyone for help.

I was at Greg's mercy. Whatever he planned to do to me would likely be over with by the time anyone even knew I was gone. I was stranded out here with a maniac who had been abducting women. Based on the photos I'd found and the fact that some of them had been missing for some time, I was guessing they were dead and soon, I would be too.

I kicked myself for being so stupid. There had been no signs that Greg was anything beyond what he seemed, but once I'd discovered those items, I should have bolted. If I'd had my gun with me, I could have protected myself. I laughed bitterly as I considered that Dylan had gone through all that trouble to make sure I was safe, and I'd been too stupid to make use of it when I needed it most.

I gave up my assault on the pole and leaned against what I suspected was a blood caked wall. Tears began falling down my face as I realized that I was going to die in a dirty, dusty seller and no one would ever know what had happened to me.

Chapter 34

Dylan

I hardly recognized the woman sitting at my reception desk on Monday morning. Dot's frizzy red hair had been cut into a layered cut that feathered her face beautifully. She stood to greet me when I came in and I could see that she was wearing a simple black skirt and a crisp button-down white shirt. A pair of faux pearl earrings and necklace completed the ensemble.

"Good morning, Mr. Hayward," she said as I approached.

"Good morning, Ms. Rose," I replied. "I trust that Sadie got you settled in okay?"

"She did," she told me.

Sadie was the head of our HR department. I'd left her a message this weekend that Dot would be coming in today as a new receptionist. I had an early meeting this morning and couldn't be here but didn't want there to be any confusion that might frighten Dot.

I nodded and headed for the steps, leaving Dot to do the job she was being trained for without any pressure from me. Inside the conference room, I met with members of several law enforcement agencies to discuss the protocols in place and what needed to be done to bring the system fully online.

We were in the final stages of getting everything up and running. The jewelry line was ready to go to market. We had a full marketing campaign built around the brand name "ResQ." All that was left to accomplish was to get police departments to embrace the tech.

"The 911 board has approved incorporating our tracing system but it will only work as well as your response time. Currently, all beacons initiated with a piece of ResQ jewelry are routed through the internal servers of my company. Whoever is manning the monitors has to notify police in whatever area is being pinged. That increases the time it takes for someone to get help."

"What is it you are looking for from us?" one of the police chiefs asked.

"I need your IT support to work with my people to install the software necessary so that when a unit pings, it goes directly to the nearest police department."

"I thought it was going to 911?" another replied.

"No. It will utilize their network, but the notification will come directly to your stations."

"That sounds like a hassle and like money we don't have."

"No. I'm funding this entire project. It will work with your existing software and if it doesn't, I will help you upgrade on my dime. I don't think it is a hassle to make sure someone who is in trouble gets help as quickly as possible."

"You know how many crank calls we get a day? If 911 didn't weed some of them out, we'd be on a constant wild goose chase."

"Not with this. There is no phone call. The jewelry is designed so that it isn't easily initiated, and it can't be turned off by anyone but a tech from my company. The moment the person wearing a ResQ piece of jewelry pushes that button, it will send an alarm to our end but will be silent on their end. We can silence that alarm, but it will continue to sound until it is shut down by an authorized person."

"I don't get it. How does it let us know what is going on if we're not getting info through 911? Just some alarm somewhere?"

"That's the point. This isn't meant to be used by people who can call 911 and get help. We're not just selling this product over the counter. It will be sold to people who understand that it is only to be used in the event that they find themselves in serious trouble where they are unable to make a phone call."

"So, some woman has a flat on an abandoned road and we get an alarm because her phone is dead?"

"I can't guarantee that won't happen, but if a woman is stranded with no phone and feels her only option is to initiate her ResQ for help, then I'd think you would want to be there. That's what *Protect and Serve* means, isn't it?"

There were some nods around the room, but also a few grumbles. It was appalling to me that some police believed helping out a woman in distress was only acceptable if she was in life-or-death circumstances.

"Listen, I know you guys don't want to waste your time and I don't want that either. This system is designed to be a last-ditch method of getting help. Will some women abuse it? Perhaps, but not that many. Women just want to be safe, and they know they will face a hassle getting their system reset if they set it off unnecessarily."

"That ain't never stopped nobody," one of the sheriffs scoffed, setting off a few chuckles around the room.

"Let's talk about it this way. How many times has your department dealt with a missing person and had no way of finding them? Someone yanks them off the street, tosses their phone or they don't have one with them. They are just gone. They end up in someone's shed or some abandoned building suffering who knows what indignities. There is no way for them to get help. This jewelry changes that."

"What if they get robbed, hit in the head, left somewhere to die?"

"This jewelry can't be easily taken. Every single piece is worn in such a way that it can't be removed without a key. For example, a bracelet. Can they cut off a hand to get it off? Sure, but it's not likely they are going to worry about a metal bracelet, even in a robbery. There is no silver, no gold. The bracelet itself is worth nothing. And if they are cutting it off to prevent identification of a body, it's already too late. That is why it is important that this signal gets to the people who can help as fast as possible. That is, you guys."

I began to see them come around. They were catching on that this wouldn't cost them anything and that it might save lives. The true test of that was in putting it to use and I needed them for that.

"Can we get a demonstration?" one of them asked.

"Absolutely. I have a member of my staff on standby via Zoom. He has one of the finished bracelets and is waiting for me to give him the word."

I clicked a few keys on my computer and a hardware developer named Thomas popped up on the large monitor behind me.

"Thomas, can you hear me?" I said.

"I can," he told me.

"I'm ready for the demo."

Thomas nodded and held up his wrist to display a metal bangle. It was designed for a woman, but Thomas was very thin, so it fit his wrist just fine. He held the bangle in place with his hand and pushed the button inward until it clicked firmly in place with the tip of his pinky.. I pointed out that this bracelet had been modified to make it easier for the demo, but final products were much more difficult to engage, preventing false alarms. Immediately, a loud alarm sounded on my computer. I put my screen up on the monitor for the law enforcement representatives present to see and pushed a button to silence the alarm.

"As you can see, the sound has been muted but the alarm continues to flash. It shows me the GPS chip number, the name of the owner, and the GPS coordinates of their location. When I click on those, it spins into a map pinpointing their location on a city map."

The screen showed where Thomas was standing but I asked him for clarification.

"Thomas, where are you standing?"

"In front of the Johnson's Foodtown. 414 Mill Street, Pulaski, Tennessee."

It matched the information on the screen perfectly.

"Thanks Thomas. You can come home now."

He nodded and killed the feed.

"That's some range," one of the sheriffs commented. "How far will it broadcast?"

"Mostly anywhere. It uses whatever communication towers are in the area to broadcast. So, unless you are out in the middle of nowhere without any kind of signal available, you can be found. It will track you as you move just like a phone, except without detection from the people who mean you harm."

"But if you get taken out of range, you're still lost."

"For now. We are working on satellite access that will remove those kinds of blackout spots. In the meantime, the onus lies in the victims' hands to press the button as soon as they realize they are in trouble. I can't stand here and tell you it is a perfect system, but I can tell you it is damn good and will only continue to get better."

By the end of the meeting, I had most of them on board and the few holdouts seemed like they might come around. I left feeling pretty good about things. Glancing over the glass railing that overlooked the balcony, I could see Dot was still at the front desk and seemed to be answering the phones without a problem. I smiled and went to my office. I didn't usually spend the day here in the office, but I felt a need to stay with Dot on her first day.

When I finally stepped out to go home, she was gone and Monica, who had been training her, was packing up her things.

"How did the new girl go?" I asked her.

"Dot? She's wonderful. A real go-getter," she said.

"Are you just saying that because I own this place, or do you mean it?" I asked.

"No, she really is great. I don't know where you found her, but she is a natural people-person."

"Fantastic," I told her. "Have a good night, Monica."

"You too, Mr. Hayward."

I left the building and headed home. Misti was on my mind again. That same feeling that had been plaguing me was still running around my brain. Despite what her text message had said, I felt there must be some misunderstanding. A phone call should straighten it out. I tried to call her again, but it went straight to voicemail.

I went out to the gym to work out, feeling a need to just zone out for a while. Rather than lifting weights, I went to the punching bag and began knocking the hell out of it. It had been a productive day, but I still felt on edge. I worked the bag until I had nothing left to give and collapsed against it, sweating and breathing heavily. I turned off the music and went back inside to shower.

When I came out, I turned on the television to watch the news while I made myself a sandwich. I was walking back across the floor from the kitchen to the den when I caught sight of the news. All the strength left my body. The plate in my hands crashed to the floor and shattered as I looked on in shock at an image of Misti on the screen. I hurried to grab the remote, turning the volume up.

"Tonight, we are getting news of another University of Tennessee student who has been reported missing. Only days after the disappearance of Mary Anne Housley, Knoxville police have received a report that 21-year-old Misti Ann Bridges of Nashville has been reported missing by her roommate. Misti is a senior at UT and the daughter of Martin Bridges, CEO of Bridges International."

There was a lump in my throat as I continued to listen.

"Misti was last seen on Friday. She was seen by fellow students attending class. A security camera on campus shows her walking home just after 2 p.m. That is the last time anyone would see her. According to reports, her roommate understood that she was going out of town with someone but when she hadn't returned for classes on Monday morning, concern grew about her whereabouts."

I cut off the television and bolted upstairs to finish getting dressed.

Chapter 35

Misti

As I lay in the little boxed-in room, all I could think about was how much I was going to miss out on by dying so young. My head ached horribly from where Greg had hit me, and I felt like some sort of fog had engulfed me. I didn't know how long I had been here or how long I had left to live. It was a sobering thought to know you were going to die.

How long would it be before anyone even started looking for me? No one knew I was anywhere but school except for Stephanie and she thought I was off with some secret lover I wouldn't reveal. That meant she wouldn't be looking for me at least until Sunday night, maybe even Monday morning. Even though I didn't have Monday classes, I'd told her that I had some work to do at the library.

I tried to clear my brain enough to make sense of my situation. Greg and I had left the little bookstore we both frequented a little after four on Friday. We'd driven an hour to get here with only one stop along the way, a little Mom and Pop grocery store off the main highway. There had only been a few people there and I couldn't say whether any of them had even noticed us.

We'd arrived at the house just past six that night and spent the evening in bed. The thought of having willingly given my body to someone capable of what I saw in those photos sickened me, but I had to push that aside in order to focus.

On Saturday morning, we'd slept in for a bit and then Greg had graded papers while I read, until he had left for whatever errand he had to run. I shuddered to think about what it might be. That had been at about 3:30 that afternoon and he'd said he'd be gone for about three hours, which put him back home at about 6:30, assuming he'd been gone that long.

I struggled to piece my thoughts together past that. I remember watching the news. I'd not looked at the clock but remembered the woman referring to it as the "news at six" so by the time I'd seen that, gotten the key to the basement, and made the horrible discovery there, it must have been about time for Greg to come back home.

Past that was where I lost all idea of how much time had passed here in the dark hole he'd tossed me into. The blow to the back of my head had sent me falling forward, leaving me with not only the wound on the back of my head but a knot on the front where I hit my head. I reached up to run my fingers across it and that's when I realized what I was forgetting.

The bracelet. My phone was gone, but I still had the bracelet on. It was hard to see where the dot was in the dark, but it was slightly raised above the pattern on the bangle. I felt around until I found it and then positioned it so that it was facing the wall. I smashed it backwards against the wall like Dylan had told me. Afraid that it didn't engage, I brought my hand back down and slid my finger back and forth across it to make sure it had stayed down like it was supposed to once engaged.

Now, I just had to hope that Dylan saw it in time. I knew the bracelet was a prototype and I had come back to school before he had finalized his designs. I hoped, for my sake, that he'd kept this one online. He hadn't been returning any of my texts lately, but I was certain that he would look for me if he thought I was in trouble.

If I hadn't been here long enough for Stephanie to notice my absence and report it, this might be my only chance for someone to find me. I was certain that I was the only one here. If he had, in fact, taken Mary Anne on Friday before we left, why wasn't she here? What had he done with her? It was a bad sign if he was only keeping the women for such a short period of time.

My stomach growled loudly, and my throat was dry. He'd not been down here to even check on me since he'd put me here. How could a man be so charming and attentive without giving any indication of the sickness that lay beneath the surface? I'd never thought for a moment that he was any danger to me. I wonder if he would have been had I not found out his secret.

I considered how secretive he'd insisted on keeping our relationship. It had made complete sense to me that he wouldn't want anyone to know that he was dating a student, so I had gone along with it. Now, I understood that it may have been for a different purpose altogether. What I wasn't clear about was if he had been having a relationship with the others before he took them too.

He obviously targeted women who looked like me, with the exception of the professor. What was it about her that had caught his attention? I had so many questions. I found myself wondering if he would answer them. Of course, if he did, I'd likely never be able to share them with anyone. A rueful laugh escaped my lips at the thought.

My stomach growled again. It was odd to think about eating when you were on a makeshift death row, but I was starving. I thought about the steaks we had picked out for our dinner and wished I had one now. I wondered if he would feed me at some point or just come down here to collect me for the slaughter.

Where did he put the women? There was no way they were alive. If they had been, why wouldn't he have them here? Or did he? Was there a part of this property I didn't know about? I couldn't imagine him taking them somewhere else when he had such a private piece of real estate.

My mind jumped back and forth from one thing to another, trying to figure out where I had gone wrong. Why was this happening? How I missed the signs. I looked at the bracelet again. I talked to it.

"Do your job please. I need for you to do your job and the sooner the better," I told it.

I was tired and weak. I needed to be strong. I needed to fight him when he came for me but first I needed to rest. I needed some sleep. Yes. I'd sleep for a while and then I would make a plan to fight.

Laying my head down on my outstretched arm, I curled up and went to sleep. For a while I felt at peace, with everything that was happening around me shut out of my thoughts. I fell into a dream.

Dylan was here, walking into the cellar and opening the door to rescue me. He was pulling me up in his arms and carrying me upstairs and out the door, putting me in his convertible.

"I found you, Misti. I found you. You're safe."

I lay my head against his shoulder and closed my eyes, breathing a sigh of relief. I was finally on my way home.

"I love you," I whispered to him. "I should have told you."

"It's okay. I love you too," he whispered, taking one hand off the wheel and stroking my hair as we drove.

The wind rippled through my hair, the fall chill caressing my skin as he drove me away from the horrors that might have awaited me at Greg's house if he hadn't gotten there in time. I smiled happily up at him, grateful to be headed home.

Then he was talking to me, his voice urgent.

"Misti. You have to wake up. He's coming for you. Wake up," he
pleaded.

Slowly, I drifted back up through the fog. Climbing toward his
words, trying to reach the top. I could hear the sound of footsteps as
I snapped out of the dream and realized I was still here. I was still on
the floor of the killing room in Greg's cellar. Wearily, I dragged myself
to my feet, prepared to put up a fight for my life.

The footsteps stopped just outside the door, waiting for something.
Perhaps listening. The door didn't open. Instead, I heard him speaking
to me through the door.

"Are you sorry for what you did, Misti? Have you had enough time
to think about how you betrayed my trust? We're really going to have
to talk about your behavior and come to some understanding about
what is and is not acceptable here. I had such high hopes for you, but
you turned out just like the rest of them."

I didn't speak. I waited. I listened. I had nothing in here to attack
him with, and my body and I felt weak. What kind of chance did I
stand against him? I didn't know, but as I heard what sounded like a
lock on the door being removed I prepared myself.

Fight or flight was what they say. I planned on doing both.

Chapter 36

Dylan

"It's pinging, Dylan!" Gloria shouted from the little room we had set up to monitor the bracelet Misti was wearing.

I ran inside, flanked by the two detectives who had accompanied us to my office to interview me while we waited and hoped that Misti was able to push the button at some point.

"Where is she?" I asked.

"I can't tell. The signal is really weak," she said.

"Let me sit down," I told her.

Gloria stood and one of the detectives tried to stop me, putting his arm on my sleeve.

"Mr. Hayward, we need to finish your interview first. You may have urgent information about where we might find Misti Bridges."

"I do have urgent information about where to find her. It's right here on this screen," I told him, yanking away from him and sitting down to look at the notifications.

It made no sense. The chip was sending out a signal, but it was so faint that it was difficult to pinpoint where it was located.

"What are you seeing?" the detective beside me asked.

"Not what I should be seeing," I said, feeling defeated. "Normally, this chip is powerful enough to tell me exactly where she is, but the signal is weak and only pinging one tower. That means she is within fifty miles of that tower."

"That's a lot of territory. You can't narrow it down?"

"No. There are very few towers out there and we don't have satellite linkups yet. Plus, there is something blocking the signal. The chip in her bracelet is my original prototype. It is powerful enough that even with just one tower, it should be clearly giving me her GPS coordinates."

"What would block it?"

I hung my head. I didn't want to say it. I didn't want to think about it. I took a deep breath and looked up at him.

"If she's underground or perhaps, underwater. Then, yes it's possible."

"But she had to push the button for the signal to start, right? So, even if either of those things are true, she had to be alive."

"Yes, at least for a while."

"Okay. I get that you are high-tech and all that, but let's add a bit of old-fashioned police work to the mix. Can you pull up a map of what is in that 50-mile radius around the tower?"

I put Gloria on an adjacent computer and had her pull up the satellite image maps and project them on the wall so we could all see it. I felt sick but I didn't have time to fall apart right now. I had to keep my shit together for Misti, no matter how she felt about me. I stood up from my chair suddenly and pulled my phone from my pocket.

"What is it?" the detective asked.

"My phone. I forgot something. Misti sent me a message. She sent it on Saturday. Are we sure she went missing on Friday?"

"No. We are sure she was last seen on Friday, but we aren't sure about exactly when she might have encountered whatever trouble has found its way to her."

"Okay, but the message was strange."

"Strange how?"

"I had called her a couple of times because I hadn't talked to her in a while. She never answered, so I left her a message. This is what I got back," I told him, handing him my phone. He read the message from Misti and made a clucking noise with his tongue.

"Ouch. What did you do to get her so angry with you?"

"That's it, Detective Brown. I didn't do anything. Misti and I hadn't had a crossword with each other, so it came out of the blue. Now, I think it wasn't her. I think whoever may have taken her sent me that message."

He looked at the phone and then called an officer waiting out in the hallway into the room, handing him the phone. "Take this to forensics and have them trace this call. See if they can find out where the phone that sent it was when the message was sent. Tell them a woman's life may be at stake so not to drag their asses."

"What about her roommate in Knoxville, Stephanie? She reported her missing. Was she able to tell you anything that might help us narrow down this search?" I asked.

"No, not really. She said that Misti had been seeing someone, but she wouldn't tell her who. She was going away with him over the weekend and told her she would be back Sunday night. When she didn't show up, she thought maybe she had just crashed at his place or something. But when she still hadn't shown up on Tuesday, she checked with her professors and found out she hadn't been in class. That's when she reported her missing to campus police," Detective Brown replied.

"What about her car? Her keys?"

"Her car is still sitting in the apartment parking lot. I don't know about her keys. We're liasoning here in Nashville but Knoxville is heading up most of this."

I reached for my phone, then realized it wasn't there. I didn't know Stephanie's number, but Misti had given it to me once in case I needed to get in touch while hers was being repaired for a cracked screen.

"Do you have the roommate's phone number?" I asked.

"No, but I can get it."

"Call her. Ask her about the keys and if they are there, have her check the gun safe to see if Misti's pistol is at home or in her car."

"She has a pistol?"

"Yes. She bought a pistol and got her concealed carry permit before she went back to school. I set it up for her at my gun range."

"I'll get on that."

He disappeared down the hall for a minute while Gloria and I continued to look over the map with the other detective. That area was mostly farmland and rivers. She could be anywhere. She flagged all of the houses and sent them to the Knoxville PD so they could start knocking on doors but that was going to be a slow process. It wasn't a heavily populated area, but there were still a number of houses to check, and they were spread out all over the place in the area.

Still, it was a place to start and that gave me hope. Gloria and I went back to the signal. It was coming and going, possibly being blocked by cloud cover that was opening up periodically to let what little signal could get through reach the tower. We began working on boosting it but that was difficult when you weren't in possession of the actual chip.

"Mr. Hayward?" the detective called out to me as he returned.

"Yes?"

"We spoke to the roommate, Stephanie Baransa. She said that Misti gave her the code to the safe in case she needed it while she wasn't home. She checked and it is still there."

My heart sank. The one thing that might have protected her and it was safe at home in a box. Fuck!

"She also told me something else. She said that Misti had been upset because you weren't returning her messages."

"What? When?"

"She said that Misti had told her she had been messaging you for weeks and gotten no response at all. I thought you said the two of you had no issues."

"We didn't and I didn't get any messages. You can look at my phone and see that."

"Messages can be erased, Mr. Hayward."

"Are you serious right now? Are you insinuating that I had something to do with this?"

"I'm just asking questions, Mr. Hayward."

"Well, ask them in the right fucking places."

"Listen, I'm not accusing you of anything. I know you were here this weekend. We've talked to your employees and Dorothy Rose. They all confirm that you were here, though it's a bit suspect that Ms. Rose went from being a server at a diner to working a job she isn't qualified for at your company and living in a house you own."

I felt the heat rising up my cheeks when he said this. My entire head must be red with the anger I felt in that moment.

"Am I under arrest, Detective Brown?" I asked.

"Why would we arrest you?" he replied dryly.

"Because you want an easy arrest so you can call it a day. Meanwhile, a woman that I love is out there with God knows who doing God knows what to her and she trusted me to get her safely back home.

I'm going to do that with or without you. So, if you are going to waste time investigating me, you can get the fuck out of my building and go do what you need to do. You have my phone. Go through it. Knock yourself out," I said through gritted teeth.

"You came to us, Mr. Hayward. You admitted that you had a sexual relationship with a girl who was less than half your age and that you put a tracking device on her. How could we not look at you?"

"It's not a Goddamned tracking device, you stupid fuck. It only tells me where she is if she wants it to and she has activated it for that purpose, knowing that it is a prototype and that the signal will come through me because it's not fully capable yet. Misti trusts me to find her so leave and let me do that."

"We'll go but if we turn up anything that points in your direction, we'll be having our next discussions down at the station with you in handcuffs."

I turned my back on him and went back to the computer. As their footsteps cleared the hallway, I opened up my laptop beside Gloria and went to work doing what I did best. I might be a legit tech bro now, but I was once useful in the army for skills frowned upon by the legal community.

Chapter 37

Misti

I was ready to pounce on Greg as soon as he opened the door, but I found that wasn't going to be possible. He left the chain on it and only opened it wide enough to slide a five-gallon bucket inside of it and close it again. I tried to push against it, but he had his body weight on it and the lock back into place in a matter of seconds.

"It's not my first rodeo down here, Misti. I know how you girls can get. You're like feral animals in a cage."

I didn't respond, so he continued.

"Since it is your first time sleeping down here instead of upstairs in my bed with me, I thought I would be nice and bring you a few things to make yourself more comfortable. I brought you a bucket in case you need to, you know, relieve yourself. Don't worry, it's clean right now. Inside it, there's a bag of food. No utensils. Sorry, you'll have to eat it with your hands. Also, a bottle of water and a small flashlight so you can see what you're eating."

"Why are you doing this to me?" I asked him.

"You know why, Misti. You betrayed me."

"No, I didn't."

"Sure, you did. We were having a good time. At least that is what I thought. Then I found out you were messaging your loverboy over in Nashville."

"What are you talking about?" I asked, wondering how he could possibly know that.

"What are you talking about?" he said mockingly. "You know good and fucking well what I'm talking about. Should I read some of them to you?"

"Greg, please let me out of here," I pleaded.

"Dylan, I miss you. I miss the way you feel inside of me," he said.

Of course. My phone. He had taken it and it had the messages I had sent Dylan on it, but how had he gotten it unlocked? I realized the answer to that was probably simple too. It unlocked with my fingerprint, which he probably got when I was knocked out.

"Greg, please."

"I had a dream about you last night. I dreamed we were in your convertible, and we went out to that field we used to lay in. We stayed there all night, making love under the stars. I miss your touch so much."

I didn't respond. He continued reading my texts to Dylan. Yes, I had sent them while I was seeing him, but it had been early on in our relationship, and I had stopped. I would say it was because I felt bad about it or that I'd lost interest after things were going so well with Greg. The truth was far worse. I'd only stopped because I never got any responses.

For a moment, I forgot about the horrible predicament I was in and thought about Dylan. I guess he had moved on and just couldn't keep talking to me anymore. I'd seen the photo of him and the judge and realized that was why he couldn't keep sexting with me. He'd moved on to someone he could actually be seen in public with, someone he could build a life with. Our summer fling had turned out to be just that, after all—a fling.

"I don't know why you won't answer me. That's so cold," Greg read to me through the door.

"Please stop," I said, my voice barely a whisper.

"Oh, my sweet Misti. I will not stop. You think this feels like torment? We haven't even gotten to the real pain yet. If listening to a few of your own lamentations gets under your skin, you're going to really hate the needles I place there."

I felt a chill run down my spine. What was he planning to do to me?

"Anyway, I have to run for now. I have to get to work and then I have a date in the city. She reminds me of you," he chided. "Eat your food and drink some water while I'm gone. We can't have you starving to death in there before we get to the fun bits. I'll be back to take care of you later."

I heard the sound of him going back up the steps and the door up top closing and locking. Tears fell down my face. I sat there for a really long time in the dark, letting the darkness wash over me like a funeral shroud. Then I remembered the flashlight. I fished around in the bucket and found it, flipping the switch on.

It was one of those big plastic kiddie flashlights that was useless as a weapon. If I hit him with it, it would just shatter into bits. It would only make him mad. It didn't even provide much light. It was really old, and the lens was yellowed. I used it to get a better look around, hoping to find something that might be of use to me. There was nothing. The room was all concrete and the pole in the corner was cemented in. Even the ceiling was solid.

I fished the bag out of the bucket and opened it to find a piece of overdone steak and a cold baked potato. It looked disgusting but I was hungry, and it was edible. I choked the dry meal down with a bit of water and listened to my stomach growl even more as the brick of food I'd ingested churned unpleasantly there.

I wondered if he really had a date. Was this what he did? Did he date women until they no longer appealed to him or until they did something he decided was a betrayal, then kill them and move on to another?

I guess it was futile to try and figure out why someone like him did what he did. He was obviously unhinged, a complete monster who hid in the disguise of a flirtatious and funny lit professor.

I think the worst part of it all was that I had been the one who had pursued him. I'd practically thrown myself at him. That must have really amused him, having potential prey do all the work for him. He hadn't needed to woo me or win me over. In fact, he'd done the opposite for a bit. He'd played hard to get, and I'd worked that much harder to get him to notice me.

I laughed out loud at my stupidity and drank some water, but I was careful not to drink it all, just in case he didn't come back for a long time. It might be all I had to keep me going. Sitting back against the back wall, I rolled the flashlight around in my hands making light patterns on the ceiling and singing to myself.

I imagined that this must be what prisoners on death row felt like, except they at least had the courtesy of being given an execution date and were guaranteed that it would be carried out in a humane manner. From what Greg had said and what I knew to be true from the pictures I had seen, that wouldn't be the case.

I rocked back and forth, humming a bedtime song my mother used to sing to me when I was small. I wished she could sing to me now. I needed her comfort. I realized that with my disappearance, certain truths about me were going to come out. She would know about Dylan. Though we had concealed our relationship from my parents, we'd made no serious effort to hide anything beyond that. Police would ask questions of her and my father.

She would tell them I had been cleaning Dylan's pool and they would question him. He would tell them the truth, because he had nothing to hide, and he would want to find me. Still, he would be a suspect, and they would comb through his life. They would find our texts. They would learn about the gun. It might already be happening. He would have gotten a signal from my bracelet by now, at least I think he would. I didn't know.

The signal here was so bad already and I was in a concrete room in the cellar. There was a chance that the one thing that might have saved me wasn't able to do its job. I didn't blame Dylan for that. It was a prototype. He'd told me it wasn't perfect. Still, I had to hope that it was getting through. I had to believe that he would find me.

I thought about the messages that Greg had read to me. In hearing them read by someone else, I realized that they were all hyper-sexual. It sounded like I was only into Dylan for the great sex but that was so far from the truth. There was so much more I felt for him. I knew that now more than I ever had. The sex was so great because there was a depth of feeling so far beyond the physical.

I began to cry again. I felt sorry for myself, and I think it was okay to do that when you were going to die before you'd had much of a chance to live.

Chapter 38

Dylan

I stared at the screen in front of me in disbelief. Why had I never seen these before? There were nearly a dozen messages from Misti that I had never seen before. Some were simply her reaching out to say hello and some were of a more provocative nature. There were messages about how much she missed me and wanted me. Finally, there were messages asking why I wasn't responding to her. I'd never seen any of these. How was that possible?

And then there was the last message—so different than all of the others she had been sending. It was full of vitriol and venom. It was unlike her, especially compared to the others. I could be tempted to say that she'd lashed out at me because I'd never responded to these very personal messages and that would be reasonable, but something else occurred to me. She'd been ignoring my messages too and though I'd given my phone to the police, I was pretty sure those two events overlapped.

I hacked into my own phone, the same way I had hacked into hers. It was easier than getting my phone back from the incompetent buffoons that were currently combing through it trying to prove I had something to do with Misti's disappearance. I pulled my own messages up on the screen and compared the timelines. I was correct. At the same time that Misti was sending me messages that I had never seen, I was sending her similar messages that went unanswered.

I had attributed this to her having moved on but now I realized that there was something else going on here. Someone was intercepting the messages between us, but how? Was it as simple as having access to her phone? They could possibly delete messages from me before she saw them, but how had they prevented me from seeing what she sent?

While I was puzzled about this, I also looked to see who else she had contact with. There were a lot of messages between her and various friends but none with someone she might have been having an affair with. In fact, there were only a handful of messages between her and members of the opposite sex, which I found surprising. Of course, Misti was adventurous. There was always the possibility that she'd been seeing a woman, but I didn't really see her getting nabbed by another woman.

I went down the list of numbers and texts to see if I saw any patterns and nothing stood out. I stopped and rubbed my eyes. I was so tired. I needed sleep, but how could I possibly sleep when Misti was out there somewhere. She had pushed the button, asking me to help her. This was exactly what I had built this tech to do and if I couldn't do it, what good was any of it? If I couldn't find and save the woman I loved, then how could anyone hope that I could help them in their hour of need?

I smiled at Gloria. She was tired too, but she was staying with me. She brought me a cup of coffee and sat down with her own, pouring over maps of the area and doing everything she could to pinpoint the signal. I looked back at my screen wearily and I saw it. There was a number that she had called several times during the last week before she went missing.

I reverse searched it and found that it was a university number. There was no way of telling which exchange, but it was unique to the

English department at the school. It might not seem out of place to some, but it stuck out to me. Why would she have called the same department so many times that week and why would she have been on the phone with them so long? One call was only a few seconds long, but a couple of them were as long as fifteen minutes.

Misti had not wanted her parents to know about us because of our age difference. They wouldn't approve and it could cause problems for me business wise, but we had never worried about calling one another or texting. I'm sure that when the police interviewed people, there would be many of them that had seen us together at locations her parents didn't frequent.

We hadn't been open about our relationship and had taken measures to conceal it from her parents, but we had never tried to sanitize it to the point that no one could discover it if they were really looking. Whoever she had been seeing before her disappearance, there had been an effort to hide it. If this person took her, it was obvious why they would want to make sure no one could connect her to them, but what would have convinced her to keep it from everyone, including Stephanie, who she told everything to.

I looked at her texts to Stephanie. I felt like shit for invading her privacy like this, but it might be my only hope of finding her. There were hundreds of texts between the two of them. I went back to the summer and scanned through them. There it was. While Misti's parents and the general public didn't know about me, her messages to Stephanie went so far as to name me. Dylan this, Dylan that. There was even one in the beginning that had my full name.

I smiled a little at this but then went quickly back to recent texts. There was not one mention of this guy by name or anything that would reveal his identity. The closest the texts came were just referring to him as the mystery man and that was mostly from Stephanie's side of the texts. She talked about sex with him which was hard for me to read but I did it anyway just in case I could find any clues there.

The last one that referred to him was her telling Stephanie that she was going to spend the weekend with "him" at his place and that she might be out of touch because the signal was always shit at his place. So, that was it. Wherever she was with him, the signal was weakened by something.

I had so many questions. I had to think. I had to dig deeper. It was right in front of me. I knew it was. As I sat there drinking coffee and contemplating what it was that I was missing, it hit me. I glanced at my watch. It was early Monday morning. I pulled Stephanie's number from the screen and used the office phone to call her. She answered, sounding a little groggy.

"Stephanie? I'm sorry. I hope I didn't wake you up," I said. "This is Dylan Hayward."

"Oh. Hello, Dylan. Are you supposed to be calling me?" she said, sounding concerned.

"What do you mean?"

"The police, they've been asking me a lot of questions about you. They took my phone. There are texts on there about you and Misti. I'm sorry. I didn't know what to do," she said.

"It's okay, Stephanie. They would have found them eventually. I don't have anything to hide but that's not why I called."

"Why did you call then?" she asked.

"Misti was seeing someone. The police here told me that you said you didn't know who he was," I told her.

"Right. She said she couldn't tell me. I think she wanted to, but she held back for some reason."

"Could that reason have been because he was one of her professors?" I asked.

"A professor? I don't—" she cut herself off and hesitated. "Fuck me. Of course. Yes. I don't know his name but when we first started the semester she told me about her English professor. I can't remember his name, but she said he was hot. At first, she mentioned him from time to time, but then she just shut up about it. I even remember asking about him again at one point and she just shrugged it off and changed the subject. It was around that time that the mystery man arrived. Holy shit, how did I miss that?"

"I think we all missed way more than we should have. Listen, Stephanie, I want you to tell the police there what you just told me. I want them all over this guy as soon as possible."

"They'll want to know about you calling me."

"That's fine. Tell them I called you. I don't care about any of that. I only care about finding Misti," I told her.

"I believe you. You know she loved you," she said, then corrected herself, "loves you."

"I love her too, Stephanie. I'm going to find her. Hang up and call the police right now. Get them on this."

"I will. Bye, Dylan."

"Bye."

I immediately pulled up Misti's email. Somewhere in there was her schedule. I remember her telling me that she'd had to drop a class on the weekend she picked up the keys to her apartment. It was the weekend we'd spent at the cabin. Memories of that weekend were too painful to recall right now but I know it was an English class she'd picked up. She had told me that she had just gotten her schedule emailed to her and had to switch classes. That's where she had gone while I was alone at the apartment with Stephanie.

"Gregory Simmons," I said aloud.

"What?" Gloria asked.

"Gloria, I need to go to Knoxville. While I'm driving, I want you to find out everything you can about Professor Gregory Simmons, he's an English professor at the University of Tennessee. Call me with anything worth noting."

"You don't have a phone," she replied. "The police took it."

"Fuck me," I replied. "I'll get one and send you the number."

"Okay," she replied.

"And Gloria, if you find out anything about where that signal is coming from, you call me about that too."

"You know I will," she replied.

I raced down the corridor and made my way toward the front doors. I had to get a phone and get on the road. As I passed by the front desk, I caught sight of Dot sitting there. I ran back to her and pulled all the cash I had out of my wallet and dropped it on the desk in front of her.

"Dot, I need your phone. Can you buy another one?"

"I can buy several with this amount of money," she said, looking down at the cash.

"Good. Do that," I replied as she handed over her phone.

"Go upstairs and find Gloria. Give her your phone number and tell her I have it with me so she can get in touch," I said as I turned and hurried out the front doors.

I jumped in my car, slapped the phone in the hands-free cradle and roared out of the garage, heading to Nashville to see this Professor Gregory Simmons for myself. If I had to, I would beat him until he told me where to find Misti.

Chapter 39

Misti

"I'm back. Did you miss me?" Gregory's voice sing-sang through the door.

It was funny how I had been so enamored of his voice as he pranced back and forth in front of the class not that long ago and now it made my skin crawl. How did I miss that he was such a monster? Surely there were clues hidden beneath the good looks and charm. Everything had seemed so perfect—until it wasn't.

"Are you not speaking to me, my darling," he said mockingly through the door.

"I'm just tired. I haven't slept much."

"I guess the cold concrete floor in there isn't very pleasant. I could get you a blanket and a pillow. Perhaps even a little mat, but you'd have to earn them."

"Earn them?" I asked, feeling disgusted already by the probable meaning of that.

"Yes. I reward good behavior. I punish bad behavior. All of them were bad in the end. You will be bad too. That's just how it always goes."

He was like a different person now. There was none of the charm and eloquence that had attracted me. It seemed like some sort of madness had set in. I'd learned in my abnormal psychology class that monsters like him experienced a high level of narcissism. They loved to talk about themselves, how superior they were, how they wielded power over less evolved people.

"What did you do to the others? Are they all dead?" I asked.

"Dead. Yes. Of course. I told you they were bad. I had to punish them."

"Tell me what you did," I said.

"Oh, you don't want to hear that," he scoffed.

"I do. I want to know about everything."

"Why?"

"I don't know. It interests me. I want to understand things from your point of view. I mean, you had reasons why you chose certain women. Why you ended their lives. Who was the first? How many have there been?"

There was silence for a moment. I thought maybe he wouldn't answer me, but finally he began to speak, and I understood he had been sitting there, quietly reliving the moment. I wondered if I was the first to ask him questions.

"Well, there is a lot to tell, and I don't think we have much time, but I suppose I could consider the last wish of the dying. So, yours is to know about me. Okay. I'll tell you." He said, pausing for a moment before continuing. "Her name was Isabella Shaw. She was a childhood friend. She used to come to our house to play and I grew to love her. We did everything together until we were about fifteen. Then, she started talking to a boy who'd moved to our school a few months earlier. Next thing I knew, she was his and I was cast aside like a toy she'd grown bored with."

"What did you do to punish Isabella for her unkindness?" I asked, careful not to blame him for his behavior.

"I waited for her one night as she was leaving dance rehearsal. She was a beautiful dancer. Her raven-colored hair was always up in a high ponytail, and it spun in the air when she whirled around. I used to sit in the back of the auditorium and watch from the shadows, at least until that last night."

"You watched her dance and then you followed her home."

"Well, not exactly. I followed her but she never made it home. About halfway, there was a new house being built. They had it all sectioned off to pour the foundation. As she approached it, I stepped out of the shadows. She was frightened, at first, but then she saw that it was just me and relaxed. I lured her over to the house site by telling her I had found something cool there."

"What happened then?" I coaxed after he paused again. I had no doubt that he was enjoying this, reliving that first victim's fear of him in his mind.

"We reached the edge of the house, and she grew agitated when she realized there was nothing to see there. I told her I had just wanted to be alone with her. We hadn't been alone together in so long. She said she didn't want to be alone with me and tried to leave. I grabbed her by the arm and shoved her."

His voice was rising like a crescendo as he described the scene for me.

"Her foot caught, and she fell backwards, hitting her head on a concrete block sitting inside the house frame. It was dark but I could see the black blood oozing from her head into the white gravel that had been spread there in preparation for the concrete to be poured. I panicked and ran."

"So, it was an accident then. You didn't deliberately kill her."

"No, not that one. I went home and lay in my bed, but I wasn't scared anymore. I was fascinated. I snuck back out of my room and went back to the building site with a small flashlight and turned it on. It was weak, casting only a pale-yellow glow across her sun kissed bronze skin. Her almond-colored eyes stared into the nothingness."

"What did you do with her body?" I asked.

He sighed heavily before responding. I had a feeling that for all of the enjoyment he seemed to get out of killing women, this one had not brought him as much joy. This one, he had loved in as much a way as a teenage boy knew how to love.

"She was astonishing, laying on the ground so beautiful and broken, her body twisted into a contorted shape from the way she had fallen. I did what I had wanted to do for quite some time. I took her virginity and gave her mine in return."

I recoiled at his words, realizing what he was saying. He had defiled her body after she was dead. Was that something he had done to all of them? Was it something he would do to me? As sick as I was about having been sleeping with someone who had killed a number of women, the thought of him enjoying my body after I was dead was even more horrifying.

"Does that shock you?"

"No. You loved her. You wanted what you felt should be yours," I said, forcing the words out of my mouth.

"Yes. Her body was already cold, beginning to stiffen. It was the most wonderful experience of my life."

"And so, you wanted to repeat it."

"Not at first. For a long time, it was just her. For years she was the only one. It wasn't until I was in college, when I was about your age, as a matter of fact. Did you know that I was engaged once?"

"No. Tell me about her."

"Her name was Carlita. Carlita Stover. She had beautiful caramel skin from working on her father's ranch in Texas. Her hair was midnight black, and her brown eyes seemed to shimmer when she looked at me. Of course, I later discovered that part was just the contacts she wore to boost her natural color. Anyway, we began seeing one another. She was my first since Isabella, so I hadn't had a lot of practice in the sex department, but she was a virgin and didn't seem to know the difference."

"What went wrong?" I asked.

"Her friends were what went wrong. I heard her talking to one of them about sex. I was horrified to hear her telling the other woman about the intimate things that happened between us. We were engaged to be married by this point and I thought that our private affairs would have remained private."

"She betrayed your trust by telling your sexual secrets."

"Worse. Her friend convinced her that I was somehow inadequate. Can you imagine that? You've had me. You know that I am nothing remotely like inadequate!" he roared.

"Yes, I know that," I told him, feeling nauseous.

"I decided that I was perhaps not adventurous enough, so I tried to spice things up but when I would check the little recorder I left near her phone table, she was there again, telling her friend things. She said I had gotten weird with her, and she wasn't sure that she wanted to marry me."

"What did you do, Greg?" I asked.

"I showed her how weird I could get if I really wanted to explore my true desires. I drugged her wine that night and tied her to the bed. I covered her with ice packets I had been keeping in my freezer so that she was much cooler than usual, but she was still too warm for what I wanted. I used a popsicle from the freezer to get her nice and ready for me and then showed her what I'd really wanted to do to her all those months we'd been dating."

I was quiet for a moment, thinking about that poor woman, helpless and forced to endure the humiliations he forced upon her. Perhaps there were things worse than post death sex, after all. Though I suspected the story wasn't over.

"What happened next?"

"She couldn't scream. I had a gag in her mouth, but I could see her face. It was full of fear and disgust. I knew she would never look at me the same again."

"So, you killed her," I finished for him.

"Yes. I strangled her. Then I untied her and removed the ice packets before adjusting the thermostat in my apartment down to its lowest setting. When she'd been there long enough. I was able to take what I wanted without her looking at me like I was some sort of monster. It felt like I was sixteen again—like I was there with my beautiful Isabella once more."

"What did you do with her body?"

"Oh, I brought her here, of course. We were in school at Penn State, but my parents lived down here, in this very house. I drove here with Carlita in a large cooler of ice in my trunk. I hid her down here while my parents were out at a movie and had fun with her for a few days before burying her out by the lake."

I began shaking uncontrollably realizing that I was sitting in a room where there had likely been countless women before me, both alive and dead. I remember him smiling thoughtfully at a patch of wild roses that grew by the lake, seemingly misplaced. Now, I knew that they were really a grave marker. He had been reliving his murder of Carlita even while sitting there with me.

"How many have there been?" I heard myself asking, but it sounded like the words were coming from somewhere outside my body.

"I don't know. A few, but we'll have to talk about him more another time. I have to go back to the city. I have class tomorrow. We've planned a little prayer vigil for you in hopes that you will be safely returned soon. Isn't that a hoot?" he said with a laugh.

"Not really. Not if you are me," I said, unable to play this game with him further.

"No. I suppose not. Completely understandable. Anyway, I'm going to make you a few sandwiches for tomorrow because I have to be elsewhere. I'm afraid that the wolves may be at my door with you, young lady. It looks like we may have to end this little courtship of ours very soon."

I heard him heading up the steps, but he didn't close the door this time. A few minutes later, he returned, and I heard the lock on the door rattling as he opened it again. He slid in a paper bag and quickly closed it again, putting the lock back into place.

"See you tomorrow, beautiful," he chirped happily as he went back upstairs. This time I heard the door close and lock. I knew my time was getting shorter.

Chapter 40

Dylan

I was relieved to find that the Knoxville police were much more on the ball than their counterparts in Nashville. I spoke with two detectives by the name of Blass and Skerrit. The information they had was much more evolved because they had been working multiple cases they believed were tied to the same killer and I was able to help them with more specifics about Misti, thanks to info Gloria had found for me while I was on my way to Knoxville.

"His name is Gregory Simmons. I'm almost certain of it. He's a professor at UT."

"We know Simmons. I spoke to him personally yesterday. Seems nice enough and we found no reason to suspect him of anything."

"Then why did you go to see him?"

"Just routine. We spoke to all of Miss Bridges' professors and friends."

"Did you know that he started working at UT not long before the first disappearance? Or how about the fact that he is currently teaching the class of one of the other victims, Professor Aria Jones?"

The two detectives exchanged glances. I could see that they hadn't picked up on that yet. She was the one victim in all of this that didn't seem to fit the pattern. She wasn't a student and she bore no physical similarity to the others, who all had long black hair, brown eyes, and dark complexions.

"Now, it makes sense. Jones didn't fit the description of his usual kind of girl because he took her for a different reason. He wanted her class!" Detective Blass said.

"But why?" Skerritt asked. "Because he had already picked out his next victim? He was trying to get close to her by teaching her class?" Skerritt pondered aloud.

"No. I don't think so. Misti only picked up that class after he was already assigned to it. There has to be another reason," I said.

"Or another victim. Perhaps she wasn't his original target," Blass replied.

Skerritt was already picking up a nearby phone and speaking to someone on the other end as he perused a file that was lying on his desk.

"I need you to run down some information for me. I need a list of students in the English lit class at UT attended by Misti Bridges. It's taught by Professor Gregory Simmons. Pull student photos for every female student in that class and call me when you have them."

He had barely put the phone back on the cradle when he was pulling on his jacket and nodding towards Blass and myself.

"Let's go," he said.

"Where are we going?" I asked.

"To see Professor Simmons again. He should be home from class by now according to the schedule he gave us before. Last time, we interviewed him in his classroom. I want to get a gander at his apartment," Skerritt replied.

"Shouldn't we get some backup?" Blass asked.

"Nah. He'll be expecting us to have more questions. Wherever Misti Bridges is, she won't be at that apartment. It's a university accommodation they rent out short term to adjunct professors like Simmons. I've been there before and it's pretty small and close-knit. Be hard to be sneaking in abducted women without anyone noticing," Skerritt told him as we walked out to their car.

"Then why are we going there?"

"To rattle his cage. If we shake it hard enough, he might just lead us to Misti and anyone else who is still alive."

"Is it a good idea to take a civilian?" Blass asked him.

"Probably not, but if Simmons lets us in for questions, he might spot something related to Miss Bridges quicker than we will. It might give us enough to get an official warrant to go back in and do a real search of his place. He doesn't know who Dylan is, so he'll just think he's one of us," Skerritt told him before twisting sideways in his seat to address me. "Just keep your mouth shut and observe. If he seems hospitable, ask him to go to the bathroom. Be discreet but look for anything you recognize as belonging to Misti. Can you do that?"

"Yes."

"Are you sure? I can't have you fucking this up by going apeshit on me and attacking the guy."

"I won't. No way am I going to screw up any chances we have of finding Mysti or any of the others."

"Tell me about you and Misti. I understand that Nashville is looking into your relationship with her too," Skerritt said.

"Yes. They'd rather waste their time looking at me than help find her."

"Just the same, tell me what I'm looking at."

"Misti lives next door to me. We had a fling over the summer."

"Bit young for you, isn't she?" Blass said.

"Yes, she is," I replied.

"End badly?" he asked.

"No, not at all. It was completely amicable. It ended because it was never intended to be serious, and it was time for her to get back to school."

"And yet, here you are. I understand you also had a tracking device on her," Skerritt interjected.

"You understand wrong. I gave her a prototype of a piece of high-tech jewelry being designed by my company. It has a chip in it that sends out her GPS coordinates."

"Like I said, a tracking device."

"No. It's not like an air tag or something. Its user activated. It can only be tracked if she asks for it to be."

"And she activated this GPS signal herself? It couldn't have been done any other way?"

"It could be, but it's not likely. The bracelet can only be removed with a special pin. It locks on the wrist and looks like a normal piece of jewelry. It's titanium, so it's too strong to be easily removed otherwise and no one looking at it would think it worth stealing anyway. The beacon on it is not easy to accidentally trigger. You'd have to know where it is and know how to initiate it. It was designed to prevent accidental deployment."

"But you aren't able to track it, which was what it was made for?" Blass asked.

"No. Wherever she is, the signal is blocked. It's there, but it's faint. We can't get a strong enough reading to narrow it down within a fifty-mile radius around a single remote cell tower right now."

"That's the area where the task force is going door to door," Skerritt added.

"We're here," Blass said, pulling into the parking lot of a brick building not far from campus. It looked more like a dormitory than apartments.

"Remember, not a word. Just observe," Skerritt told me as we got out of the car. "And keep yourself under control."

"Got it. Don't worry about me. I'm not going to do anything that puts Misti in more danger."

The detectives exchanged another glance but said nothing. I knew exactly what they were thinking. Misti might already be dead. I refused to accept that. I would never accept it unless I saw her lifeless body for myself. I stood behind them as they knocked on Simmons' door. For a moment, I didn't think he was going to answer, but then he was there, smiling broadly at the three of us.

"Detectives. Back with more questions?" he asked.

"Yes, if you don't mind. Can we come in?" Blass asked, already insinuating himself inside the door frame.

The Detectives sat on the sofa facing Simmons while I stood nearby, taking advantage of his focus on them to look around a bit. Nothing stood out to me. If Misti had been here, she'd left no traces. However, I was guessing she either had never been here or he'd made sure there was no trace of her left behind. You didn't get by with taking multiple women and never getting caught if you weren't careful, but everyone made a mistake eventually and his was taking someone I loved.

In the middle of the detective's questions, he stopped and looked at me, scrutinizing my face. He seemed to be sizing me up and it was in that moment that I knew I was right. Professor Gregory Simmons recognized me. He recognized me because he'd seen photos of me, and those photos had to have been on Misti's phone. She had taken several while we were together. Playful little snapshots of me laughing or being silly. She'd never done that with him. He wouldn't have let her even if she'd have wanted to do so.

"I didn't catch your name," he said to me. "Are you a detective too?"

"No," I said, not offering my name.

"What part do you play in all of this? What do you contribute to finding my lost student?"

"I'm her friend. I'm just assisting with the search," I told him.

He smiled and nodded, a flicker of something in his eye. Smug prick. Yeah, he knew me and now, I knew exactly what he was. He was a sick fuck and he had Misti. The only questions that remained were where and if it was too late to get her back.

I let the detectives continue their questioning while I pulled out Dot's cell phone and texted Stephanie to send a message to Misti's number right now. A moment later, there was a slight beep from the laptop nearby. I tried not to react, but he heard it, and he knew that I did too. When we were gone, he would check it and find a message from Misti's roommate just telling her that she missed her and wanted her to come home.

The detectives finished up their interview, only asking him about the comings and goings of certain students to keep him from realizing they were onto him. As he walked us to the front door, he looked me in the eye and said he wished me luck in finding my friend safe and sound.

"I'll find her and when I do, the person who took her will regret they ever saw my face," I told him, wanting desperately to choke the ever-living fuck out of him.

The detectives hurried me out. Making sure we were all the way back to the car before saying anything about the case.

"Well, did you see anything?" Blass asked.

"No, but I heard something. He doesn't have Misti's phone, at least not at his apartment, but he does have access to it. I had her roommate Stephanie send a message that would seem like she is just grieving and missing Misti, but when she sent it, his computer beeped on the desk nearby. He's spoofed her phone. He's been keeping tabs on her communications for a while."

"That seems a bit far-fetched. You got all of that from one beep?" Skerritt said in disbelief.

"No. I learned something odd when I talked to Stephanie the other day."

I told them about the messages I'd never gotten. I couldn't understand why they were never received, but now I did. He had software that allowed him to intercept her messages. All of her messages were being filtered through him. He decided what she got and what she didn't.

"Her phone has probably been physically destroyed by this point. He wouldn't want it to give up her location, but he's still intercepting her messages. Is that enough for a warrant to dig through his place?"

"It might be. I don't think we'll find any trace of the women there, but if what you are saying is true, we might be able to at least tie him to them through that."

Skerritt was straight on the phone to his IT guy, asking him to draft a warrant with the correct lingo based on what I had told him, and hand deliver it to the judge for signature. The sand in our hourglass was dropping fast.

Chapter 41

Misti

"How many have there been?" I asked Greg.

"I don't know. I've never counted. Do you want me to give you a number? You want me to tell you about each and everyone?"

"Yes."

"Why?" he asked.

"Because I want to understand. I want to know why you felt they should die, why you feel that I should die. I want to know how they died and where you buried them."

"You planning to write a book? Sadly, you probably could. You are an excellent writer. I've seen your potential in your class submissions. Okay. I'll give you that. Let me get my things. It will help me remember," he said.

I sat quietly. I could hear him opening the dumbwaiter and what sounded like him retrieving his box of photos and trophies. The sound of a chair scraping across the floor of the cellar as he likely sat down at the dusty little table that held a basket of lids to jars. I assumed that someone used to do some canning and stored the jars down here.

"You know the police came to see me earlier today. I wasn't sure that I should come back here after they left. They seem to suspect me and the man with them, he certainly does. Of course, there is nothing there for them to find. I've completely sanitized the place since you were last there. I gave it a good cleaning that would make a crime scene cleaner jealous after we started meeting at the bookstore and coming here."

"Did you plan our meeting there?" I asked, only now realizing it had likely not been chance at all.

"Of course I did, but I thought you wanted to talk about the others," he said.

"I do."

"Okay, but I'll have to give you the quick tour. I'm afraid that tonight will be our last night together. It's time for me to move on. I fear that if they are onto me, it is only a matter of time before they discover my mother's house."

"I understand. Tell me about the women," I said, wanting to make sure that he didn't decide to move the timetable forward. I didn't know that buying myself another day would do me any good in the end, but I wasn't exactly in any hurry to die.

I listened to him go through the names of the women he had murdered. I could hear him shuffling through the items in the box, reliving their deaths, enjoying them. Either he had a phenomenal memory or there was a list I hadn't seen in the box.

There had been five years between the time he murdered Isabella and Carlita. There had been another six years before he took his next victim. He was capable of controlling himself for periods of time and then something triggered him to kill again. Was it an internal need or was it something external? What had happened recently that he'd lost control and started taking so many lives?

Every woman Greg had murdered since the first had been because he felt betrayed in some way. Most were lovers who had lost interest. He had been patient. The killings weren't crimes of passion, they were vengeance. When he was 27, he took his third victim, but she was a woman he had dated within a year of killing Carlita. She had left him for a man she met at work, but he knew if he killed her, he'd be the primary suspect.

So, he waited. He'd waited for over five years to kill Helen Carlton. He'd moved to another city and started dating someone else, but he had continued to keep tabs on Helen in covert ways. There was no trail of him stalking her, but he had done exactly that. When he felt the time was right, he took her. He hadn't had access to this house at the time, so he'd held her in an old factory he'd scoped out for just that purpose.

"I kept her there for nearly a week, showing her what she was missing. It wasn't exactly as romantic as I would have liked, but I did the best I could. I brought her nice meals and wine. She eventually caught on to the fact that the wine was laced with sedatives and started refusing to drink it, so I had to force it down her throat at knifepoint."

"Why did you drug her? Were you afraid she would get away?"

"Oh, heavens no. But she was a screamer you see, and it was a turn off. I just wanted her to be still," he said.

"I like for you to be still. It is as though you are absent. Distant and full of sorrow. So, you would've died..." he said, quoting Neruda.

I felt sick that he was equating a beautiful poem that was centered around the love for a woman and a longing for her tranquility to the sickness he had inflicted on a woman who may have once cared for him.

"I just wanted her to be quiet, but then I discovered that it made her so deliciously still. It was like she was dead. A little foreplay with some ice cubes and she was ripe for the taking."

I wanted to scream at him, tell him what an inhuman bastard he was, but I knew I had to remain calm if I wanted to stay alive. A part of me still believed this wouldn't happen to me. Somehow, I would survive this.

The stories that followed were pretty much the same, except I noticed they had continued to escalate. He'd gone from killing women who he had met organically to seeking out women for the purpose of killing them. They came from the many places he'd lived over the last thirty years since he'd taken his first victim, but all but one had something in common. They reminded him of his beloved Isabella.

The other common thread was that he had sexually assaulted each and every one of them either while simulating death or post mortem—both, in some cases. Yet, he'd not touched me since he'd put me in this room. Why was I different? Or had that changed with his latest victims? It seemed I was about to find out.

"I'm afraid that our time grows short so I will just lump the women I've killed here into a single discussion. Unlike the others, they meant nothing to me. They were whores willing to jump into bed with their professor for good grades. I was a fantasy for them. I suppose a lot of students think of having sex with a professor as a conquest. I wasn't willing to give them that."

"You weren't dating them when you abducted them?"

"Oh, heavens no. They caught my attention because they reminded me of Isabella, sure, but I took them on my terms, not theirs. They threw themselves at me and I ignored them. I was trying so desperately to be good. Then I saw one of them walking home one night. She was alone and no one was around. She was grateful to me when I stopped and offered her a ride. I suggested we finally get to know one another better and so we did. I kept her here for three days until I tired of her and then I slit her throat mid-coitus. It was beautiful."

I felt ill. I wasn't sure how much more of this I could stand to listen to, but I knew I had no choice if I didn't want to risk him stepping up his timetable.

"The next three were quicker. I felt invigorated by them. I didn't keep them. I plucked them up off the street when they least expected it and brought them here, taking what I wanted from them and then disposing of their bodies."

"And the professor that you killed? She wasn't like the others."

"No. I just needed her class. I had finished up my time here and would have to move on, but I'd met someone, and I wasn't ready to give her up. I thought it might be too obvious if I killed the woman I had been replacing and she was a new mother. I didn't want to cause her child the pain of being orphaned so young. So, I set my sights on someone else."

"Did you bring her here too?"

"I did, but not like you think. She wasn't a good woman. She drank too much. I followed her to a local bar and when she left, quite inebriated, I grabbed her from the parking lot. I brought her here, but only to kill and bury her. She held no interest for me otherwise. She was old and reeked of whiskey."

"And the woman you killed her to stay near? Mary Anne Housley, right?"

"Yes, the beautiful Mary Anne. She looked more like my Isabella than anyone and she seemed to be really into me, but I gained access to her phone and realized she'd been playing with me all along. She was seeing someone else behind my back. It wasn't even someone she might have loved or cared for. It was another professor. She was fucking both of us for grades," he said with disgust.

"Why did you wait to take her?" I asked.

"Why, I did that because of you. If not for you and your deceit, Mary Anne would still be alive."

I didn't know if that was true or not, but it swept over me in waves of repulsion that he might have killed her because of something I had done. How could I have caused such a thing?

"Oh, look. It's late and I need to get to sleep. I'm going to stay with you here tonight because I'm afraid I may be followed in if I attempt to make it back here again from the city. Get some sleep and I will see you in the morning. We can finish our little chat over breakfast and make arrangements for our last night together. I can't wait to be inside you again."

I didn't respond. I felt numb. I felt disgusted. Mostly, I felt a sense of terror that I couldn't begin to describe.

Chapter 42

Dylan

I checked into a local hotel near the police station and ducked out for some supplies to set up a makeshift research station. I'd learned a few things today. I knew that Misti was not at Simmon's apartment but that he had her somewhere. I refused to believe that she wasn't still alive, but I didn't think she had much time left. Simmons was wily enough to know we were onto him.

I put up an easel with a large corkboard balanced on it and pinned a map of the fifty-mile area around the Grandview cell tower. Gloria was able to narrow the signal down too. There were other towers in that area, but it was the biggest—the most powerful. Whatever was weakening the signal was allowing enough of it to reach that tower to at least register but its exact location was masked.

Based on the fact that he had somehow managed to subvert messages going to and from Misti's phone, he had at least a few computer skills beyond what normal people possessed. He was not a match for mine, though. I began working on accessing his network through his router. I'd gotten a good look at it while we were there and knew exactly how to get into it. It would take a bit to tunnel in, so I got it rolling and then went to look at the map.

I put a pin in the tower and used a pencil and string to mark off the 50-mile radius around it. I turned back as my computer started beeping. My attempt to hack his system failed. He'd shut it all down before I could get in.

"Fuck!" I yelled, throwing a glass on the table at a nearby wall. It shattered, pieces of it falling to the floor. I stared at them helplessly for a moment before shaking off my momentary paralysis. I didn't have time for anger. I could be furious later. Right now, I had to find Misti.

The phone rang and I snatched it up. "What have you found, Gloria?"

"We sent some guys out to the cell tower and added some boosters to enhance the signals coming into it. It's still not good but we've been able to pinpoint it a bit more. It's coming from within ten miles of that tower from the east."

"Brilliant. Good work. Anything else?"

"Yes. I got access to the county's property records for the area. I didn't find anything for the name Gregory Simmons but I've sent you the login data so you can look at whatever you need."

"Thank you, Gloria. Have you been home? Have you gotten any rest?"

"Not yet."

"Go get some sleep. Let someone else take over for a while."

"I'll sleep when you do. Dot is here. She's taking good care of me with food and letting me nap a little when I need to."

"Dot, huh?" I said, smiling for the first time since this had all started. "Bye, Gloria."

I hurried to the map and reduced my radius to ten miles around the tower, focusing on the east side of it. I felt a sense of renewed hope as I noted that there weren't as many houses to consider now. It was mostly rural properties. Farms and vacant land. Assuming Misti was still alive and being held somewhere, I looked for a place that would explain the reduced signal.

Using the county property database, I pulled up all the properties in that area, going through them one by one. I put pins in those with dwellings present, focusing on those with basements, silos, storm shelters or other features that might reduce a signal. I'd tested the GPS chip in such situations and knew what caused the weakened signal.

Misti was likely underground, but she wasn't buried. If she had set the signal before being put into a grave or a lake, the initial signal would have been strong enough to get out and then been reduced. Even beneath the dirt or underwater, the signal would have still carried with more strength. Wherever he was keeping her, it had a structure around it with walls of concrete or metal that were heavy enough to partly block the signal.

I was quickly working my way through the properties on the list, putting blue pins in those that I could discount and red pins marked possibilities. When I was done, there were only four houses. I began looking at their ownership. Two belonged to families that lived there and listed farming as their trade. It was unlikely that Simmons would have access to any structures on their land based on the details I was seeing.

That left only two. One was an abandoned farm. The only possible structure on it that might block a signal was a well that sat behind a house that had burned down the year before. It was likely covered with a heavy cap to prevent access, but Simmons could have removed that with a pulley or something similar. I shuddered at the thought of Misti cowering at the bottom of some cold dark well waiting for help to come and losing hope.

The other was a house owned by a woman named Angela Guilian. It had an old wine cellar beneath it. Looking into Angela Guilian's information, I discovered that she no longer lived in the house. A change of address had been filed by a senior care home for insurance purposes within a year of her taking possession of the home. I called the care home and found that she was still alive and being cared for by her son.

"I need to get in touch with someone about the home she owns in Grandview. There's been a problem there."

"I'm sorry, I'm not allowed to give out Mr. Simmon's personal information."

I hung up without another word, glancing back at the property data on my screen. Angela Guilian had inherited the property from her father, Mr. Gregory Guilian. She had named her son, who I assumed carried his father's surname, after her father.

"I've got you, motherfucker," I hissed, not bothering to shut anything down as I grabbed my phone and ran out of the room to my car. On the way, I called Detective Skerritt. He answered on the first ring.

"The Guilian farm just outside of Grandview. That is where he is holding Misti. I'm sending you the address. I'm headed there now."

"Don't do anything stupid, Hayward. I'm sending units and I'm on my way, too. Do not go blazing into that house. You let us do our jobs," he said, but I didn't care. I ended the call and roared down the highway as fast as my fucking Mercedes would go.

It felt like it was taking forever to get to the house, but I finally arrived. There was a long gravel drive that disappeared into a heavy thicket of trees. I had no desire to announce myself. Instead, I pulled into a grove of trees that sat adjacent to the drive and began running toward the trees, slipping into them quietly.

My heart thudded against my chest as I grew closer. I wasn't scared, not for myself, but I was terrified of what I might find inside or that I would fail and that I would find I was too late. As I grew closer, I could see the house through the trees. There was a Jaguar parked in the driveway. I recognized it from our visit to Simmon's apartment. It had seemed very out of place sitting outside the bland little dwelling.

There was no sign of Simmons or Misti. The house seemed quiet. I glanced at my watch. It was almost 6 p.m., still a couple of hours before sunset and I couldn't wait for the cover of darkness. If Misti was in there and she was still alive, I would tear him limb from limb to get to her.

My phone buzzed in my pocket as I stood in the trees waiting. It was Gloria. I pulled it out and held it up to my ear but whatever she was saying was garbled. I looked at the phone and realized I had very little signal. It was a cheap phone. I was still using the one Dot had loaned me, but it had worked fine up until now.

There was something about this place that ate communication signals. Whether it was a natural phenomenon or a manmade effort, it explained the poor signal. If she was in the cellar listed in the property records for this house, it was a wonder any signal had gotten through at all.

I debated how to best proceed, but not for long. I edged around closer to the house, staying in the trees for as long as I could before quickly making my way across the yard and flattening myself up against a wall near a window. I listened for any indication that there was someone inside before peering through the window. My heart stopped as I took in what was happening inside.

Chapter 43

Misti

"Well, beautiful. It looks like it's time," Gregory said as he came down the stairs and approached my door.

"Wait. You still haven't told me about Mary Anne. You said you would finish first. You said she would be alive if not for me. I want to know why."

"Oh. That. I was seeing Mary Anne when I met you at the drop and add for my class. I knew you would be a temptation, but I was able to set that aside before classes began. Then, you pursued me. I resisted for a while, but I soon found I couldn't think about anything but you. I decided to see how things went with us and when they seemed to go well, Mary Anne was in the way."

"She found out?"

"Yes. She was in my office one day when you called. I had told you not to call me. I told you that I didn't want anyone at school to connect us beyond the classroom, but you called me anyway. I let it go since you're a student and sometimes students call the office to sort out issues but you knew better. Anyway, she was waiting for me outside my door to go to lunch. I didn't know she was there when you and I were talking about our weekend plans."

"And she confronted you about it," I said.

"Yes. She started to make a stink and I lied to her. I told her that she had misunderstood what she had heard and that we were making plans for you to stay at the house that weekend with a friend. She didn't know who was on the other end of the line, so she only heard my side of the conversation about what to bring and such. I told her I would prove it to her."

"So, you brought her here to show her there was nothing to worry about."

"Not quite. It was an unexpected hiccup, but I couldn't afford for her to be mad and go blabbing all over school. I told her you were meeting us here to get keys and such and she was welcome to meet you. She believed me and met me off campus. When we got to a little shopping center where I left the professor's body, I pretended I had a flat and pulled over. It was empty just like it was the night that you were left there by that horrible guy you went out with."

"You knew about my date with Tucker? How?"

"You told me. Don't you remember?"

I thought about this and couldn't remember it. The only person I remember telling about that horrible experience was Stephanie. Had he been stalking me even back then?

"Maybe. So, you stopped at the shopping center and what? You killed her?"

"Yes. I strangled her and put her in the trunk of the car."

"In broad open daylight?"

"Yes. The road isn't well traveled, and that shopping center isn't just closed, it's shut down permanently. It gave me just enough cover to accomplish what I needed to do and get back to campus for my last class and in time to pick you up for our trip."

The gravity of what he was saying hit me. He was lying about me causing Mary Anne's death. Perhaps the timing of her death was on me, but he would have killed her no matter what. That was simply what he did. What really bothered me was realizing that he was saying that Mary Anne's dead body had been in the trunk of his car while we were in the front, laughing and talking about what a great time we were going to have.

"Anyway, that is where my story comes to an end, at least for you. I've already made arrangements to leave as soon as we're done here. But first, I want to spend our last night together enjoying you the way I always wanted to but didn't think you'd enjoy."

"Meaning?"

"I've put together a little romantic setup in the living room. There's a nice roaring fire for ambiance, but you won't really feel much of it in the ice bath I've prepared for you there. One of the great things about this old place is the abundance of items from its earlier years. My great-grandfather had one of those old metal tubs that you fill with hot water to bathe. I've filled it with ice water for you."

I didn't respond. I knew he would open that door soon and I would have to be prepared to fight my way out or suffer the indignities of those that came before me in his little hellscape. I had no weapons unless you counted the bucket of piss and shit I'd been forced to share space with in my concrete prison cell. I could throw it on him. It might slow him down, but it wouldn't stop him.

I looked down at the fucking useless bracelet on my wrist. I didn't know if it was putting out a signal, but if it was, no one had come for me. I remembered the pointed locking mechanism inside. It hadn't been razor sharp, but I was betting it could do damage if I could strike a well placed blow. The only problem was that I didn't have a key.

"No more questions, Misti?" Greg said from outside the door.

"Where will you go after you've killed me, Greg?" I asked, wanting to keep him talking.

"I don't know. We'll see. But now it's time to finish our time together," he told me. "I just need to grab my tools and I will be right
with you."

I remembered the pins in my hair. It had been pinned up in a loose
bun when this had started and was still partly that way. I began feeling
around to find one lost in my thick locks and finally landed on one
holding onto a strand of hair close to the back. I quickly pulled it out
and stripped off the little plastic piece that covered the sharp tips and
then bent both sides of it outward.

I felt a sense of relief when it was small enough to go into the tiny
hole that triggered the bracelet release. Thank goodness I didn't use
the larger kind of pins. It took a little work to get the thin metal to
push the latch inside, but the bracelet clicked open. I pulled it apart,
running my finger over the pointed side of the clasp in the dark room.
The flashlight had died a long time ago.

That made me remember what he said. He told me he had looked at
Isabella's body with a flashlight that gave off a dim yellow light. Could
this be the same one? Had he kept it all this time? Was he getting some
sick little extra thrill by giving it to me to use in this hole?

In the darkness of the room, I could see the light on the beacon
dimly flashing. It had not been visible outside the bracelet but seemed
vivid without any light present. I looked at it sadly. No matter what he
had felt for me in the end, I knew that Dylan would be devastated that
this device he had created to save women like me had failed. Perhaps,
in the end, he could at least be happy that I'd been able to repurpose
the hard titanium casing as a weapon.

I'd either fight my way free or at least leave a mark that Greg would
remember me by for the rest of his life. I held it in an iron grip, poised
above my head in preparation for him to open the door. I heard the

chain on the door rattle and the sound of the lock being snapped open. Then the door was slowly opening. I didn't hesitate.

Shoving my weight against the door from my side to knock him off balance, I came bounding out through the opening and pounced on him. I brought the bracelet down before he could get an arm up to stop me. It connected with his right eye, making a sickening wet plopping noise.

"You fucking bitch!" he shouted as he stumbled backward, his hand covering his now bleeding and damaged eye. I knew I had to react before he could recover the upper hand. I grabbed the closest thing I could find, a broken wooden ax handle leaning against a nearby wall.

I brought it down heavily on his head, missing but quickly recovering and swinging again. I managed to make contact with a sickening thud the second time and then immediately swung again. I had lost all sense of humanity as I swung a third time in an effort to save myself. He went down as I struck him heavily against the left side of his head.

I didn't hesitate. While he was moaning on the floor, I ran up the steps and tried to open the door. He had locked it from the inside. My heart felt like it was beating out of my chest, and I threw my weight against it with no success.

Maintaining my grip on the ax handle, I hurried back down the steps to look for his keys. They weren't on the table or anywhere on the floor that I could see so I knew they had to be in his pocket. He was still moving but disoriented on the floor, but I needed those keys to get out of here.

I was going to have to get those keys or die.

Chapter 44

Dylan

My heart sank as I saw the line of police cars flying down the driveway to the house. It was good that they were here, but I was afraid that their very loud entrance would send Simmons over the edge and Misti would be dead before they got inside.

I hurried out to them, my hands over my head. I was quickly looking down at the barrels of several guns pointed at me as I appeared. Skerritt and Blass appeared from a car and approached, motioning for the officers to lower their weapons.

"What are you doing here, Hayward? I told you to let us handle this."

"Yeah and then you come barreling in here with guns blazing and sirens blaring. If you're going to be fucking cowboys, then get in there before he kills her," I yelled at him, furious.

"Stay out here and let us handle this," he told me, motioning for other officers to join him as he and Blass unholstered their weapons and approached the house.

I watched as they entered the house and began going room to room looking for Misti and Simmons. I could see them through the windows on the first and second floors as they cleared rooms and moved to the next, but I knew she wasn't upstairs. She was in the cellar. I was certain of it.

"Fuck this shit," I growled hurrying toward the front steps. An officer yelled for me to stand down, but I ignored him. "Fucking shoot me. I'm going in."

I was barely in the door when I heard Misti screaming. It was horrible to hear but also comforting because it told me that she was still alive. Armed officers approached the door with caution before one of them began ramming his way through it with a small bar. He immediately backed out, dropped the battering ram, and held his hands up to show he had no weapon.

Simmons ascended the steps holding Misti tightly by the arm in front of him. He held a large bowie knife to her throat as they emerged. My heart sank as I saw the fear on her face as she looked wildly around at the police. I didn't call attention to myself for fear of setting Simmons off. Instead, I moved behind an officer and waited to see what they would do.

"If you want her alive, you will lower your weapons. I'm going to go out to my car now and Misti is coming with me. You are not to follow me, or I will cut her lovely throat and enjoy watching her bleed out."

"You don't have to do this Professor Simmons. We just want Misti. Let her go and we can talk about how to resolve this so that no one gets hurt."

"Do you think I'm an idiot? Without her, you will not think twice about shooting me in the head. She's coming with me. When I'm safely away, I will leave her somewhere for you to find."

"Alive?" Skerritt asked.

"Alive," he replied, still backing through the house toward the door.

I saw Misti's face as she caught sight of the tub of ice and the look of horror that flashed across her eyes. It was all I could stand. I spotted a back door that was open and slipped out of it away from the carnage unfolding in the front room of Simmons' mother's home.

"He's bringing her out," I told the police who were waiting outside to secure the perimeter.

All of their eyes were on the front door as Simmons emerged, trying to keep his eye on the cops following him and the ones behind him.

"Tell them to put their guns down," he warned Skerritt. "Tell them to put their guns down and move away from my car. I swear to you I will slice her open like a juicy cantaloupe if you don't."

Skerritt gave the order for the officers outside to stand down, but he and the ones with him remained vigilante, even with their weapons lowered. Their eyes were peeled on him, waiting for an opening. Now, their backs were turned to me as he pulled her toward the Jag. I moved forward, not sure what I was doing, but knowing that there was no way I was letting him leave here with her.

Hidden by the car and with all eyes on him, no one noticed me creeping in closer to the Jag. I grabbed the utility knife that I kept in my pocket for emergencies and pulled it open, using all my strength to puncture the front right tire. He wasn't going to get very far on that even if he made it into the car.

The front tire hissed as it deflated, the noise blending into the chaos surrounding us. I moved toward the back of the car and hit that tire, as well. He might force the cops to put a spare on while he held Misti at knifepoint, but he damned sure wasn't going to have two spares. His only option would be to force them to give him a cop car that could be remotely disabled.

I watched as he pulled Misti closer to his car. I remained crouched nearby, out of sight of the cops and him. All I needed was a chance.

I didn't want to risk Misti in the process, but I had to stop this. I couldn't let him take her. I couldn't lose her.

"Here's what you are going to do," he snarled as he reached the passenger side of his car, oblivious to the rapidly deflating tires on the opposite side. "You're going to put your guns down on the ground while I get in this car and leave this property. If you follow me, she's dead. If you even try to follow me, she's dead. Getting the picture?"

"It doesn't have to be like this," Skerritt told him. "There is no reason to hurt her. You've hurt so many already. Why not let this one go? Why not end this thing with knowing you showed mercy on one of these poor innocent women?"

"Innocent? Innocent? Is that what you think? None of them were innocent. This one certainly isn't. She pursued me. She begged for my attention and then, when she got it, she betrayed me by reaching out to some old fuck she was banging during the summer. I thought she was the one. I believed we had a solid relationship. She's nothing more than a whore who didn't deserve my attention in the first place."

"I don't know about all that. People change their minds. Feelings fade, but at the end of the day, that shouldn't be a death sentence. She should be able to move on without paying for a bad relationship with her life."

"Oh? Is that what you think? You don't think I'll pay for this bad relationship with my life? We both know that the moment I let her go, I'll pay the price with a bullet to the head. No judge. No jury. Just execution by a jury of cops with itchy trigger fingers. I'm afraid I'm going to pass on that," he said, moving closer to the car and opening the door.

Simmons began pulling Misti inside, crawling across the seat with the knife pushed into her neck forcefully enough that a tiny bit of blood trickled down her skin. I was infuriated by it as I moved slowly around the car and caught sight of it. I could see that Skerritt had caught sight of me from the direction of his gaze, but it was only momentary, and he was quickly focused back on Simmons, not wanting to call attention to my presence.

I felt like screaming, they were letting him leave with her. They were letting him take her after we'd worked so hard to find her and save her. What was going to happen to her once she was in that car and he discovered he couldn't go anywhere?

Chapter 45

Misti

My mind was racing. I was so close to being free, but for all their efforts even this massive police presence couldn't save me as long as Greg had me in his grasp. Our heads were too close to take a shot and the knife in his hands was razor sharp as it rested against the soft flesh of my neck. I could feel where it was biting in, the warm blood trickling down my neck.

As he began pulling me into his car, I tried to figure out how to put enough distance between us that someone could get a shot in. He'd made them put their guns down, so I'd have to create enough room and hope that someone with quick reflexes reacted to the opportunity. I focused my gaze on the older cop who seemed to be calling the shots. I didn't believe in telepathy, but I felt certain that holding his gaze might relay my intentions to him, preparing him to make a move as soon as he saw a shot.

In all honesty, if he missed and shot me in the head, it was better than the plans Greg would likely have for me if he managed to get me out of her and alone again. I hadn't missed the tub of ice that he'd prepared for me before I'd attacked him. And he was in pain now, without a doubt. He was going to lose that eye and I was the one who had caused it.

If nothing else, I'd learned from our discussions just how unforgiving he was. He would kill me for the damage I'd done, but first he would make me suffer. What he had done to the others would likely look like a cake walk compared to what he would do to me. The only reason I wasn't dead or on my way to dead already was that I was his only hope of getting out of here.

I maintained eye contact with the cop who was talking to him. He squinted his eyes at me slightly and I knew he understood. Greg glanced at another cop who sneezed nearby, and the cop shook his head ever so slightly at me, warning me not to do whatever it was I was trying to do, but he wasn't the one being held at knifepoint.

Greg opened the door behind him, fumbling momentarily as he pulled me in behind me, dragging me along as he slid across the passenger seat toward the driver's side of the car. It was now or never. I steeled myself for whatever would happen next. Worst case scenario, he'd cut my throat. That would still be better than other things he could come up with if we were alone. I'd rather die here and now than let him touch my lifeless body in the disgusting ways he'd told me about in the cellar.

As he moved to slip beneath the wheel, he momentarily lost his grip on me, the knife slipped away from my neck, and I shoved my shoulder and arm forward in an attempt to knock it free from his hand. He reacted quickly, too quickly, holding on to the knife as he attempted to regain control over me. His grip on me tightened as I struggled to lurch forward out of the car.

Then, as if he materialized from nowhere, Dylan was there. He grabbed me by the waist and hauled me forward, breaking Greg's grip on me. It was as if he threw me, hurling my body out of the car and onto the ground outside the car. Cops rushed forward from all directions to pull me up and get me safely away from the car. I turned to see that Dylan was in the car, holding Greg's wrist as he tried to plunge the knife into his neck. They struggled and Greg's arm was forced downward.

It was hard to see what was happening as the two men fought in the front seat. My heart sank. I was safe but now Dylan was the one in danger. I was terrified. Suddenly, I saw Dylan lunge forward, a loud grunt escaping his throat and then he seemed to collapse. Blood was visible as it began to seep from between them and across the floor mats of the Jag.

I realized I was holding my breath as I watched the police force move slowly to the car, surrounding it with guns drawn. After a moment, there was movement. Dylan emerged from the car, drenched with blood, and staggered toward me. I ran to him, catching him in my arms and holding on to him.

"God, no," I cried. "Someone get some help. Call him an ambulance."

"Shh. It's okay," he whispered, finally straightening up and pulling me closer into his arms. "It's not my blood."

I pulled away, wide-eyed, as I looked him over and realized he had no holes in his clothing. We both turned as the police pulled Greg from the car and laid him on the ground. His chest heaved up and down as blood poured from his side. Skerritt pulled the radio to his belt and called for an ambulance.

"This is KPD12. We need an ambulance to respond to the current location. One victim recovered at the scene. We also need body transport for one," he told them, clipping his radio back onto his belt.

Dylan and I looked at him and he shook his head as if to say we shouldn't ask. It was evident that, without medical intervention, Greg would bleed out before an ambulance reached us. For all purposes, he was already dead. It was over.

"How are you here?" I asked.

"You called me," he told me, looking toward my wrist.

"It's in the cellar. I didn't think the signal was getting out and I had to use it as a weapon instead."

"The signal was weak. It took a bit to find you."

"But you did find me. I don't want to think about what would have happened if you hadn't," I told him, laying my head on his chest, and closing my eyes.

"Hayward, I thought I told you to stand down and let us do our job," Skerritt said as he approached us.

"Yeah. I know you haven't known me that long but even in such a short period of time, you should have learned that I don't listen to people who try to tell me what to do."

"I can see that, and I would bust your balls about it a bit longer, but if not for your stubbornness, we might still be looking for this guy and having to talk to another family about why we can't find their daughter."

"Can we go?" I asked.

"Not yet. An ambulance is coming to check you out and we'll need to ask you both some questions. Your family is already being notified that you've been found safely. They are waiting in a hotel here in Knoxville for news, so we'll get you back to them as soon as possible."

"Thank you."

"Don't thank me. Thank this man. If he hadn't been so determined to find you, things might have turned out differently."

I smiled up at Dylan and then turned back to the detective.

"Detective?" I said.

"Yes?"

"I'll save you some time. There are no bodies in that house, but you will find photos and other evidence in the cellar. There is an old dumbwaiter behind the right end of the wine rack. I don't know where the bodies are, but all of the women he took are dead and at least one of them is buried on the property. She's been there a long time under a batch of roses."

"Do you know about more?" he asked.

"Yes. I know a lot more than I care to know, but I had to keep him talking to keep him from killing me sooner than he tried. I have a lot of information that I want to make sure you have, because I don't think some of these women are even on your radar as his victims."

"Well, then we have a lot to talk about," he said.

In the distance, I could hear a siren wailing. The ambulance was on the way. A few moments later, I saw it blasting down the limestone gravel road that led to the house. The ambulance was already parked and tending to my wounds when a somber black hearse rolling slowly in at a much less hurried pace.

"Go get checked out and then we'll talk a bit," Skerritt said.

Dylan walked with me to the ambulance, standing close by as they bandaged my wounds from where Greg had hit my head and sliced into my neck. His face looked pale as he waited for them to patch me up.

"We're going to need to take you to the hospital and let a doctor look at those head wounds just to be safe," the paramedic said.

"Not yet," I told them. "I have a story to tell and I'm not leaving until I finish. I'll go to the hospital when I'm done."

"We can't wait for you to do interviews," he said in a dry tone.

"I didn't ask you to," I told him, stepping out of the back of the ambulance, and walking toward Detective Skerritt.

Dylan and I rode to the station with him while the other police tended the scene. In a small room with fluorescent lights, I began recounting the stories Greg had shared with me. I gave them names and approximate dates, locations, and whatever else I could remember. Much of it they would be able to match up with the trophies Greg had kept, I tried to fill in what they couldn't easily see.

"You'll make yourself available if we need you again?" he asked.

"I will be available to you for the rest of my life," I replied. "I want every woman Greg Simmons killed to finally be able to rest in peace. None of them deserved this."

"You didn't deserve this," Skerritt responded.

"I know," I told him, shaking his hand before leaving the interview room to find Dylan, who was being interviewed separately.

A few minutes later, Detective Blass escorted him down the hall to the lobby. I stood to greet him.

"You ready to go to the hospital?" he asked.

"No. I want to go home. I want to see my parents," I told him.

"Then let's get you there," he said, kissing me on the forehead and holding me close.

We walked out of the police station and caught a cab to the hotel where Mom and Dad were waiting. They weren't terribly surprised to see Dylan as much of the events that had taken place had already been conveyed to them by the police. They hugged us both and we all went to their room to put the horrible events of the last few days behind us.

I walked into their suite and went to the shower. I needed to cleanse myself of the filth from my ordeal. When I stepped out, Dylan was waiting for me. He led me to the bed and we both lay down. Dylan pulled me tightly to him and held me close as I fell asleep.

Epilogue

Dylan

In the years after Misti's ordeal, I'd wanted to give Misti some space after the horrible events she had endured, but she'd had other ideas. We'd both spent a lot of time on numerous police interviews explaining some of the things that had taken place during her abduction in addition to what we knew about the others who had been taken.

Her parents weren't exactly thrilled to find out about our relationship, but they came around. Misti was a grown woman and I had been the one they credited for saving her, so they kept any thoughts they had about our age difference to themselves and just let us be.

In the beginning, things were tough for her. She had nightmares and often woke up screaming in her sleep. As time passed, the bad dreams seemed to ease, and she began to regain a bit of her former self.

It had taken a lot for her to work up the courage to even leave the house. For nearly a year, she'd gone no further than moving between her parents' house and mine. So, I was surprised when she popped up one day and said she wanted to go back to school. I would never discourage her from it, but my heart sank at the idea of her being away from me again, even with a much-improved ResQ bracelet on her arm. It was part of our latest line, which was selling like hotcakes after word got around of how she was found and rescued.

Of course, I had scrapped the original batch in favor of an improved model. The new generation of bracelets featured a boosted signal capability and an improved clasp with a sharper point to serve as a weapon in a crunch.

"I'm sure UT will give you credit for where you left off, considering what happened," I'd said, almost choking on the words.

"I don't want to go back to UT. There are too many bad memories there now. I'm going to stay here in Nashville and pursue a degree in criminal psychology at Vanderbilt instead of finishing my mechanical design degree."

"That sounds like something you will be brilliant at."

"I think so too. I want to understand what creates men like Greg Simmons. I want to do what I can to stop men like him before they take lives."

I'd smiled and kissed her, holding her close to me as we stood there in the cool evening air by the pool she used to come over and clean. In some regards, she was forever changed. In other ways, she was still the vivacious girl I'd fallen in love with.

We'd long ago discussed the events that'd happened to her. I'd told her that I hadn't ignored her messages, Greg had intercepted them. We'd forgiven each other for imagined transgressions and embraced one another again. Though she'd moved into her own place to attend school, she rarely stayed there. Most nights, she was curled in my arms in the quiet of my bedroom. There was no formal declaration of commitment between us. We'd simply started being together with no desire to be apart.

Over the years, both of us gave a number of interviews about Gregory Simmons. Misti never painted herself as a victim. Instead, she spoke of the women who had not survived him. She advocated for women who had suffered at the hands of men. Often, by her side sat another woman who knew what it was like to be traumatized by a violent man.

Dorothy Rose had not only completed her high school GED, but she had also gone on to achieve a master's degree in criminal science. It had been years since she'd sat at the reception desk of my company, but she still lived in the house I had loaned her, only now, she owned it and spent her days as a victim's advocate at a local program for women. She never told anyone what I had done for her, per my request. Only she, Misti and I knew how we had met and become friends.

"In my darkest hour, a man arrived to save me, and I was skeptical because the men I had known had only ever hurt me. But I took a chance and it changed everything. I will forever be grateful to him for giving me back the smile I had lost years before," Dot once told an audience the three of us were addressing. She had punctuated her remarks by giving me the largest smile I had ever seen from her, and it was exactly what I had always wanted from her.

Outside of public requests for interviews, none of us ever talked about what had brought the three of us together, but Misti and I were committed to one another for life and Dot was a part of our lives until she passed away many years later.

As life goes, we had experienced some rough patches along the way, but overall, our life together was nothing short of amazing.

~The End

Book 2 in the series coming soon....

https://amazon.com/author/rachelkstone

bookbub.com/authors/rachel-k-stone

youtube.com/channel/UCbZdQqxw7X0FtMONGRm
mlqg

facebook.com/authorrachelkstone

instagram.com/rachelkstoneauthor/

goodreads.com/author/show/23254854.Rachel_K_Ston
e